The
Ax

The AX

Donald E. Westlake

Thorndike Press • Chivers Press
Thorndike, Maine USA Bath, England

This Large Print edition is published by Thorndike Press, USA and by Chivers Press, England.

Published in 1997 in the U.S. by arrangement with Warner Books, Inc.

Published in 1997 in the U.K. by arrangement with the author's agent.

U.S. Hardcover 0-7862-1191-1 (Cloak & Dagger Series Edition)
U.K. Hardcover 0-7540-3095-4 (Chivers Large Print)

The text of this Large Print edition is unabridged.
Other aspects of the book may vary from the original edition.

Set in 16 pt. Plantin by Al Chase.

Printed in the United States on permanent paper.

British Library Cataloguing in Publication Data available

Library of Congress Cataloging in Publication Data

Westlake, Donald E.
   The ax / Donald E. Westlake.
    p. cm.
   ISBN 0-7862-1191-1 (lg. print : hc : alk. paper)
   1. Large type books. I. Title.
  [PS3573.E9A9 1997b]
   813'.54—dc21   97-24789

This is for my father,
Albert Joseph Westlake, 1896–1953

The old superstition about fiction being 'wicked' has doubtless died out in England, but the spirit of it lingers in a certain oblique regard directed toward any story which does not more or less admit that it is only a joke. Even the most jocular novel feels in some degree the weight of the proscription that was formerly directed against literary levity: the jocularity does not always succeed in passing for orthodoxy. It is still expected, though perhaps people are ashamed to say it, that a production which is after all only a 'make-believe' (for what else is a 'story'?) shall be in some degree apologetic — shall renounce the pretension of attempting really to represent life. This, of course, any sensible, wide-awake story declines to do, for it quickly perceives that the tolerance granted to it on such a condition is only an attempt to stifle it disguised in the form of generosity. The old evangelical hostility to the novel, which was as explicit as it was narrow, and which regarded it as little less favourable to our immortal part than a stage-play, was in reality far less insulting. The only reason for the existence of a novel is that it does attempt to represent life.

Henry James, *The Art of Fiction*, 1888

If you're doing what you think is right for everyone involved, then you're fine. So I'm fine.

Thomas G. Labrecque, CEO
Chase Manhattan Bank

1

I've never actually killed anybody before, murdered another person, snuffed out another human being. In a way, oddly enough, I wish I could talk to my father about this, since he did have the experience, had what we in the corporate world call the background in that area of expertise, he having been an infantryman in the Second World War, having seen "action" in the final march across France into Germany in '44–'45, having shot at and certainly wounded and more than likely killed any number of men in dark gray wool, and having been quite calm about it all in retrospect. How do you know beforehand that you can do it? That's the question.

Well, of course, I couldn't ask my father that, discuss it with him, not even if he were still alive, which he isn't, the cigarettes and the lung cancer having caught up with him in his sixty-third year, putting him down as surely if not as efficiently as if he had been a distant enemy in dark gray wool.

The question, in any case, will answer itself, won't it? I mean, this is the sticking point. Either I can do it, or I can't. If I can't, then all the preparation, all the planning, the files I've maintained, the expense I've put myself to (when God knows I can't afford it), have been in vain, and I might as well throw it all away, run no more ads, do no more scheming, simply allow myself to fall back into the herd of steer mindlessly lurching toward the big dark barn where the mooing stops.

Today decides it. Three days ago, Monday, I told Marjorie I had another appointment, this one at a small plant in Harrisburg, Pennsylvania, that my appointment was for Friday morning, and that my plan was to drive to Albany Thursday, take a late afternoon flight to Harrisburg, stay over in a motel, taxi to the plant Friday morning, and then fly back to Albany Friday afternoon. Looking a bit worried, she said, "Would that mean we'd have to relocate? Move to Pennsylvania?"

"If that's the worst of our problems," I told her, "I'll be grateful."

After all this time, Marjorie still doesn't understand just how severe our problems are. Of course, I've done my best to hide the extent of the calamity from her, so I shouldn't blame Marjorie if I'm successful in keeping her more or less worry-free. Still, I do feel alone sometimes.

This has to work. I have to get out of this

morass, and *soon*. Which means I'd better be capable of murder.

The Luger went into my overnight bag, in the same plastic bag as my black shoes. The Luger had been my father's, his one souvenir from the war, a sidearm he'd taken from a dead German officer that either he or someone else had shot, earlier that day, from the other side of the hedgerow. My father had removed the clip full of bullets from the Luger and transported it in a sock, with the gun itself traveling in a small dirty pillowcase he'd taken from a half-wrecked house somewhere in muddy France.

My father never fired that gun, so far as I know. It was simply his trophy, his version of the scalp you take from your defeated enemy. Everybody shot at everybody and he was still standing at the end, so he took a gun from one of the fallen.

I too had never fired that gun, nor any other. It frightened me, in fact. For all I knew, if I were to pull the trigger with the clip in place in the butt, the thing would blow up in my hands. Still, it was a weapon, and the only one to which I had ready access. And there was certainly no record of its existence, at least not in America.

After my father died his old trunk was

moved from his spare room to my basement, the trunk containing his army uniform and folded duffel bag and a sheaf of the orders that had moved him from place to place, way back then, in the unimaginable time before I was born. A time I like to think of as simpler and cleaner than ours. A time in which you knew with clarity who your enemies were, and *they* were who you killed.

The Luger, in its pillowcase, was at the bottom of the trunk, beneath the musty-smelling olive-drab uniform, its clip lying beside it, no longer concealed in that long-ago sock. I found it down there, the day I made my decision, and brought it out, and carried gun and clip up to my "office," the small spare room we used to call the guest room before I was at home all the time and in need of an office. I closed the door, and sat at the small wood table I used as a desk — bought last year at a lawn sale offered by some particularly desperate householder about ten miles from here — and studied the gun, and it seemed to me clean and efficient-looking, without rust or obvious injury. The clip, this small sharp metal machine, felt surprisingly heavy. There was a slit up the rear of it, through which could be seen the bases of the eight bullets it contained, each with its little round blind eye.

Touch that eye with the firing mechanism of the gun, and the bullet leaps off on its only journey.

Could I just insert clip into gun, point, and pull the trigger? Was there risk involved? Afraid of the unknown, I drove to the nearest bookstore, one of the chains, in a mall, and found a little manual on handguns, and bought it (another expense!). This book suggested I oil various parts, and so I did, with Three-in-One oil. The book suggested I try dry-firing the gun — pull the trigger without the clip or any bullets in place — and I did, and the click sounded authoritative and efficient. It seemed that I did have a weapon.

The book also suggested that fifty-year-old bullets might not be entirely trustworthy, and told me how to empty and reload the clip, so I went to a sporting goods store across the state line in Massachusetts and with no trouble at all bought a little heavy box of 9-millimeter bullets and brought them home, where I thumbed eight of them into the clip, pressing each sleek torpedo down against the force of the spring, then sliding the clip up into the open butt of the gun: *click*.

Fifty years this tool had lain in darkness, under brown wool, wrapped in a French

13

pillowcase, waiting for its moment. Its moment is now.

I practiced with the Luger, driving away from home one sunny midweek day last month, April, driving thirty-some miles westward, across the state line into New York, until I found a deserted field next to a minor winding two-lane blacktop road. Hilly woods stretched upward, dark and tangled, beyond the field. There I parked the car on the weedy verge and walked out across the field with the gun a heavy weight in the inside pocket of my windbreaker.

When I was very close to the trees, I looked back and saw no one driving past on the road. So I took out the Luger and pointed it at a nearby tree and — moving quickly so as not to give myself time to be afraid — I squeezed the trigger the way the little book had told me, and it *shot*.

What an experience. Not expecting the recoil, or not remembering having read about the recoil, I wasn't prepared for how violently the Luger jumped upward and back, taking my hand with it, so that I almost hit myself in the face with the thing.

On the other hand, the noise wasn't as loud as I'd expected, not a great bang at all, but flatter, like an automobile tire blowout.

I did not, of course, hit the tree I was pointing at, but I did hit the tree next to it, making a tiny puff of dust as though the tree had exhaled. So the second time, now at least knowing the Luger was operational and wouldn't explode on me, I took more careful aim, with the standing stance the book had recommended, knees bent, body angled forward, both hands gripping the gun at arms' length as I sighted down the top of its barrel, and that time I hit *exactly* the spot on the tree I was aiming at.

Which was nice, but was somewhat spoiled by the fact that my concentration on aiming had made me again pay too little attention to recoil. This time, the Luger jumped out of my hands entirely and fell onto the ground. I retrieved it, wiped it carefully, and decided I had to conquer this matter of recoil if I were going to make use of the damn machine. For instance, what if I ever had to fire twice in a row? Not so good, if the gun is on the ground or, worse, up in my own face.

So once again I took the standing stance, this time aiming at a tree farther off. I clenched the grip of the Luger *hard*, and when I fired I let the recoil move my arm and then my whole body, so that I never really lost control of the gun. Its power trembled and shivered through my body, like a wave, and made me feel stronger. I liked it.

Of course, I was well aware that in giving all this attention to the physical details, I was not only providing proper weight to the preparation but was also avoiding, for as long as possible, any thought of the actual object of the exercise, the end result of all this groundwork. The death of a man. Though that would be faced soon enough. I knew it then, and I know it now.

Three shots; that was all. I drove back home, and cleaned the Luger, and oiled it again, and replaced the three missing bullets in the clip, and stored gun and clip separately in the bottom drawer of my filing cabinet, and didn't touch them again until I was ready to go out and see if I were actually capable of killing one Herbert Coleman Everly. Then I brought it out and put it into my overnight bag. And the other thing I packed, in addition to the usual clothing and toiletries, was Mr. Everly's resumé.

Herbert C. Everly
835 Churchwarden Lane
Fall City, CT 06198
(203) 240-3677

MAJOR WORK EXPERIENCE

Management

Responsible for inflow of pulp paper from Canadian subsidiary. Coordinated functions of polymer manufacturing arm, Oak Crest Paper Mills, with Laurentian Resources (Can). Maintained delivery schedules for finished product to aerospace, auto, lighting and other industries. Oversaw 82-person manufacturing department, coordinated with 23-person delivery department.

Administration and Personnel

Interviewed and hired for depart-

17

ment. Wrote employee analyses, recommended raises and bonuses, counseled employees where necessary.

Industrial
23 years' experience, paper mills, paper products sales, with two corporations.

EDUCATION   BBA, Housatonic Business College, 1969

REFERENCE   Human Resources Division
Kriegel-Ontario Paper Products
PO Box 9000
Don Mills, Ontario
Canada

There's an entire new occupation these days in our land, a growth industry of "specialists" whose function is to train the freshly unemployed in job-hunting, and specifically how to prepare that all-important resumé, how to put that best foot forward in the increasingly competitive struggle to get a new job, another job, the next job, a *job*.

HCE has taken such an expert's advice, his resumé reeks of it. For instance, no photo. For those applicants over forty, one popular theory holds that it is best not to include a photo of oneself, in fact not to include anything at all that points specifically to the applicant's age. HCE doesn't even give the years of his employment, limiting himself only to two unavoidable clues: "23 years" and his college graduation in 1969.

Also, HCE is, or at least he wants to appear to be, impersonal and efficient and businesslike. He says nothing of his marital status, or his children, or his outside interests (fishing, bowling, what you will). He limits himself to the issues at hand.

It is not the best resumé I've seen, but it's far from the worst; about middling, I would say. About good enough to get him an interview, if some paper manufacturer should be interested in hiring a manager-level employee with an intense history in the production and sales of specialized polymer paper products. Good enough to get him in the door, I would say. Which is why he must die.

The point in all this is to be absolutely anonymous. Never to be suspected, not for a second. That's why I'm being so very cautious, why in fact I'm driving a good twenty-five miles toward Albany, actually crossing into New York State, before turning south to make my way circuitously back into Connecticut.

Why? Why such extreme care? My gray Plymouth Voyager is not after all particularly noticeable. I'd say it looks rather like one vehicle in five on the road these days. But what if, by some remote chance, some friend of ours, some neighbor of ours, some parent of a schoolmate of Betsy or Bill, happened to see me, this morning, eastbound in Connecticut, when Marjorie has been told I'll be westbound in New York or even airborne by now, toward Pennsylvania? How would I explain it?

Marjorie would think at first I was having an affair. Although — except for that one time eleven years ago that she knows about — I have always been a faithful husband, and she knows that, too. But if she thought

I were seeing another woman, if she had any reason to question my movements and my explanations, wouldn't I eventually have to tell her the truth? If only to relieve her mind?

"I was off on a private mission," I would finally have to say, "to kill a man named Herbert Coleman Everly. For us, sweetheart."

But a secret shared is no longer a secret. And in any event, why burden Marjorie with these problems? There's nothing she can do beyond what she's doing, the little household economies she put into place the instant the word came I'd be laid off.

Yes, she did. She didn't even wait for my last day on the job, and she certainly wouldn't have waited until my severance pay was gone. The *instant* I came home with the notification (the slip was yellow, not pink) that I was to be part of the next reduction in force, Marjorie started the belt-tightening. She'd seen it happen to friends of ours, neighbors of ours, and she knew what to expect and how — within her limits — to deal with it.

The exercise class was cancelled, and so was the gardening workshop. She cut off HBO and Showtime, leaving only basic cable; antenna TV reception is virtually impossible in our hilly corner of Connecticut.

Lamb and fish left our table, replaced by chicken and pasta. Magazine subscriptions were not renewed. Shopping mall trips ceased, and so did those wandering slow journeys pushing a grocery cart through Stew Leonard's.

No, Marjorie is doing her job, I couldn't ask for more. So why ask her to become part of *this?* Particularly when I still can't be sure, after all the planning, all the preparation, that I can do it. Shoot this person. This other person.

I have to, that's all.

Having driven back into Connecticut, well south of our neighborhood, I stop at a convenience store/gas station to fill the tank and to take the Luger out of my suitcase, putting it under the raincoat artfully folded on the passenger seat beside me. There's no one around at the station except the Pakistani nestled behind the counter inside, surrounded by girly magazines and candy, and for one giddy second I see *this* as the solution to my problem: banditry. Simply walk into the building there with the Luger in my hand and make the Pakistani give me the cash in his till, and then leave.

Why not? I could do that once or twice a week for the rest of my days — or at least until Social Security kicks in — and continue to pay the mortgage, continue to pay for Betsy and Bill's education, and even put lamb chops back on the dinner table. Just leave home from time to time, drive to some other neighborhood, and rob a convenience store. Now *that's* convenient.

I chuckle to myself as I walk into the station with the twenty-dollar bill in my hand and exchange it with the surly unshaven fellow in there for a one-dollar bill. The absurdity of the idea. Me, an armed robber. Killer is easier to imagine.

I continue to drive east and a bit south, Fall City being on the Connecticut River not far north of where that minor waterway enters Long Island Sound. My state road atlas has shown me that Churchwarden Lane is a winding black line that moves westward out of the town, away from the riverside. I can come to it, according to the map, from the north, on a back road called William Way, thus avoiding the town itself.

The houses in the hills northwest of Fall City are mostly large and subdued, light with dark shutters, very New England, on large parcels of well-treed land. Four-acre zoning is my guess. I wind slowly along the narrow road, seeing the affluent houses, none of the affluent people or their affluent children visible at the moment, but their signs are ev-

23

erywhere. Basketball hoops. Two or three cars in wide driveways. Swimming pools, not yet uncovered for the summer. Gazebos, woods walks, lovingly reconstructed stone walls. Extensive gardens. Here and there a tennis court.

I wonder, as I drive along, how many of these people are going through what I'm going through these days. I wonder how many of them now realize just how thin the ground really is, beneath those close-cropped lawns. Miss a payday, and you'll feel that flutter of panic. Miss every payday, and see how *that* feels.

I realize I'm concentrating on all this, these houses, these signs of security and contentment, not only to distract myself from what I'm planning, but to make me firm in my intention. I'm *supposed* to have this life, just as much as any of these damn people on this damn winding road, with their names on their designer mailboxes and rustic wooden signs.

The Windhull's.
Cabett.
Marsdon.
The Elyot Family.

William Way does T at Churchwarden Lane, as the map shows. I turn left. The mailboxes are all on the left side of the road, and the first one I see is numbered 1117. The next three have names instead of numbers, and then there's 1112, so I know I'm moving in the right direction.

I'm also coming closer to the town. The road is mostly downhill now, the houses becoming less grand, the indicators now more middle class than upper middle. More appropriate for Herbert and me, after all. What neither of us wants to lose, because it's all we've got.

The nine hundreds, and at last the eight hundreds, and there's 835, identified only by number, HCE apparently being the modest sort, who doesn't flaunt his name at the brim of his property. The mailboxes are still all on the left, but Everly's house is surely that one on the right, with an arbor vitae hedge along the verge of the road, a blacktop driveway, a neat lawn with two graceful trees on it, and a modest white clapboard house surrounded by low evergreen plantings and set well back; probably late-nineteenth century, with the attached two-car garage and the enclosed wraparound porch added later.

A red Jeep is behind me. I continue on, not too fast, not too slow, and about a quarter mile farther down the road I see the mailman coming up. Mail woman, actually, in a small white station wagon plastered with

US MAIL decals. She sits in the middle of the front seat, so she can steer and drive with left hand and foot, and still lean over to reach out the right side window to the mailboxes along her route.

These days, I am almost always home when the mail is delivered, because these days I have a more than casual interest in the possibility of good news. Had there been good news in my mailbox last month or last week or even yesterday, I wouldn't be here now, on Churchwarden Lane, in pursuit of Herbert Coleman Everly.

Isn't he likely to be at home as well, watching out the front window, waiting for the mail? Not good news today, I'm afraid. Bad news today.

The reason I've given this full overnight trip to the Everly project is because I had no idea how long it would take me to find and identify him, what opportunities I might have to get at him, how much time would be spent tracking him, waiting for him, pursuing him, before the chance of action would present itself. But now, it seems to me, the likelihood is very good that I'll be able to deal with Everly almost at once.

That's good. The waiting, the tension, the second thoughts; I hadn't been looking forward to all that.

I turn in at a driveway to let the Jeep go by, then back out onto the road and head uphill once more, back the way I'd come. I pass the mailperson, and continue on. I pass 835, and continue on. I come to an intersection and turn right, and then make a U-turn, and come back to the Stop sign at Churchwarden. There I open my road atlas, lean it against the steering wheel, and consult it while watching for the appearance of the mailperson's white station wagon. There is almost no traffic on Churchwarden, and none on this side road.

The dirty white car; coming this way, with stops and starts. I close the road atlas and put it on the seat behind me, then make the left turn onto Churchwarden.

My heart is pounding. I feel rattled, as though all my nerves are unstrung. Simple movements like acceleration, braking, small adjustments of the steering wheel, are suddenly very hard to do. I keep overcompensating, I can't fine-tune my movements.

Ahead, a man crosses the road from right to left.

I'm panting, like a dog. The other symptoms I don't object to, I half expect them, but to pant? I'm disgusting myself. Animal behavior . . .

The man reaches the mailbox marked 835.

I tap the brakes. There's no traffic visible, either ahead or behind. I depress the button, and my driver's side window silently rolls down. I angle across the empty road, hearing the crunch of tire on roadway now that the window is open, feeling the cool spring air on my cheek and temple and hollowly inside my ear.

The man has withdrawn letters, bills, catalogues, magazines; the usual handful. As he's closing the front lid of the mailbox, he becomes aware of my approach and turns, eyebrows lifted in query.

I know him to be forty-nine years old, but to me he looks older. These past two years of unemployment, perhaps, have taken their toll. His mustache, too bushy for my taste, is pepper and salt with too much salt. His skin is pale and drab, without highlights, though he has a high forehead that should reflect the sky. His hair is black, receding, thin, straight, limp, gray at the sides. He wears glasses with dark rims — tortoise? — that look too large for his face. Or maybe his face is too small for the glasses. He wears one of his office shirts, a blue and white stripe, under a gray cardigan with the buttons open. His khaki pants are baggy, with grass stains, so he's perhaps a gardener, or helps his wife around the place, now that he has so much free time. The hands holding his mail are surprisingly thick, big-knuckled, as though he's a farmer and not a white-collar worker after all. Is this the wrong man?

I pull to a stop next to him, smiling out of the open window. I say, "Mr. Everly?"

"Yes?"

I want to be sure; this could be a brother, a cousin: "Herbert Everly?"

"Yes? I'm sorry, I —"

. . . don't know me, I think, finishing the sentence for him in my mind. No, you don't know me, and you never will. And I will never know you, either, because if I knew you I might not be able to kill you, and I'm sorry, but I really do need to kill you. I mean, one or the other of us must die, and I'm the one who thought of it first, so that leaves you.

I slide the Luger out from under the raincoat and extend it partway through the open window, saying, "You see this?"

He looks at it, expecting no doubt that I want to sell it to him or tell him I just found it and ask if it's his, or whatever happens to be the last thought that crosses his brain. He looks at it, and I squeeze the trigger, and the Luger jumps up in the window space and the left lens of his glasses shatters and his left eye becomes a mineshaft, running deep into the center of the earth.

He drops backward. Just down and back, no fuss, no lunging, just down and back. His mail frets away from him in the breeze.

I make a sound in the back of my throat like someone trying to pronounce that Vietnamese name. You know the one: Ng. I put the Luger on top of the raincoat and drive on down Churchwarden, my trembling finger on the window button until the window completely shuts. I turn left, and then left again, and two miles later I finally think to put the Luger under the raincoat.

My route is now planned out. A few miles farther on, I'll find Interstate 91, which I'll take north through Hartford and on up into Massachusetts at Springfield. A little north of that I'll turn west on the Massachusetts Turnpike, heading once again for New York State. Tonight I'll stay in an inexpensive motel near Albany, paying cash, and tomorrow afternoon I will return home jobless from my interview in Harrisburg, Pennsylvania.

Well. It seems I can do it.

2

I did it their way for eleven months. Or six-teen, if you count the final five months at the mill, after I got the yellow slip but before my job, as they said, ceased to go forward, the period of time when the counseling was done, and the training in resumé writing and the "consideration" of "options." This entire charade as though we were all, the company and its representatives and the specialists and the counselors and yours truly, as though we were all working together on some difficult but worthy task, the end result of which was supposed to be my personal contentment. Sense of fulfillment. Happiness.

Don't go away mad; just go away.

Earlier, for a year or two, there had been rumors of the downsizing to come, and in fact two smaller winnowings of staff had taken place, but they'd merely been the pre-liminaries, and everyone knew it. So, when the yellow slip was presented to me with my paycheck in October of 1995, I wasn't as shocked as I might have been, and I wasn't even at first all that unhappy. Everything seemed so businesslike, so well-thought-out, so professional, that it was more like being nurtured than weaned. But I was being weaned.

And I had plenty of company, God knows. The twenty-one hundred people at the Belial mill of Halcyon Mills was reduced to fifteen hundred seventy-five; a reduction of about one-fourth. My product line was dropped entirely, good old Machine No. 11 sold for scrap, the work absorbed by the company's Canadian affiliate. And the long lead-time — or so it seemed, then — of five months not only gave me plenty of time to look for another job but meant I would still be on salary through the Christmas season; nice of them.

The severance package was certainly generous enough, I suppose, within what is considered generous and rational at the moment. We discontinued employees received a lump sum equal to one month of salary for every two years of employment, at the present wage for that employment. In my case, since I'd been with the company twenty years, four as sales director and sixteen as product manager, I received ten months' pay, two of them at a somewhat lower rate. In addition, the company offered to maintain our medical insurance — we pay twenty percent of our medical costs, but no insurance premiums — for one year for every five years of employment, which means four years in my case. Full coverage for Marjorie and me, plus coverage for Billy for two and a half years until he's nineteen; Betsy's already nineteen, and so is uninsured, another worry. Then, five months from now, with Billy's nineteenth birthday, he's also without insurance.

But that isn't all we got when we were severed. There was also a single flat payment to cover vacation time, sick time and who knows what; it was figured out using a madly complex formula that I'm sure was scrupulously fair, and my check came to four thousand, seven hundred sixteen dollars and twenty-two cents. To tell the truth, if it had been nineteen cents, I doubt I would have known the difference.

I think most of us, when we get the chop, see our coming unemployment as merely an unexpected vacation, and assume we'll be back at work with some other company almost immediately. But that isn't how it happens now. The layoffs are too extensive, and are in every industry across the board, and the number of companies firing is much larger than the number of companies hiring. More and more of us are out here now, another thousand or so every day, and we're chasing fewer and fewer jobs.

You put together your resume, your education and job history, your life, on a page. You buy manila folders and a roll of first-class postage stamps. You carry your resumé down to the drugstore with the copying machine, and run off thirty copies at a nickel each. You start circling in red ink the likeliest help wanted ads in the *New York Times.*

You also subscribe on your own to your trade journals, the magazines your employer used to subscribe to for you. But the magazine subscriptions are not part of the severance package. *Pulp* and *The Paperman*; those are the journals of my trade, both of them monthly, both rather expensive. When they were free, I rarely read them, but now I study them cover to cover. After all, I have to keep up. I can't let the industry move on without me.

Both of these magazines carry help wanted ads, and both carry position wanted ads. In both of them, more positions than help are wanted.

At least I was never fool enough to spend money on a position wanted ad.

Over the years of my employment, I became quite specialized in one kind of paper and one method of manufacture. That was a subject I really knew — and still know — all about. But back at the beginning, twenty-

five years ago, when I started out as a salesman for Green Valley, before I switched over
to Halcyon, I was marketing all kinds of
industrial paper, and I learned them all. I
learned *paper;* the whole wild complex subject.

I know many people think paper is boring,
so I won't go on about it, but in fact paper
is far from boring. The way it's made, the
million uses . . .

We even eat paper, did you know that? A
special kind of paper-source cardboard is
used in many commercial ice creams, as a
binder.

The point is, I do know paper, and I could
take over almost any managerial job within
the paper industry, with only minimal training in a particular specialty. But there's so
many of us out here, the companies don't
feel the need to do even the slightest training.
They don't have to hire somebody who's
merely good, and then fine-tune him to their
requirements. They can find somebody who
already knows their precise function, was
trained in it by some other employer, and is
eager to come to work for *you,* at lower pay
and fewer benefits, just so it's a *job.*

I studied the ads, I sent out my resumés,
and most of the time nothing at all happened. No response. No answer to all the

questions you naturally ask: Is my salary request too high? Did I phrase something poorly in the resumé? Did I leave something out I should have mentioned?

Here's my own resumé. I decided to go for absolute simplicity and truth and clarity. No fudging my age, and no unnecessary crowing about my skills and training. But I included my college interests, because I think it's good to suggest you're well rounded. I think so. Who knows?

BURKE DEVORE
62 Pennery Woods Road
Fairbourne, CT 06668
(203) 567-9491

WORK HISTORY

1980–present   Product Manager, Halcyon Mills Responsible for manufacture and sales, polymer paper specialty products.

1975–1979   Sales director, Halcyon Mills Coordinated sales force in areas of specialized paper applications.

1971–1975   Salesman, Green Valley Paper & Pulp. Learned and described complete product line. Top salesman 19 of 45 months.

1969–1971   Bus driver, city of Hartford, CT.

| 1967–1969 | US Army, Information Specialist, learned typing, radio skills. |

EDUCATION
BA, Northwest Connecticut State University, 1967. American history major. Debate team. Track.

Occasionally, that resumé draws a response, and briefly my heart lifts. I get a phone call or a letter, usually a phone call, and an appointment is made. It's usually somewhere in the northeast, though once it was Wisconsin and once it was Kentucky. Wherever it is, you pay your own transportation costs. You want to get to that meeting.

You shower thoroughly, you dress carefully, you try to find the balance between self-assurance and easy geniality. You don't want to be full of yourself, but you don't want to be a toady either. You meet and chat and discuss. You might even tour the plant with the interviewer, showing your familiarity with the machine, the line, the work. Then you go home, and you never hear another word.

From time to time there would be a small news item in *Pulp* or *The Paperman*, when a mill announced hiring so-and-so for such and such a management position; with that usual smirking headshot of the lucky bastard. And I'd read it, and realize it was a position I'd interviewed for, and I couldn't help it, I'd have to study and study that guy's face, his eyes, his smile, the tie he wore. Why him? Why not me?

Sometimes it would be a woman's picture there, or a black man's picture, and I'd decide it was quota time, they were hiring politically and not commercially, and in a strange way that would make me feel better. Because it wasn't *my* failure then. If it was a woman or a black man they wanted, and they were just going through the motions with people like me, there was nothing I could do about it, was there? No blame, then.

But other times I did feel the blame. Why him, why that guy with the sloppy grin or the huge ears or the rotten haircut? Why not me? What did he do or say? What was on his resumé, that wasn't on mine?

That was what started me, that was the first question. What do they have on those resumés? What edge do they have? That's what led me to take out my ad.

3

Yesterday I killed Herbert Coleman Everly, and today I come home from my interview in Harrisburg, Pennsylvania, and when I walk into my house at four in the afternoon Marjorie is waiting for me in the living room. She's pretending to read a novel — she borrows novels from the library, now that we have fewer magazines and less television — but she's really waiting for me. It's true she doesn't know the full extent of our trouble, but she does know there's trouble, and she realizes I'm worried.

Before she can ask, I shake my head. "Not a chance," I say.

"Burke?" She gets to her feet, dropping the novel behind her in the chair. "You can't be sure," she says, to encourage me.

"Oh, yes, I can," I say, and shrug. I don't like lying to Marjorie, but there's no other choice. "I'm getting to know the interviewers by now," I tell her. "This one just didn't like me."

"Oh, Burke." She puts her arms around me, and we kiss. I feel a certain stirring, but it doesn't last, it's like an underwater

41

echo. Not a submarine, but a submarine's refraction.

I said, "Any mail?" Thinking of Everly.

"Nothing . . . nothing that mattered," she says.

"Well."

There are a lot of men now, in my position, who take out their frustrations on their families, particularly on their wives. A lot of wife-beating going on these days, among the middle-class unemployed. I admit I've felt that nasty urge myself, the urge to destroy, to release the frustration by just lashing out at the nearest target.

But I love Marjorie, and she loves me, and we've always had a good marriage, so why should I let this external thing tear us apart? If I'm going to lash out, if I'm going to destroy, I should make my violence more productive than that. And I will.

In doing what I did yesterday, apart from any other benefits to be derived (I hope, in time), I made it even more certain that I would never attack my girl. Never.

"Well," I say again, and we share a companionable and rueful smile, and I carry my suitcase away to the bedroom, as Marjorie returns to her novel.

Knowing she'll stay put in the living room with her book, I carry the Luger and Everly's resumé to my office and stow them in my filing cabinet. Then I go back to the bedroom, unpack, strip and take a long shower, my second of the day. In the shower, I permit myself at last to think about Herbert Everly.

A man, a decent man, a nice man, rather like me. Except he's unlikely to have killed anyone. I feel terrible about him, and about his family. I had trouble sleeping last night, I was racked with guilt much of the day, I thought seriously about giving the whole thing up, abandoning the entire project with it barely begun.

But what choice do I have? I stand in the hot water, clean and cleaner, and go over it all again in my mind. The equation is hard and real and ruthless. We're running out of money, Marjorie and I and the kids, and we're running out of time. I have to be employed, that's all. I'm no self-starter, I'm not going to invent a new widget, I'm not going to found my own paper mill on a shoestring. I need a job.

There are too many of us out here, and I have to face the fact that I am never going to be anybody's first choice. If it were just the job, just the knowledge and experience, just the capacity and the expertise, just the willingness and the proficiency, no problem.

43

But there are too many of us going after too few jobs, and there are other guys out there just as experienced and willing and capable as I am, and then it comes down to the nuances, the ineffables.

Amiability. Sound of voice. Smile. Whether or not you and your interviewer are fans of the same sport. What he thinks of your choice of necktie.

There is always always *always* going to be somebody just that tiny bit closer to the ideal than I am. In this job market, they don't have to take second best, and I have to either accept that fact or I'm going to be very unhappy for a very long time, and drag my family down with me. So I have to accept it, and I have to learn to work within it.

I finish my shower, and dress, and go into my office. I look at my list, and I think it would probably be best not to kill two people in the same state within just a few days of each other. I don't want the authorities to start looking for patterns.

On the other hand, I don't have much time. I've started the operation now, and I have to move briskly to the end of it, before something happens to spoil it all.

Here's one, in Massachusetts. Next Monday, I'll drive north.

4

Technically the computer belongs to the whole family, but it's really Billy's, and a year ago it moved into his room in acknowledgment of that truth. I'd made it a gift to the family at Christmas, 1994, the year before I was downsized, when we were still financially okay. The money was going out, in mortgage and taxes and schooling and food and gasoline and clothing, plus all of those things we hardly thought about but no longer spend money on, like rental tapes of movies, but the money was also coming in, adequately to cover expenses, the ebb and flow nicely attuned, like the inhale and exhale of a healthy body. So buying a computer for the family was extravagant, but not *that* extravagant.

Charles Dickens said it, in *David Copperfield*: "Annual income twenty pounds, annual expenditure nineteen nineteen six, result happiness. Annual income twenty pounds, annual expenditure twenty pounds ought and six, result misery." He didn't say what the result was when you dropped annual income to zero, but he didn't have to.

The point is, the computer entered our

lives when we thought we could afford our lives, and is still with us, in Billy's room, on the wheeled metal table purchased for it at the same time. His room is small, and crammed chock-a-block, as teenage boys' rooms tend to be, but oddly enough it's neater now that the computer and its table have been inserted there. Or maybe he just hasn't been able to buy so many things recently, hasn't been able to add to the pile of his possessions.

Well. When all this began, in February, almost three months ago, my second step, even before I had any idea what the plan was or that there would be a plan, was to go into Billy's room and sit down in front of the family computer and, from the wealth of available typefaces and sizes, create letterhead stationery. (My first step had been to take a post office box in a town twenty-some miles from home.)

B. D. INDUSTRIAL PAPERS
P.O. BOX 2900
WILDBURY, CT 06899

The post office box was actually 29, but I added the zeroes to make both the local post office and, by extension, B. D. Industrial Papers, seem more imposing. I made a joke of it with the clerk in the post office, who found the idea amusing and said she'd have no trouble putting 2900 mail into box 29, since in fact there were only sixty-eight boxes in the entire branch.

My next step was to write my ad, basing it on the ads I'd been circling in the help wanted sections for over a year:

MANUFACTURING
LINE MANAGER

Northeast paper mill w/specialty in polymers, capacitor tissue & film require individual w/strong specialty paper bkgrnd to head new product line mnfctring on rebuilt electrolytic capacitor paper machine. Minimum 5 yrs mill exp. Competitive salary, benefits. Send resume & salary history to Box 2900, Wildbury, CT 06899

Then I phoned the classified ad department of *The Paperman*, which it seemed to me usually carried more such advertising than *Pulp*, and arranged for them to run my ad, which would cost forty-five dollars to appear in three consecutive monthly issues. The woman I spoke to said there would be no problem if I paid with a money order rather than a company check, after I explained we were a small mill with little experience of hiring outside our own geographic area and would be paying for this ad from petty cash.

Then I went back to the Wildbury post office and bought the money order and signed it Benj Dockery III, with a very sloppy handwriting unlike my own. The copy machine at the drugstore gave me fine letterhead stationery from the original I'd put together at the computer, and I used it to send the wording of the ad plus the money order to *The Paperman*. Benj Dockery III signed the letter as well.

The ad ran first in the March issue, out the last week in February, and by the first Monday in March, when I drove up to check, box 2900 had received ninety-seven replies. "Those zeroes sure attract a lot of mail!" the postal clerk said, and we laughed about it together, and I explained that I was trying to start up a trade journal about trade journals. This was the response to an ad I'd run in selected magazines.

(I didn't want anyone to suspect I might be engaged in some sort of mail fraud, and start an inspector after me. What I was doing was probably not illegal, but it could be extremely embarrassing, and harmful to my employment chances, if it got out.)

"Well, I wish you luck with it," she said, and I thanked her, and she said, "More and more people are becoming their own boss these days, have you noticed?" and I agreed.

That first flush of mail soon dropped off to a steady trickle, kicking up again in the few days after each issue of *The Paperman* was published. The May issue, the last one with my ad, is still current, and I've had two hundred thirty-one responses so far. I'm guessing there'll be another ten to fifteen, and that will be the end of it.

It was fascinating to study those resumés, to see how much fear was in them, and how much gallantry, and how much grim determination. And also how much cocksure bloated self-important ignorance; *those* people are not competition, not for anybody, not until they've been roughened up by life a bit more.

Back in the transition period at Halcyon, when part of my workday was to sit through ongoing training in how to be unemployed, one of our advisors, a stern but hearty woman whose job it was to give us pep talks laced with harsh reality, told us a story, which she swore was true. "Some years ago," she said, "there was a downturn in the aerospace industry, and a lot of bright engineers found themselves unemployed. A group of five of them in Seattle decided to come up with some innovation of their own, something marketable, and after a lot of brainstorming and memos they did create a new variant on a kind of game, something that had real potential. But the idea needed seed money, and they didn't have any. Already in Seattle they'd learned that, when everybody is trying to sell the second car, nobody wants to buy one. They tried every contact they could think of, relatives, friends, former co-workers, and finally they were put together with a group of venture capitalists based in Germany. These financiers liked the engineers' idea, and were very close to agreement on funding them. All that was left was a face-to-face meeting. The financiers, three of them, flew from Munich to New York, and the engineers flew from Seattle to New York, and they met in a hotel suite there, where everyone got along very well. It looked as though the engineers were going to get the money and start their company and be saved. And then one of the financiers said, 'Let me just get the schedule clear. When we give you this money, what are you going to do to begin with?' And one of the engineers said, 'Well, the *first* thing we're going to do is pay our back salary.' And that was the end of it. The engineers went back to Seattle empty-handed, as well as empty-headed. Because," this counselor told us, "they didn't know the one thing you have to know if you're going to survive and prosper. And that one thing is: Nobody invited you. Nobody owes you a thing. A job and a salary and a nice middle-class life are not a *right,* they're a prize, and you have to fight for them. You have to keep reminding yourself, 'They don't need me, I need them.' You have no demands. You have your skills, and you have your willingness to work, and you have the brains and the talents and the personality God gave you, and it's up to *you* to make it happen."

I have taken that message to heart, perhaps more than she intended. And I have seen the resumés written by the people who did not have the benefit of her breed of advice, the people who still think like that benighted engineer: The world owes me a salary.

Maybe a quarter of the resumés stink of that self-importance, that aggrieved sense that things *ought* to work out right. But the problem with most of the resumés is a simpler one that that; their aim is wrong.

I wrote an ad that *I* could respond to, that was absolutely appropriate to my experience, without being overly specific and narrow. There is such desperation out there, however, that people don't limit themselves to the job openings where they might stand some chance. Clearly, they're sending out the resumés wholesale, in hopes that lightning will strike. And maybe sometimes it does.

But not in the paper business. Not in the specialized kind of industrial use of paper in which *I'm* the expert. These people are amateurs, when it comes to my field, and they don't worry me.

But some of the others do. People whose qualifications are very like mine, perhaps even a touch better than mine. People with a background like mine, but an education that looks in the resumé just a little more distinguished. The people that I would be second best to, if my ad had been real and I'd sent my own resumé in response.

People like Edward George Ricks.

TO WHOM IT MAY CONCERN

My name is Edward G. Ricks. I was born in Bridgeport, Conn., on April 17, 1946. I was educated in Bridgeport schools and took a degree in Chemical Engineering at Henley Technical College, Broome, Conn., in 1967.

In my Navy service — 1968 to 1971 — I performed as a printing technician on the fleet aircraft carrier *Wilkes-Barre*, where I was responsible for putting out the ship's daily newspaper as well as producing all orders and other printed material on the ship, and where I first combined my chemical background with an interest in specialized forms of paper.

Subsequent to the Navy, I was hired by Northern Pine Pulp Mills, where I worked in product development from 1971 until 1978. When Northern Pine merged with Graylock Paper, I was promoted to management, where I held responsibility for a number of product lines.

From 1991 until spring of 1996, I was in charge of the polymer paper film product line at Graylock, where the customers were almost entirely defense contractors. With the recent military cutbacks, Graylock dropped that product line.

I am now at liberty to present my experience and expertise to another forward-looking company in the specialized paper industry. I have been based in Massachusetts since 1978, but have no objection to relocation. I am married, and my three daughters are at this writing (1997) all at university.

Edward G. Ricks
7911 Berkshire Way,
Longholme, MA 05889
413 555-2699

5

I would hire him, before I hired me. That degree in chemical engineering is a real bone in my throat.

And the self-assurance of the man. *And* he was twenty-five years with the same employer, so he must be a good and faithful employee (just as they, of course, are a bad and faithless employer, which doesn't matter).

The form of his resumé is the only thing against him, and it isn't enough. That to-whom-it-may-concern business is just too artificial, and so's the restrained chattiness. The pomposity grates, his being "at liberty to present" himself, and having three daughters "at university," as though they're all at Oxford and not some community college. The man is undoubtedly a prig and a bore, but he's perfect for any job that I would be very good for, and because of that I hate him.

Monday, May 12th. Over breakfast I tell Marjorie I'll be doing library research today, a thing I actually do spend time at occasionally, searching through recent magazines and newspapers for leads to jobs that might be opening up but that aren't yet in the help wanted columns.

Mondays and Wednesdays are when Marjorie has one of her two part-time jobs. We sold the Honda Civic last year, so I'll have to drive her to Dr. Carney's office and then pick her up again at the end of the day. She is our dentist's receptionist now, two days a week, and is paid a hundred dollars a week off the books. On Saturday afternoons she's cashier at the New Variety, our local movie house, her other part-time job, where she's paid minimum wage on the books, taxes are deducted, and she brings home nothing. But she feels better getting out of the house, doing something, and the perk is that we get to go to the movies for free.

Today, though, is Dr. Carney. I drive Marjorie to the mall where his office is located, and leave her there at ten. Now I have eight hours to drive to Massachusetts, see what the situation is with EGR, and get back to the mall to pick up Marjorie at six.

But first I have to return to the house, since I didn't dare carry the Luger with me while Marjorie was in the car. At home, I put the gun in a plastic bag from the drugstore, carry it out to the car, and put it on the passenger seat beside me. Then I drive north.

It's forty-five minutes northbound, up into Massachusetts, then a right turn at Great Barrington, and another thirty minute drive to Longholme. Along the way, I keep remembering last week's event with Everly, which now seems to me about as clean and perfect as such an experience could ever be. Will I be that lucky again today? Can I merely once again follow the mail carrier, and have EGR delivered into my lap?

(I have no idea, of course, what happened after I left Everly last week, and I think it would be dangerous to try to find out. The shooting was not important enough to be written up in the *New York Times*, and the only other paper I normally read, the *Journal*, our local weekly, does not extend its reach as far as Fall City. Our cable service doesn't carry local channels, but I doubt Everly made the TV news.)

My Massachusetts road atlas shows Longholme about twenty miles west of Springfield and north of the Massachusetts Turnpike. Berkshire Way is another wiggly black line — suggesting hills again — extending out of the town proper, this time northward. It's a long sweep around for me to avoid the town and stay on country roads, but I think it's worth the time and trouble. Still, it's almost twelve o'clock when I finally make the turn onto Berkshire Way.

This is decidedly more rural, with a few actual farms along the way. The private homes are mostly large but unpretentious, as though the residents don't feel they have anything to prove to their neighbors. The countryside is more open, with cleared fields and wide valleys rather than the tumbled woodsiness of Connecticut. It doesn't feel suburban, probably because it's just a little too far from New York and Boston and Albany and every other northeastern urban center.

7911 Berkshire Way turns out to be a modern house on a traditional plan, on the right side of the road as I come along. Probably built after World War II, when the boys came home to create us baby boomers, so that fifty years later we could all be shunted off the social order.

I'm a bit surprised at the house and disappointed with EGR, with his daughters "at university," which does not imply yellow aluminum siding and green fake shutters and a TV satellite dish as prominent as an erection right next to the house. There are scrubby plantings around the base of the building and a few small specimen fruit trees haphazardly placed, but nothing has been planted along the line between scraggly

58

lawn and roadside.

The wide door of the two-car garage is lifted open as I drive by, and there are no cars in there. Nobody home. Damn.

I drive on. A quarter mile farther, a convent school provides a handy parking area in which to turn around. I drive back, looking for an inconspicuous place to park. Unlike the last time, the mailbox is on the same side of the road as the house, so I'll have less warning when EGR comes out to get his mail. If he's home. If he comes out to get his mail. If the mail hasn't already been delivered.

Next beyond the Ricks house, back the way I'm now going, is an empty field, strewn with shrubs and low pines, with a For Sale sign — white letters on red, phone number added in black Magic Marker — on a post near the road. Next beyond that is another house similar to EGR's, built around the same time, probably by the same builder, onto which a few additional rooms were pasted over the years. Stucco was applied at some point, instead of aluminum, and painted the color of squash. A large metal For Sale sign from a local real estate agent stands on the unmowed lawn, and the place has an abandoned air to it, as though the family has gone away to live somewhere smaller, less expensive, closer to the Welfare office.

I turn at this decamped home, enter the driveway, stop, and back turning out of it, so that I'm parked off the road in front of the house, with a clear view beyond the offered field to the front of EGR's place. I've been careful not to block the view of the For Sale sign with my Voyager, because I want the occasional passerby to assume I'm waiting for the agent.

I'm getting hungry, but I don't want to give up my vigil, lose my opportunity to finish the day's work. In my mind's eye, a car pulls in at the driveway over there, a man gets out of it, he crosses to the mailbox, I drive forward, and it's all over.

Does he get his mail while still in his car? And then does he drive into the garage before getting out of the car? And does he close the garage door immediately? And do I follow him, the Luger in my hand, or under my jacket?

I can only guess at any of these things. I can only wait to see what happens, and see what I do in response.

Three hours go by, and nothing happens, and I'm getting very hungry indeed. I may be out of work and desperate, but I'm still not used to missing meals. Still, the thought remains, that if I leave my post, EGR will appear immediately, and will be safely inside his house before I return.

Twenty past three. A Windstar minivan, gray, very like my Voyager, drives slowly past me, and what attracts my attention is that the heavyset middle-aged woman at the wheel of it is glaring at me. Glaring. I blink at her, not understanding her hostility. She drives on by, and then she stops at that mailbox just up ahead, in front of EGR's place. Would this be Mrs. Ricks?

Apparently. I see her slide over to the right side of the Windstar, open the mailbox, pull out the mail. Then she drives on into the garage, and the door slides down.

So. It could be that she wasn't exactly showing hostility, after all, but merely close observation. If she did make the assumption I'm hoping for, that I'm a prospective buyer waiting for the Realtor, maybe she was just frowning at me, studying me, as a potential neighbor.

But the question is, where's her husband? She closed the garage door, so she's not expecting him to drive in any time soon. Was he at home all this time? Maybe he's sick today, got a spring cold.

Or maybe he's out on a job interview, won't be back for a couple of days.

It's getting late. I'm very hungry, and I also have to get back to the mall to pick up Marjorie at six. I can see now that nothing is going to happen here today. A wasted day.

I can't have too many wasted days. This whole operation has to be done as quickly and cleanly as possible, without sloppiness or unnecessary risk, to get it over with before the equations change. Still, nothing is going to happen here today.

Now what? Tomorrow, oddly enough, I have a job interview of my own, in Albany, with a man from a package and label manufacturer, an outfit that specializes in the labels that wrap around tin cans. I don't have much hope, since labels are really some distance out of my line, and surely there are label experts who've been downsized in the last few years, but you never know. Lightning might strike.

Well, if it does, I won't be back here on Berkshire Way any more, will I? And EGR will never know what a lucky man he is.

But if lightning doesn't strike, what then? I can't come back up here on Wednesday, that's Marjorie's other day with Dr. Carney, and the next time I come here I'd better leave home a lot earlier. Clearly the mail had already been delivered when I first got here today.

Thursday, then. I'll be back here Thursday. Unless, of course, by Thursday I'm becoming an expert in tin can labels.

6

When I first got my hands on that great pile of resumés, with more coming in, and still more, what I felt, I now realize, looking back on it, was a kind of gleeful power. I'd put something over on these people, the competition, I'd learned their secrets and they didn't even know I was there, in the darkness, in the shadows, in the corner, in the box number, watching them. I was like a miser with his gold, hunched over the file folders of resumés in my office, secret even from Marjorie, no one knowing the power I had, no one knowing the coup I'd accomplished.

But that first euphoria had to wear off, and it did, leaving only questions in its wake. What would I *do* with these things? How, after all, could the resumés help me? Or would they merely serve to discourage me, as when I would look at this sheet or that sheet and see someone just slightly better-looking for the job than I am. *Look* at all these people out here, all of them worthy, all of them accomplished, all of them willing. Look how many there are, and look how few the berths they're all steering toward.

So I went from secret pleasure at my cleverness in amassing this hoard of resumés to just as secret depression. I might have given up then, given up everything — this is before my current plan, of course — I might have given up all hope of finding a new job and maintaining my claw-hold on my life, this life, I might have given in completely to despair, if only there had been any other choice.

But there wasn't. There wasn't, and there isn't. I kept going then, only because there was nothing else to do. And who knows how many of these people in these resumés are in the same state? Going forward with no hope, but only because there's nothing else to do. We're like sharks, in that way; if we don't keep swimming, we'll merely sink.

Suicide is not an option, I wouldn't consider it for a second, though I know some of these people have considered it and some of them will do it. (This world we live in began fifteen years ago, when the air traffic controllers were all given the chop, and suicide ran briskly through that group, probably because they felt more alone than we do now.) But I don't want to kill myself, I don't want to *stop*. I want to go on, even when there's no way to go on. That's the point.

In any event, I was feeling just about as

low as I've ever felt, I was having real difficulty just to rouse my energy enough to send out my own resumés. But just then an article in *Pulp* caught my eye and got my brain working once more.

It was one of those inside-a-corner-of-our-fascinating-industry pieces, the sort that used to make my eyes glaze over when I was working for Halcyon, but which now I read slowly and carefully, even underlining certain trenchant sentences, because I need to keep up with the industry. Don't ever permit yourself to become yesterday's man, that's one of the basic rules.

Well, this particular piece in *Pulp* was about a new process at a plant over in New York State, at a town called Arcadia. The company, Arcadia Processing, was a wholly owned subsidiary of one of the biggest paper companies in America, one of the outfits that make their millions in toilet paper and tissues. But Arcadia was a success story in itself, so the owners were leaving it alone.

For much of this century, Arcadia had specialized in turning out cigarette paper made from tobacco leavings, the shreds and stems that are left over after the manufacture of cigarettes. Early in the twentieth century, a couple of different processes were developed to make paper out of that stuff — it's hard to do, because tobacco fibers are so short — and this tobacco-paper was initially used to strengthen the end of cigars, to make them chewable. Later, a variant on that paper was bleached and aerated so it could be used as the paper around ordinary cigarettes, and this is the product Arcadia produced.

A few years ago, it seems, Arcadia's management came to the conclusion it was no longer a good idea to be tied so closely to the fortunes of the tobacco industry, and so they looked for another area in which to diversify. The area they found, I read to my astonishment, was just the polymer paper specialty that I'd been working on the last sixteen years!

The article writer went on to say that, rather than compete with mills that had already been in that business, and feeling they had a superior product with a new manufacturing method (wrong about that; it was precisely the system we'd installed at Halcyon back in '91), they'd gone offshore for their customers. Aided by NAFTA, they'd found Mexican manufacturers who were delighted by their products and could afford to buy them. With Mexican customers already in hand, they'd spread their sales force farther south, and now had customers all through South America as well.

It was a true success story, one of the few around these days, and there was something very bittersweet about reading it. But one part of the piece really snagged my attention, and that was the brief description of and interview with one Upton Fallon, production line manager. Fallon, who was known by his middle name, Ralph, answered questions from the writer about the production process and about his own background; he'd been there all along, starting almost thirty years ago on the tobacco-paper machine, apparently straight from high school.

Upton "Ralph" Fallon had my job. I read the piece, and I read it again, and there was no doubt in my mind. He had my job, and in a fair contest *I'd* get it, not him. Of course, there wasn't as much information about him in the article as there would be in his resumé — he didn't *need* a resumé, the bastard, he already had my job — but there was enough stated and implied so I could get a good solid reading on the guy, and I was better than him. I knew I was. It was obvious. And yet, he had my job.

I couldn't help it, I couldn't help day-dreaming about it. If he were to be fired, for getting drunk or having an adulterous affair with a girl on the shop floor, say. If he were to come down sick, with some wasting disease like multiple sclerosis, and have to leave the job. If he were to die . . .

Yes, why not? People die all the time. Automobile accidents, heart attacks, kerosene heater fires, strokes . . .

What if he were to die, then, or just become too sick to stay on the job? Wouldn't they be glad to see *me,* so much more qualified for exactly the same position?

I could kill him, if that's what it took.

I thought that, mostly as hyperbole, in the daydream. But then I thought it again, and I wondered if I meant it. I mean, really meant it. I knew how bad my situation was, I knew how unlikely things were to improve, I knew how surely things were going to get even more desperate, I knew how expensive Betsy was in college and Billy would be, graduating this year from high school. I knew what my expenses were, my outgo, and I knew my income had stopped, and now I saw the one man who stood between me and safety. Upton "Ralph" Fallon.

Couldn't I kill him? I mean, seriously. In self-defense, really, in defense of my family, my life, my mortgage, my future, myself, my *life.* That's self-defense. I don't know this man, he's nothing to me. He sounds like a jerk, to tell the truth, in this interview here. If the alternative is despair and defeat and grinding misery and growing horror for Marjorie and Betsy and Billy and me, why *shouldn't* I kill him, the son of a bitch? How could I *not* kill him, given what's at stake here?

Arcadia. Arcadia, New York. I looked it up in the road atlas, and it was so *close.* It was like an omen. Arcadia was probably no more than fifty miles from here, just across the state line, barely in New York at all, maybe ten miles in. *Commuting* distance, I wouldn't even have to relocate.

Pulp magazine and the road atlas open on my desk. Silence in the house, the kids at school and that being a day when Marjorie was at Dr. Carney's office. Daydreaming.

That's when I thought first of the Luger, remembered it at the bottom of my father's trunk. That's when I first imagined myself pointing that gun at a human being, pulling the trigger.

Could I do it? Could I kill a man? But people do that, too, every day, for far less. Why wouldn't I be able to, with the stakes so high? My *life;* the stakes don't get higher than that.

Daydream. I'd drive over to Arcadia, New York, the Luger beside me in the car. Find the mill, find Fallon — don't have his picture, not printed in *Pulp*, but that can be solved somehow, we're only daydreaming here — find him, and follow him, and wait for the opportunity, and *kill him*. And apply for his job.

Which is where the daydream broke down, and came crashing down at my feet. That's where I went again from pleasure to misery. Because I knew what would happen next, if reality were to follow my daydream this far, if Upton "Ralph" Fallon were actually gone from that job, through his own actions or mine.

Of course I'm better than he is, in any contest between us for that job it would be *my* job, no question. But the contest isn't between us, and never can be. The contest, once Fallon is out of the way, is between me and that stack of resumés over there.

Somebody else would get my job.

I went down through the stack again, winnowing them, picking out the ones I feared, and that first time I was so pessimistic that I pulled out over fifty resumés as being people with a better shot at that job than I had. Which was wrong, of course, overstating them and underestimating me, that was merely the despondency doing my thinking for me. But the problem was still overwhelming. And real.

I was so blue by then I couldn't stand to

be in the office any more. I left the room, and killed some time cleaning out some old trash in the garage — once we'd sold the Civic, the space it used to take up began immediately to fill with junk — and my mind kept circling back to Upton "Ralph" Fallon, fat and happy, smug and secure. In *my* job.

I couldn't sleep that night. I lay in bed, beside Marjorie, thinking, mourning, frustrated, miserable, and it wasn't till first light outlined the bedroom windows that I at last fell into fitful sleep, full of troubled dreams, nightmares out of Hieronymus Bosch. I'm glad I don't remember my dreams; their echoes are bad enough.

But I finally did fall away into that restless sleep, and when I rose to cold consciousness three hours later, I knew what to do.

7

Thursday. I'm on the road by eight-fifteen
A.M., telling Marjorie I have some follow-up
to do on Tuesday's job interview in Albany,
and that I might be late this evening, coming
home.

The interview. Well, of course I didn't get
that job, I won't be learning the intricacies
of tin can labels after all, so here I am once
again, on the way to Longholme.

I didn't get that job, and I didn't expect
to get it. Just another failed interview. But
this time, there was a bit more to it. This
was the first interview I've gone on since I've
added this second string to my bow, the plan
(if I can make it work, make the whole complicated thing work, and not lose my determination), and as a result of that, I guess, I
somehow saw Tuesday's interview differently from the ones before it. I saw it more
dispassionately, is what it was. I saw it from
outside.

And what I saw only increased my desperation. I saw that Burke Devore, *this* Burke
Devore, this man I've become in half a century of life, is not friendly.

I don't mean I'm unfriendly, I don't mean

I'm some snarling sort of misanthrope. I simply mean not friendly *enough*. Back in my young days, in school and then in the Army, I could always build up enough enthusiasm to be a part of the gang, part of the group, but it was never really natural to me. The four years I spent as a salesman, on the road for Green Valley, selling their industrial papers, I did learn how to be a salesman, grinning, cheery, shaking hands, slapping backs, making people feel I was glad to see them, but it was always hard.

Hard. I'm not a natural glad-hander, hail-fellow-well-met, I never was. Studiously, in those salesman days, I would collect new jokes and memorize them and retail them around to my contacts. Earnestly I would have a vodka or two with lunch, to loosen me up for my afternoon calls. I was drinking much too much in those days, and if I'd gone on being a salesman I'd probably be dead of cirrhosis by now.

That's what made the line so perfect for me, the product line, me the manager. Running that, in charge of that, I was expected to be amiable but a little aloof, friendly but always in command, and that suited me right down to the ground.

What I'm supposed to do now, I realized on Tuesday, is be a salesman once again.

The resumé merely gets me in the door, if it even does that much. My whole work history, my entire life till now, is simply the sales tool to get me in the door. And the interview is my sales pitch, and what I'm there to sell is me.

I'm not good enough at it. Whatever salesman skills I laboriously developed in the old days are gone now, atrophied. An ill-fitting suit, long ago given away.

Am I going to start memorizing stupid jokes again, telling them to the interviewers? Kidding with the secretaries? Giving people hearty compliments about their watch, their desk, their shoes? I just don't know how to get *back* to that person.

Those resumés in the filing cabinet in my office; a lot of *those* people are salesmen. You bet they are.

I'll do it once, when the time comes. I'll do it with the interviewer for Arcadia Processing, after the unfortunate demise of Upton "Ralph" Fallon. I'll tell that fellow jokes, you know I will. I'll praise his necktie, compliment his secretary and turn beautifully sentimental over the family photos on his desk. I'll *sell*, by God.

But not yet. That is then, and this is now, and now is the road to Longholme. I know that road better than I did on Monday, and traffic is light, so it's quite early, just quarter to ten, when I stop the Voyager in that same spot in front of the squash-colored stucco house for sale.

And the first thing I see is that the flag is up on EGR's mailbox, which means he has put letters in there to be picked up, which means the mail hasn't been delivered yet today. I didn't bother to drive past the house before coming to rest here, and from this angle I can't see whether the garage door is open or closed, but I do see the mailflag up, and I know it means the mail is yet to be delivered, so there's a chance, a hope, that today EGR himself will come out to get it. The Luger is on the seat beside me, under the folded raincoat, waiting. The both of us wait.

For twenty minutes, nothing happens. There's very little traffic along Berkshire Way, mostly delivery vans and pickup trucks. I see them out ahead, or in my rear-view mirror, and they pass, and they're gone.

And then all at once there's a vehicle braking to a stop right behind me, abruptly large in my mirror, gray, familiar. I stare at it, afraid, with that awful immediate certainty that I've been caught, disaster has struck, exposure, condemnation, Marjorie and the kids staring at me in shock — "We never knew you!" — and a woman in an open gray zippered jacket leaps out of that vehicle and runs toward me.

The woman is the one who glared at me Monday: Mrs. Ricks! What on earth is she doing? Is she a mind reader?

It's a cool day, cloudy, and the Voyager's windows are shut. The woman runs up next to me, yelling, gesticulating, hugely angry and upset about something. But what? I can hear her yelling, but I can't make out the words. I stare at her through the glass, afraid of her, afraid of the whole situation, afraid to open the window.

She shakes her fist at me. She screams in rage. She suddenly cuts away, and runs around the front of the van, and yanks open the passenger door, and thrusts her head in at me, blotchy red face, tear-streaked cheeks, and she yells, "Leave her alone!"

I gape at her. "What?"

"She's only eighteen! How can you take advan— Don't you have any *shame?*"

"I'm not —" She's mistaken me, she's got me mixed up with somebody, it's just wrong, but I'm too flustered to correct her: "I'm not, you've got the, this isn't —" Then what am I doing here, if not stalking her daughter?

"*Listen* to me!" she screams, drowning me out. "Don't you think I could talk to your *wife*, whatever Junie says? Don't you have any self-respect? Can't you, can't you, can't you just *leave her alone?*"

"I'm not the man you —"

"You're killing her father!"

Oh, God. Oh, let me out of this, let me away from here.

My silence is a mistake. She's going to reason with me now, she's going to convince this married middle-aged swine to stay away from her eighteen-year-old daughter. "There are doctors," she says, trying to be calm, supportive. "You could talk with —" And now she's going to sit beside me in the van, and she sweeps the raincoat off the seat, out of her way, and we both stare at the gun.

Now we both experience true horror. She stares at me, and in her eyes I see the entire tabloid scenario. The lust-crazed older lover is here to slaughter his nymphet's parents.

I lift a hand. "I —" But what can I say?

She *screams.* The sound caroms inside the car, and the force of it seems to drive her backward, out of the vehicle and away. She turns, and runs along the road, toward her house, screaming.

No no no no no. She's seen me, she knows my face, she saw the Luger, none of this is happening, none of this can happen, everything's destroyed if this happens. I grab the

Luger and jump out of the Voyager (at least, unlike her, I think to slam the door on my way), and I run after her.

I'm a sedentary man, I've been a manager for sixteen years, sitting at my desk, walking along the line, riding my car to and from work. Even more sedentary since I was chopped. I'm healthy enough, but I'm no athlete, and running uses me up right away. Long before I get to that yellow aluminum house, I'm gasping for breath.

But so is she. She's also out of shape, and she's trying to run and scream at the same time. *And* flail her arms. She had a good lead on me, but I'm catching up, I'm catching up, I'm not so far behind her when we veer to run angling across her unlovely lawn toward the front door of her house, and she's screaming, "Ed! Ed!" and before she gets to the house I catch up with her, and I hold the Luger directly behind her head, bobbing as we both run, and I fire once, and she drops straight down onto the lawn, like a bundle, like a duffel bag, and the momentum flings her jacket halfway up over her head, covering the hole the bullet made.

Exhausted, spent, I sink to one knee beside her, and look up to see the front door opening, the astonished face of what must be her husband, Ed, EGR, my EGR, his astonished face is in the doorway, staring out, and I raise the gun and shoot, and the bullet punches into the aluminum beside the doorframe with a muted twang.

He slams the door, already turning, running away into the house.

Reeling, almost fainting, I force myself to my feet, I lunge forward to the door, I yank the handle, but it's locked.

He'll be in there right now, dialing 911. Oh, God, this is terrible, this is a mess, this is a disaster, how did I ever think I could do these things, that poor woman, *she* wasn't supposed to —

I can't let this happen. He can't telephone, he can't, I won't permit it, I have to get to him, I just have to get to him.

The garage door is open. Around that way, through the house, find him, *find* him. I stagger like a drunk as I run along the front of the house and through the gaping open broad doorway. There, to my right, is the closed door to the house. *That* won't be locked. I hurry to it, the Luger dangling at the end of my right arm, and just as I reach the door it opens and *he runs out!*

What was he doing? What did he have in mind? Was he going to try to drive away from here, was he so rattled he never thought of the telephone? We stare at one another, and I shoot him in the face.

Much sloppier, this one, blood everywhere, face ruined, body a tangled unknotted mess on the garage floor, one arm flung backward through the open doorway into the house.

No one else at home? Daughters all at university? Or with their unacceptable lovers? How I *hate* them for making this confusion, driving that woman to mistake me for someone else, attack me, harangue me, discover the gun. Where's the neatness this time, the efficiency, the impersonality?

I'm shaking all over. I'm sweating, and I'm cold. I can barely hold on to the Luger, which I now put away in the inside pocket of my windbreaker, then trot along holding it in place with my left forearm.

I don't know if there's traffic, I don't know if a thousand people are watching me or no one. I only know there's the lawn, with that terrible dead sack on it, and there's the empty field, and there's the Plymouth Voyager.

I drive away, gripping the wheel hard because my hands are shaking. My whole body is shaking. I force myself to drive for ten minutes away from there, away from that neighborhood, staying within the speed limit, obeying all the traffic rules. Then at last I allow myself to pull off onto a dirt road and there, out of view, let the shaking have me. The shaking and the fear.

The sight of that woman's face. The memory of her running, and my hand holding up the gun, and then she falls. Her husband, goggle-eyed, made stupid by terror and grief.

This is horrible. Horrible. But what could I have done? From the instant she pulled away that raincoat, what could I have done differently?

What have I started here? What road am I on?

8

Once I knew what I had to do, after that sleepless and despairing night, I went back through the resumés three times more, and each time I was increasingly cold and critical and realistic. *This* person? Competition for *me?* Education excellent, work record outstanding, but not in my field. A real find for some employer, but not for Arcadia Processing. Not for *my* job.

And so gradually I whittled the people down to six. Six resumés from people who, because of their work history and their education and their geographical location, were my true competition. I had to count location because I knew most employers would. They don't like to pay moving expenses unless they absolutely cannot find a qualified individual who already lives within commuting distance. So the bright stars in Indiana and Tennessee I decided not to worry about. Their competition was closer to home.

I realized from the beginning the irony in what I planned to do. These people, these six management experts, Herbert Coleman Everly and Edward George Ricks and the others, were not my enemy. Even Upton

"Ralph" Fallon was not my enemy, I knew that. The enemy is the corporate bosses. The enemy is the stockholders.

These are all publicly held corporations, and it is the stockholders' drive for return on investment that pushes every one of them. Not the product, not the expertise, certainly not the reputation of the company. The stockholders care about nothing but return on investment, and that leads to their supporting executives who are formed in their image, men (and women, too, lately) who run companies they care nothing about, lead work forces whose human reality never enters their minds, make decisions not on the basis of what's good for the company or the staff or the product or (hah!) the customer, or even the greater good of the society, but only on the basis of stockholders' return on investment.

Democracy at its most base, supporting leaders only in return for their sating of greed. The ever-present nipple. That's why healthy companies, firmly in the black, lush in dividends to stockholders, nevertheless lay off workers in their thousands; to squeeze out just a little more, look just a little better for that thousand-mouthed beast out there that keeps the executives in power, with their million-dollar, ten-million-dollar, twenty-million-dollar compensation package.

Oh, I knew all that when I started, I knew who the enemy was. But what good does that do me? If I were to kill a thousand stockholders and get away with it clean, what would I gain? What's in it for me? If I were to kill seven chief executives, each of whom had ordered the firing of at least two thousand good workers in healthy industries, what would *I* get out of it?

Nothing.

What it comes down to is, the CEOs, and the stockholders who put them there, are the enemy, but they are not the problem. They are society's problem, but they are not my personal problem.

These six resumés. These are my personal problem.

9

The murders of the Rickses make the TV news, of course, being so much more dramatic than the death of Herbert Everly. Nine hours after I killed them, I sit in my living room with Marjorie, and we watch my crimes described by a solemnly excited blonde woman in a good green suit. Betsy and Billy are not with us. They never watch the news, not being interested in anything much beyond their immediate lives. At this moment, before dinner, I believe Betsy is on the phone, as she often is, and Billy is on the computer, as *he* usually is, while Marjorie and I watch my murders on the news, and Marjorie says, "Oh, Burke, that's horrible."

"Horrible," I agree.

It's strange, but someway or other I don't entirely recognize my actions from the blonde woman's recountal. The facts are essentially right; I did chase the wife across the lawn and shoot her there, and I did intercept the husband in the garage and shoot him there, and I did leave without a trace, without witnesses, without clues in my wake.

But somehow the tone is all wrong, the

sense of it, the feeling of it. These words she uses — "brutal" "savage" "cold-hearted" — give completely the wrong impression. They leave out the error that caused it all. They leave out the panic and confusion. They leave out the trembling, the sweating, the icy fear.

But there's more to the story, all at once. They have a suspect! The police are questioning him, even now, at this very minute.

He's seen being led from an office building on a community college campus. He's a tweedy slope-shouldered middle-aged man with a gray widow's peak and large bifocals. He isn't handcuffed, but he's closely surrounded by beefy state troopers, one of whom puts his hand atop the suspect's head as he's urged into the backseat of a white state police car.

His name is Lewis Ringer, and he's a professor of literature at that community college. He is also the unacceptable lover of June Ricks, eighteen-year-old youngest child of the murdered couple. He is the man her mother thought I was, and I look more closely at that quick glimpse of him from building to police car, the second and third times they show it. I too wear large bifocals, and I too have a gray widow's peak, but other than that I don't see the similarity at all. Mrs. Ricks was a very stupid woman. I try not to think that she got what she deserved, but that thought does hover around the boundaries of my brain.

We also see the daughter, and what a piece of work *she* is. Not at all like our Betsy. June — or Junie, as her mother had called her when yelling mistakenly at me — is a sly, sullen, secretive girl, pretty in a foxlike way, full of sidelong glances and flickering smiles. Clearly, she's delighted to have caused such emotional upheaval in a man as to lead him to murder her parents, though just as clearly she can't admit to either the delight or the belief that in fact Ringer did it. The camera leaves her as fast as it decently can.

And then we see Lew Ringer's wife, tear-stained and stunned, briefly in the doorway of a modest house on a modest town street. She stares at the media on her lawn, and slams the door, and that's the end of the item. We move on to northern Ireland, where the murders are much more frequent, with far less reason.

After the news, and before dinner, while Marjorie goes to the kitchen, I retire as usual to my office. It is time to decide which of my resumés is next. I have four to go, and then Mr. Fallon.

But somehow I can't think about any of

that. I can't even open the file drawer and take out the folder with those resumés. There's a great discouragement holding me down.

I try to talk myself out of this inertia. I tell myself I've gotten away with everything so far, I'm not suspected by anybody, or even thought about. I tell myself this is a good beginning, even if the second expedition was so much sloppier and more emotionally exhausting than the first. But why couldn't it turn out at the end that that one had been the worst of them, and that from then on they'd all been easy, as easy as Everly?

But it doesn't work. I am discouraged, and nothing will bring me out of it. I can't stop now, I know that, or everything till this point will have been in vain. I *have* to go on, now that I've come this far. And I have to do it all soon, and I remind myself *why* I have to do it all soon.

The fact is, these vast waves of dismissal move through industries, one after another. A swath is cut through the auto industry, and then everything is calm there for a while. A bloodletting among the phone companies is followed by peace. The computer industry will sacrifice its thousands, and then rest.

Well, the paper industry had its most recent downsizing two years ago, when I got the chop. All of these resumés in my files come from people laid off at just around the same time, in a period from six or seven months before me to a period six or seven months after me. This is the group, this is the labor pool, these are the people I have to concern myself with.

But the reductions are cyclical, and eventually return. If I don't move ahead briskly, rid myself of the competition, rid myself of Fallon, and get established in that job, I may suddenly find a whole new wave of resumés flooding the mails. And there they'll be, a whole new batch of people after my job, and some of *them* will be real competition, too. Fresh competition.

Six is a lot, but six I think I can handle. Seven, if you count Fallon. But a dozen? Two dozen? Impossible.

No, I have to do it *now*, move forward, choose the next one, go out there, *get* him, keep the momentum alive.

And here's another thought. What if Fallon dies ahead of time, without my help, before I'm ready? If that happens, and one of these four still on my list gets that job, what then?

And yet, I remain immobile. Discouraged. I just sit here, at my desk, not even looking at the file cabinet. I keep seeing, in my mind's eye, that woman struggle ahead of me, across the lawn, the two of us plodding like a couple of cows, the Luger bobbing in the air behind her head, at the end of my arm.

Marjorie calls, "Dinner!"

I turn off the light, and leave the office, and shut the door.

10

For a while, before the beginning, even when I knew absolutely and positively what I should do, I did nothing. For a while, even though I theoretically and intellectually understood that my plan was my only possible hope, I did nothing. I thought it, I planned it, I prepared for it, but I didn't yet believe it.

I did the make-work stuff instead. I studied the Luger. I bought a book to help me understand it, and I read the book cover to cover. I cleaned and oiled the gun. I bought it bullets. I took it into a field and shot trees.

I even saw Ralph Fallon one time, though I don't believe he would have noticed me. What I did, back before I was actually in motion on this thing, as a part of my make-work, my fakery, my stalling, I drove one day over to Arcadia, just to look it over. That's how it happened.

There are no large highways between our part of Connecticut and that part of New York. I took my time, studying the road atlas, wanting to find the best route because I intended this someday to be my commute to work. The roads went through little suburban towns and even smaller farm villages, past dairy herds grazing and cornfields being plowed for this spring's crop, and I thought how nice it would be to make this drive, routinely, roundtrip, five times a week. Not much traffic, beautiful countryside. And at the far end, a job I could love.

Arcadia itself turned out to be a sweet old town, very small, a cluster of twenty or so clapboard homes on the slopes flanking a small but lively stream called the Jandrow, a tributary of the Hudson. Mills are built along streams, because they need a lot of water, and the bustling Jandrow clearly provided all the water this mill could want. There was a dam, just upriver from the mill buildings. The main road through town, east-west, dipping down one slope on its way in, crossed over that dam and then climbed up the far slope and away.

Other than the mill, there was little commercial activity in Arcadia. Up the western slope, overlooking the mill, there was a luncheonette where you could also buy newspapers and cigarettes and a few minor grocery items. Farther up the slope, at the edge of town, was a Getty gas station. That was it.

I got to Arcadia around noon, and decided to eat something in Betty's, the luncheonette. It was only after I was seated at the counter, the only person there not with others at a table, and after I'd ordered a BLT and coffee, that I realized from the conversations behind me that the twenty or so people at the tables were all from the mill.

Had I made a stupid mistake coming here? Would these people remember me, much later, after everything was finished and I had Upton "Ralph" Fallon's job? Would they suspect what I'd done? Had I ruined my chance to put the plan into effect, even before I'd started?

(I think, during this period of time, I was probably unconsciously trying to find some excuse not to go forward with the plan, even though *there was no other plan.* There was no other plan, and there still is no other plan.)

But there I was, I'd already placed my order, and the one sure way to be conspicuous was to run out now, before my food arrived. So I sat hunched between my shoulders, looking at nothing but the array of items on the counter along the wall ahead of me, and from time to time I heard bits of conversation from the tables behind me. Shoptalk, some of it, shoptalk I recognized. Shoptalk I could easily, gladly, have joined. I hadn't realized until that moment just how much I'd missed being around that world.

Oh, how I would have liked to sit at one of those tables and just let the shoptalk wash over me.

Well, I couldn't. I sat where I was, at the counter, and the buxom waitress brought my BLT, and doggedly I ate. While behind me, from time to time, people would call in a joshing way to somebody called Ralph, and Ralph would answer, with that kind of hillbilly cracker voice that's more rural than regional. Not an accent, exactly, but something twanging in the mouth that makes them sound as though they have false teeth even if they don't.

I snuck a look around my shoulder at one point, and this Ralph was at a table by the window, and he was a rawboned rangy guy of about my age, but thinner. He looked like that oldtime singer/songwriter, Hoagy Carmichael. His voice, though, with that cracker twang, wasn't as musical.

Their lunch break was finished. All at once they all needed their checks, and the waitress was very busy for a few minutes, writing out the checks, ringing up totals on the cash register. The groups all left, and walked in little clumps downhill, and I turned to watch them through the windows, talking together, having a last cigarette (there wouldn't be smoking allowed inside the mill).

The waitress moved around between me and the windows, clearing tables, and I said to her, "That fellow that was sitting over there. Was that Ralph Fallon?"

"Oh, sure," she said.

"I thought so," I said. "I met him years ago, but I just wasn't sure. Doesn't matter. I'll take my check, when you've got the chance."

Driving home that day, through the pretty countryside, the memory of those lunchtime conversations circling in my head, I knew I had to do it. I had to go forward. I couldn't live without my life any longer.

That was the day, when I got home, I took out Herbert Everly's resumé, and looked at his address, and turned to my road atlas.

11

Lew Ringer has killed himself! Who would have guessed?

It's Monday now, four days since my terrible experience at the Ricks house, and Marjorie and I are watching the six o'clock news, and this has just been announced. Lew Ringer hanged himself in his garage, sometime last night. Lew Ringer is dead.

The police are saying this pretty well wraps up the case. They'd been just about certain Lew Ringer was their man, right from the beginning, but they hadn't had enough solid physical evidence to pin it on him, and without that solid physical evidence they'd had no choice but to let Ringer go on Saturday afternoon, when his lawyer demanded it.

The principal piece of physical evidence they still didn't have was the gun Ringer had used. It was a nine millimeter, they knew that much, but they hadn't yet found the gun nor the dealer from whom Ringer must have bought it. The assumption now among the authorities was that he'd picked it up some time ago, probably in some southern state using false identification, and that he'd thrown it away, after he'd done the double killing, in a nearby river or lake.

In any event, without the gun or any other evidence tying Ringer to the crime, and with Ringer's lawyer making such a fuss, eventually on Saturday the police had had to let him go, though they did keep a very close eye on him, including a police car parked twenty-four hours a day in front of his house. (That was partly also to keep at bay the crowds of the curious.)

His empty house, as it turned out. When Ringer got there Saturday afternoon, his wife had already left that morning, having announced to the media in a tearful press conference Friday evening that she was returning to her parents in Ohio, where she would begin divorce proceedings.

The police theory was that, with the departure of his wife, with June Ricks having so clearly turned against him (she'd told several reporters that she thought Ringer had killed her parents for love of her, and that she believed he really did love her but had gone too far), with the police so strongly on his trail, and with the awful knowledge of the crimes he'd committed, he simply had not been able to face the world any longer, and that's why he'd hanged himself, in his garage, in the space where his wife's car used to be, sometime last night.

Watching this news item, looking at the faces, listening to the words, it seems to me nobody's sorry Lew Ringer is dead. Everybody's pleased it ended this way, I think, because it makes less work for everybody and less doubt in anybody's mind. He was accused of killing Mr. and Mrs. Ricks, his inamorata's parents, and then he killed himself. QED.

The last four days, I've continued to do nothing, not even to *think* about anything. My despondency and discouragement have held me in a tight and smothering grip. Here I've come this far, and yet I just haven't been able to take one single step farther. The wind has been knocked out of me.

But there's something about Ringer's suicide that's making a change in me, I can feel it. Something about the glee and relief of everybody connected with that case, from the police spokesman to the blonde woman reporter, from the furtive and cunning Junie to the anchorman at his desk. The Ricks case is over, and everybody is pleased. No investigation any more, no search for the gun, no hunt for witnesses, no consideration of any other motive. Turns out, I didn't kill them!

After the news, while Marjorie goes to the kitchen to ready dinner, I return to my office for the first time since Thursday. I sit at my desk, I open the file drawer, I take out the folder with the remaining resumés. I study them, and it seems to me the best thing for me to do now is move my activity as far away physically as possible from the first two incidents.

Here he is, in north central New York State. Good, a different state again, though I won't be able to do that every time.

Lichgate, New York, according to my road atlas, is north of Utica, probably three hundred miles from here. That would put him two hundred fifty miles from Arcadia, too far to commute, but a relocation within New York State wouldn't be complex. He remains a threat.

I could drive there this Thursday morning. Five or six hours to get there. Stay overnight. See what happens.

12

When I was a boy, I was for a while a science fiction fan. A lot of us were, until Sputnik. I was twelve when Sputnik flew. All the science fiction magazines I'd read before then, and the movies and TV shows I saw, assumed that outer space belonged by natural right to Americans. Explorers and settlers and daredevils of space were all Americans, in story after story. And then, out of nowhere, the Russians launched Sputnik, the first space vehicle. The Russians!

We all stopped reading science fiction, then, and turned away from science fiction movies and TV shows. I don't know about anybody else, but, as I remember it, I turned my interest after that to the western. In the western, there was never any doubt who would win.

But before Sputnik turned my whole generation away from science fiction, we had read a lot of stories that talked about something called "automation." Automation was going to take the place of unintelligent labor, though I don't think it was ever phrased quite like that. But simple assembly line stuff is what they meant, the kind of dull deadening repetitive labor that everybody agreed was bad for the human brain and paralyzing to the human spirit. All that work would be taken over by machines.

This automated future was always presented as a good thing, a boon to mankind, but I remember, even as a child, wondering what was supposed to happen to the people who didn't work at the dull stupefying jobs any more. They'd have to work somewhere, wouldn't they? Or how would they eat? If the machines took all their jobs, what would they do to support themselves?

I remember the first time I saw news footage of a robot assembly line in a Japanese auto factory, a machine that looked like the X-ray machine in the dentist's office, jerking around all by itself, this way and that, welding automobile pieces together. This was automation. It was fast, and although it looked clumsy the announcer said it was much more precise and efficient than any human being.

So automation did arrive, and it did have a hard effect on the workers. In the fifties and sixties, blue-collar workers were laid off in their thousands, all because of automation. But most of those workers were unionized, and most of the unions had grown strong over the previous thirty years, and so there were great long strikes, in the steel mills, and in the mines, and in the auto factories, and at the end of it all the pain of the transition was somewhat eased.

Well, that was long ago, and the toll that automation was going to take on the American worker has long since been absorbed. These days, the factory workers are only hit sporadically, when a company moves to Asia or somewhere, looking for cheaper labor and easier environment laws. These days, it's the child of automation that has risen among us, and the child of automation hits higher in the work force.

The child of automation is the computer, and the computer is taking the place of the white-collar worker, the manager, the supervisor, just as surely as those assembly line robots took the place of the lunch-bucket crowd. Middle management, that's what's being winnowed now. And none of us are unionized.

In any large company, there are three levels of staff. At the top are the bosses, the executives, the representatives of the stockholders, who count the numbers and issue the orders and make the decisions. At the bottom are the workers on the line, the people who actually make whatever is being made. And between the two, until now, has been middle management.

It is middle management's job to interpret the bosses for the workers and the workers for the bosses. The middle manager passes information: downward, he passes the orders and requirements, while upward he passes the record of accomplishment, of what has actually happened. To the suppliers he passes the information of what raw material is needed, and to the distributors he passes the information of what finished product is available. He's the conduit, and until now he has been an absolutely necessary part of the process.

Once you bring in the computer, you no longer need middle management. Of course, you still need a *few* people at that level, to serve the computer, to run specific tasks, but you no longer need the hundreds and thousands of managers that were still needed only yesterday.

People like me.

As the computer takes our jobs, most people don't even seem to realize why it's happening. Why was I fired, they want to know, when the company's in the black and doing better than ever? And the answer is, we were fired because the computer made us unnecessary and made mergers possible and our absence makes the company even stronger, and the dividends even larger, the return on investment even more generous.

They still need some of us. This is a transition we're in now, where middle management will shrink like a slug when you pour salt on it, but middle management won't completely disappear. There will just be fewer jobs, that's all, far fewer jobs.

But *my* job, the one Upton "Ralph" Fallon is holding for me, that one still exists. A human being or two is still needed to run the production line, to be above the working stiffs but capable of communication with them, so the bosses won't have to deal directly with people who play country music on their car radios.

Fallon is my competition, all right. And the six resumés I've pulled out of the stack are my competition. But this is a sea change taking place in our civilization right now, and *all* of middle management is my competition. A million hungry faces will be at the window soon, peering in. Well educated, middle-aged, middle class.

I have to be firmly in place, before the flood becomes overwhelming. So I have to be strong, and I have to be determined, and I have to be quick. Thursday, I have to drive into New York State and find Everett Boyd Dynes.

EVERETT B. DYNES
264 Nether St.
Lichgate, NY 14597
315 890-7711

EDUCATION: BA (Hist) Champlain College, Plattsburgh, NY

WORK HISTORY

I have worked in the paper industry for 22 years, in sales, design, customer relations and management. I have worked in the area of polymer paper specialized applications for 9 years, during which time I have dealt with customers and designers, and have also run a product line, where my responsibilities have included interfacing with design and production teams and being in charge of a 27-person production line crew.

EMPLOYMENT HISTORY

1986–present —	Production line manager, Patriot Paper Corp.
1982–1986 —	Customer relations and some design, Green Valley Paper
1977–1982 —	Salesman, all product lines,

1973–1977 —	Whitaker Paper Specialties Salesman, industrial product lines,
1971–1973 —	Patriot Paper Corp. Salesman, Northeast Beverage Corp,
1968–1971 —	Syracuse, NY infantryman, US Army, one tour in Vietnam

PERSONAL HISTORY

I am married, with three nearly-grown children. My wife and I are active in our church and our community. I have been a Boy Scout scoutmaster, when my son was of the appropriate age.

INTENTION

It is my hope to join a forward-looking paper company that can fully utilize my training and skills in all areas of paper production and sale.

13

The New York State Thruway is an expensive toll road. It goes north from New York City to Albany, then turns west toward Buffalo. In that western part, it runs along just to the south of the Mohawk River and the Erie Canal. Just to the north of river and canal is a state road, Route 5, which is smaller and curvier, but doesn't cost anything. I am on Route 5.

I was never in Vietnam. Until I shot Herbert Everly, I'd never seen a human being dead because of violence. It irritates me that Dynes, old EBD, has to put right there, in his resumé, that he was in Vietnam. So what? Is the world supposed to owe him a living, a quarter of a century later? Is this special pleading?

I was stationed in Germany, in the Army, after I got out of boot camp. We were in a communications platoon in a small base east of Munich, on top of a tall pine-covered hill. A foothill of the Alps, I suppose it must have been. We didn't have much to do except keep our radio equipment in working order, just in case the Russians ever attacked, which most of us believed wasn't going to happen. So my eighteen months in the Army in Germany was spent mostly in a beer haze, down in Mootown, which some of us called Munich, I have no idea why.

Mootown. And while the guys in Vietnam called the kilometer a click — "We're ten clicks from the border" — we in Germany were still calling them Ks — "We're ten Ks from that nice gasthaus" — though the Vietnamese influence was getting to us, and Ks were becoming clicks in Europe as well. Nobody wanted to be in Vietnam, but everybody wanted to be thought of as having *been* in Vietnam.

Like this son of a bitch, EBD. Twenty-five years later, and he's still playing that violin.

On a midmorning Thursday in May, there isn't that much traffic on Route 5, and I'm making pretty good time. Not quite as good as the big trucks I can see from time to time across the river on the thruway, but good enough. The little towns along the way — Fort Johnson, Fonda, Palatine Bridge — slow me some, but not for long. And the scenery is beautiful, the river winding through the hills, gleaming in spring sun. It's a nice day.

Mostly it's just river, there to my left, but some of it is clearly manmade, or man altered, and that would be remnants of the old Erie Canal. New York State is bigger than most people realize, being a good three hundred miles across from Albany to Buffalo, and in the early days of our country this body of water to my left was the main access to the interior of the nation. Back before there was much by way of roads.

In those days, the big ships from Europe could come into New York Harbor, and steam up the Hudson as far as Albany, and off-load there. Then the riverboats and barges would take over, carrying goods and people on the Mohawk River and the Erie Canal over to Buffalo, where they could enter Lake Erie, and then travel across the Great Lakes all the way to Chicago or Michigan, and even take rivers southward and wind up on the Mississippi.

Some years ago, I was watching some special on TV, and the announcer described something as being a "transitional technology." It was the railroads I think he was talking about. Something. And the idea seemed to be, a transitional technology was the cumbersome old way people used to do things before they got to the easy sensible way they do things now. And the further idea was, look how much time and effort and expense was put into something that was just a temporary stopgap; railroad bridges, canals.

But everything is a transitional technology, that's what I'm beginning to figure out. Maybe that's what makes it impossible sometimes. Two hundred years ago, people knew for certain they would die in the same world they were born into, and it had always been that way. But not any more. The world doesn't just *change* these days, it upheaves, constantly. We're like fleas living on a Dr. Jekyll who's always in the middle of becoming Mr. Hyde.

I can't change the circumstances of the world I live in. This is the hand I've been dealt, and there's nothing I can do about it. All I can hope to do is play that hand better than anybody else. Whatever it takes.

At Utica, I take Route 8 north. It goes all the way to Watertown and the Canadian border, but I don't. I stop at Lichgate.

A factory town on the Black River. Prosperity, and the factory, left this town a long time ago; more transitional technology. Who knows what used to be manufactured in that great brick pile of a building that molders now beside the river. The river itself is narrow but deep, and very black, and is crossed by a dozen small bridges, all of them at least sixty years old.

Bits of the ground floor of the old factory have been kept more or less alive, converted to shops — antique, coffee, card — and a county museum. People making believe they're at work, now that there is no work.

My road atlas doesn't include a town map of Lichgate. It's after one when I get to town, so first I have lunch in the Red Brick Cafe, tucked into a corner of the old factory building, and then I buy a map of the area in the card shop down the block.

(I know it would be easier simply to ask directions to Nether Street, but what's the chance I would be remembered, as the stranger who asked the way to Nether Street just before the murder on Nether Street? Very strong chance, I should think. The idea of seeing myself on TV in an artist's rendition from eyewitness accounts is not appealing.)

From the name, I would have guessed Nether Street would run along beside the river, that being the lowest part of town, but on the map I see it's a street that borders the southern city line eastward over to the river. When I drive over there, I see that the hill the town is built on slopes down to the south, this way, and Nether Street got its name because it runs along the base of that hill.

112

This area is neither suburban nor rural, but an actual town, and this a residential area, old and substantial, the houses mostly a hundred years old, built back when the factory was still turning out whatever it was. They are wide two-story houses on small plots, made mostly of native stone, with generous porches and steep A roofs because of the very snowy winters.

When these houses were built, the managers would have lived here, middle management from the factory, although I don't think they called it middle management back then. But that's who they would have been, along with the shop owners and the dentists. A solid comfortable life in a stable neighborhood. None of those people would have believed for a second that the world they lived in was transitional.

264 is like its neighbors, wide and solid and stone. There are no mailboxes out by the roadside here, but mail slots in front doors or small iron mailboxes hung beside the door. The mailman will walk. And the roadside isn't a roadside, but a curb.

There's a sidewalk as well, and when I first drive down the block a father is using that sidewalk to teach his scared but game daughter how to ride a two-wheeler. I see them, and I think, Don't let that be EBD.

But in the resumé he described himself as having "three nearly-grown children."

Most of these houses have garages that were added decades after the houses were built, and most of them are free-standing, beside or behind the house and not attached to it, though here and there, because of those rough winters, people have built enclosed passageways to connect house with garage.

264 has a detached garage, an old-fashioned one with two large doors that open outward, though right now they're closed. It's on the right side of the house, and just behind it, with a blacktop driveway that's crumbling here and there, overdue for a touchup. In the driveway is an orange Toyota Camry, a few years old. No one is visible anywhere around the house.

Three blocks farther on, closer to the river, Nether Street crosses a main north-south road, and there's a gas station. I stop there, fill the tank, and use the pay phone to call EBD.

A male voice answers, on the third ring: "Hello?"

Trying to sound very cheerful and friendly, I say, "Hi, Everett?"

"Yes, hello," he says.

"This is Chuck," I say. "By golly, Everett, I didn't think I'd ever track you down."

"I'm sorry," he says. "Who?"

"Chuck," I say. "Everett? This *is* Everett Jackson."

"No, I'm sorry," he says. "You've got the wrong number."

"Oh, *damn*," I say. "I'm sorry, I beg your pardon."

"That's all right. Good luck," he says.

I hang up, and go back to the Voyager.

There's no trouble parking in this neighborhood. Parked cars take up about half the curb space on the westbound side, facing away from the river, as I am now. There's no parking at all on the other side, where EBD's house is, the street not being that wide. It would have been laid out before there were cars.

The horse: a transitional technology.

I park almost a block away from 264, in front of a house with a For Sale sign on the lawn and no curtains in the windows. Today I'm not trying to pretend I'm a potential buyer, I simply don't want a housewife peering out at me from behind her blinds, wondering who that is, just sitting there in his car in front of her house.

EBD is home. Sooner or later he'll come out. The Luger is under the raincoat on the passenger seat. If he drives off in the Camry, I'll pull up beside him at a red light and shoot him from the car. If he comes out to mow his lawn, I'll walk across the street and shoot him there. One way or another, when he comes out, I'll shoot him.

On the drive, all the long time coming up, I never thought about EBD or what I had to do here. I just thought about historical forces and all that stuff. But now, seated in the Voyager, watching the front of that house, all I think about is EBD. Quick and clean, and get it over with. Get the bad taste of the Ricks experience out of my mouth. Make this one simple, like Everly.

Quarter to four. The father and daughter and bicycle have long gone. The mailman has walked down the block, pushing his three-wheeled cart with the long handle. Clouds have come in from the west, and it's getting cool inside the Voyager.

I am patient. I am a leopard in the shadow of a boulder. I can stay here, without moving, until the night comes. And then, when it's dark, if he still hasn't emerged from his house, I will go in after him.

That is, I will circle the house on foot, I will look in the windows, I will find him and shoot him. I won't actually go indoors unless it's absolutely necessary, and even then with extreme caution. I have no desire to meet the wife, or the three almost-grown children.

I'll adapt myself to circumstance, but I am determined . . .

Movement, at 264. The door is opening, obscured by the shadow of the wide porch roof. A man comes out, pauses to call to someone inside, pulls the door shut, comes down off the porch. He stops there, on the slate walk that makes a part in his lawn, and looks up. Will it rain? He adjusts his windbreaker collar, pulls his cloth cap down more firmly on his head. He continues to the street, turns, and walks this way.

It's my man, EBD. The right age, coming from the right house. He's walking toward me, on the far side of the street. I can pick up the Luger, hold it against my leg, walk across the street, ask directions. He will turn aside, pointing, head raised. I will shoot him in the near eye.

My left hand is on the door handle, my right reaches under the raincoat for the Luger. Half a block away, EBD pauses and waves at a house. He stops. He speaks.

I frown and peer, and now I can see a couple seated on the porch there. I'd never noticed them before. Have they been there all along? This light is difficult, with the sun gone.

I can't do it, not in front of witnesses. My

left hand leaves the handle, my right comes empty out from under the raincoat.

Across the way, EBD touches his cap and walks on. He walks past me, on the other side of the street, no parked cars over there to block my vision. He's a tall man, gaunt, with rounded shoulders. His head is thrust forward and down, so that when he walks he looks at the sidewalk directly in front of himself. His hands are in his windbreaker pockets.

Those people on the porch; a couple, I think. Still there. When I start my car, they'll notice me. I have to wait here as long as possible, I have to try to minimize any connection between the passing of EBD and this car driving away.

I see EBD in my outside mirror, walking steadily away. He's more than a block off by now, and still moving steadily on. I can risk losing sight of him for a minute or two.

I start the Voyager. Without looking at the people on the porch, I drive forward, away from EBD. I drive briskly but not crazily down to the corner, where I turn right. I drive rapidly down that block and turn right again, and then a third right, which brings me back to Nether Street.

Only a few major streets go through here, north to south; the rest, including the street

I'm now on, end at Nether. I stop at the Stop sign there, then make the left turn onto Nether, and EBD is perfectly plain, still walking along, out ahead.

Where I got the gasoline and made the phone call, up ahead on the right, is the intersection with Route 8, my road up. Diagonally across Route 8 from the gas station there is a diner. I can park in its lot, and trail EBD from there. How far can he be going, on foot?

I drive slowly by him, and he simply walks methodically along, a man with a destination but in no real hurry to get there. I continue on.

The diner, called SnowBird, faces Route 8, with its blacktop parking lot in front of it and spreading around to its left side, away from Nether Street. There's a traffic light at the intersection, and it's red against me when I arrive. I stop and wait.

In my mirror, EBD walks diagonally across Nether Street behind me, and keeps coming.

The light turns green. I turn left onto Route 8 and then right into the diner's parking area. I drive on around to the side, and take a space near the front corner, where I can watch the intersection. The parking area's almost empty.

I switch off the ignition, and look up, as again the light turns red for Route 8, and EBD comes walking across the road. He almost looks as though he's coming to *me*.

No. He's coming to the diner. He crosses the parking lot, goes up the three brick steps to the entrance, goes into the glass-enclosed vestibule — the severe winters up here have surely caused that to be built there — and I can see him as he pushes open the inner door and goes inside.

All right, this is easy. He's here for a late lunch or a mid-afternoon snack. When he's finished, I'll see him as he comes out to the vestibule. I'll have time to start the engine, lower the window, pick up the Luger. As he comes down those brick steps, I'll drive by and stop in front of him. I'll call his name, and when he looks at me, I will shoot him.

There are exits from the parking lot both onto Nether Street and Route 8. Depending which way the traffic light is green, after I shoot EBD I'll take one or the other of those exits, and head straight down Route 8. No witness will have any idea what was going on.

I'll be home for the eleven o'clock news.

Four-fifty. He's been in there almost an hour. Does he have a girlfriend in there?

120

How much longer do I have to wait? How long can you spend in a diner, in the middle of the afternoon? He wasn't carrying a newspaper, but I suppose he could have a paperback book in a pocket of his windbreaker. Maybe his wife is doing the housecleaning, and he's agreed to stay away from home for a few hours.

I have to find out what's going on. I make sure the Luger is completely concealed by the raincoat, and then I get out of the Voyager to find that the day has become raw, with a sharp wind rushing down Nether Street from the west. I lock the car, and walk into the diner, and he isn't there.

I have a mad instant of dislocation, something out of a melodrama. He's snuck out a back entrance and into a waiting car and he's off . . .

Doing what? An assignation with that girlfriend I'd given him earlier? Is he robbing banks while waiting for a new job to come through? (I'd thought of that.)

Is he after *me?*

All of which is ridiculous. He's undoubtedly in the restroom, and I see the sign for it down to the left, so I go to the right, find a place at the counter, take the menu out of the metal rack that sticks up there.

There's only five people in the place, three

solitaries drinking coffee along the counter, and an elderly couple having dinner in a booth. I think, when he comes out of the bathroom, why not just shoot him here? Who would be able to identify me, in the shock and suddenness of it? I'll have to go back to the Voyager, get the Luger, wear the raincoat — it's chilly enough for that, anyway — and then come back and wait till he comes out of the men's room, and do it right then.

No. Wait. Wait until he's seated again, wherever he's sitting, that would be best.

He comes out of the swing door behind the counter. He's wearing a green apron and he's carrying a plate of fish and chips, which he places in front of a customer down to my left.

He works here.

I'm so stunned I'm still sitting there when he comes over to me. "Afternoon," he says. He has a pleasant smile. He looks like a nice guy, with an honest glance and an easygoing manner.

Middle management, and he's working the counter in a diner. It won't pay his mortgage on that house three blocks from here. I'm sure it helps, the way Marjorie's days at Dr. Carney's office help, but not enough. And it isn't the same thing as your own real life back.

I'm still stunned. I don't know what to do, what to think, what to say, where to look. He keeps smiling at me: "Know what you want?"

"Not yet," I say. I'm stammering. "Give me a minute."

"Sure," he says, and goes on down the counter to ask somebody else if he'd like a refill. The answer's yes, and he reaches for the glass coffee pot.

Don't get to know them. That's what I told myself when I started this. *Before* I started this. Don't get to know them, it'll be that much harder to do what you have to do. It will be impossible to do what you have to do.

He's a counterman in a diner. That's all he is. I don't know him, I don't have to know him, I'm not going to know him.

He's back. "Decided?"

"I'll, uh, I'll have the BLT. And french fries."

He grins. "Comes with fries," he says. "We're top drawer here. Comes with fries and cole slaw, little slice of pickle. Okay?"

"Sounds good," I say.

"And coffee?"

"Yes. Forgot that. Right. Coffee."

He goes away to the kitchen, and I struggle to control myself. He hasn't noticed anything yet, or at least nothing he can't put down to highway daze, the result of somebody traveling alone for hours in a car.

But what am I going to do now? How long does he work here? Am I going to have to sit in the Voyager in that parking lot for eight hours? Six hours? Twelve hours?

He comes out through the swing door, goes to get a cup and saucer and spoon and the glass coffee pot, brings them all over to me, pours me a cup of coffee. "Milk and sugar on the counter there."

"Thanks."

He puts the pot back on its electric burner while I add milk to my coffee. Then he comes back, leans against the work counter behind him, folds his arms, gives me a friendly smile, says, "Passing through?"

I hate having to look at him, talk to him, but what else can I do? "Yeah," I say. "Pretty much." And then, because I'm beginning to realize this isn't going to be as quick as I'd hoped, I say, "Is there a motel anywhere around here?"

"None of the chains," he says. "Not close, anyway."

"I don't need a chain. I don't much like chains."

"Neither do I," he says. "You have that feeling, there's no human touch to it."

124

By God, I don't want a human touch between *us*, but what can I do? "That's right," I say, just hoping to cut the conversation short.

He unfolds his arms, points away to my right, lifting his head. I look at his near eye. I wish I had the Luger with me now, wish I could get this over with now. "About a mile and a quarter south," he says, "on Route 8, there's a place called Dawson's. I've never stayed there myself, of course, you know, I'm local, but I'm told it isn't bad."

"Dawson's," I say. "Thanks."

I look away, but I can feel him considering me, thinking me over. He says, "You looking for a job?"

Surprised, I look back at him, and he's so naturally sympathetic that I tell him the truth: "Yes, I am. How'd you know?"

"I've been there," he says, and shrugs. "Still am, really. I can see it in a fella."

"Isn't easy," I say.

"Not around here, anyway," he says. "I'm sorry to have to tell you that, but there just isn't much of anything happening around here." He gestures at his own territory, his side of the counter. "I was lucky to get this."

This is an opportunity to get my question answered. I say, "You work a full shift?"

"Almost," he says. "Eight hours a day, four days a week. Four to midnight."

Eight hours. Four to midnight. He'll be coming out at midnight. In the dark, I won't see his face, he could be just anybody. In the dark, I'll shoot him. "Well, it's something, anyway," I say, referring to the job.

He grins, but shakes his head. "Not my regular line of work," he says. "I was twenty-five years in the paper business."

Being ignorant, I say, "Newspaper?"

"No no," he says, amused, shaking his head. "Paper manufacturing."

"Oh."

"I was a salesman, and then a manager," he says. "Years in a white shirt and necktie. And then one day, I got the boot."

"It happens," I say, and there's a ding from the kitchen. "It happened to me, too," I find myself saying, though I shouldn't prolong this conversation, I really shouldn't do it.

"That'll be yours," he says, meaning the ding from the kitchen, and he goes away, and I take the minute of respite to tell myself I can't relax into this thing, I can't let us be just a couple of regular guys talking over the news of the world together. I've got to keep that distance, for my own sanity I've got to keep that distance. For my future. For everything.

And aside from all the other considerations, I've already lied to him, pretended I didn't know anything about the paper industry, because I didn't want him thinking about the coincidence of me being here, a guy with the same work history as his. But that means I *can't* let the conversation go on. What am I going to do, invent some whole new life story, in a whole new industry?

He comes back, with my BLT and all the extras on a thick white oval china plate, and puts it down in front of me. "Refill on that?"

My coffee cup's half full. "Not yet," I say. "Thanks."

"Any time."

He goes away to deal with other customers, and I gnaw at my BLT. I'm not hungry, partly because I just ate four hours ago, but mostly because of the situation. I want to be out of here, on my way home. But I *need* this to be *over,* and then I'm out of here, and on my way home.

He's back, taking that stance again, arms folded, back against the work counter. "What line were you in?" he asks.

I panic for just a second, but then I say, "Office supplies," because I do remember something about that industry, from my first years as a salesman for Green Valley Paper

& Pulp. "Memo pads, order sheets, accountancy forms, things like that. I was middle management, ran the production line." Then I force a chuckle, and say, "For all I know, we bought from you folk."

"Not from us," he says. "We did specialized papers, industrial uses." Another grin, another headshake. "Very boring, for anybody outside the business."

"You probably miss it," I say, because I know he does, and I can't help saying it.

"I do," he agrees, but then shrugs. "It's a crime," he says, "what's happening these days."

"The layoffs, you mean?"

"The downsizing, the reductions in staff. All those rotten euphemisms they use."

"They told me," I say, "my job wasn't going forward."

"That's a good one," he agrees.

"Made me feel better," I say. I'm holding the sandwich, one triangular quarter of the sandwich, but I'm not eating.

"You know, I've been thinking about it," he says. "I haven't had much to do, the last couple years, except think about it, and I think this society's gone nuts."

"The whole society?" I shrug and say, "I thought it was just the bosses."

"To let the bosses do it," he says. "You

128

know, there's been societies, like primitive peoples in Asia and like that, they expose newborn babies on hillsides to kill them, so they won't have to feed them and take care of them. And there's been societies, like the early Eskimos, that put their real old folk out on icebergs to float away and die, because they couldn't take care of them any more. But this is the first society ever that takes its most productive people, at their prime, at the peak of their powers, and throws them away. I call that crazy."

"I think you're right," I say.

"I think about it all the time," he says. "But what do you do about it? Beats me."

"Go crazy, too, I guess," I say.

He gives me a broad grin at that. "You show me how," he says, "and I'll do it."

We chuckle together, and he goes off to run up the elderly couple's check on the cash register.

While he's gone, I force myself to eat most of the food and drink the rest of the coffee. I can't have more of this conversation, I just can't.

When I see him coming back down the counter, headed toward me, I make that squiggle in the air that means I want my check, so he about-turns, goes to where he keeps the book, and adds it up.

He has a couple more things to say, just chatting, but I barely answer him. Let him think I'm suddenly in a hurry. I pay the check, and I leave him too big a tip, even though it's stupid to do that, I mean, really stupid any way you look at it.

When I'm going out the first door, he calls, "See you around." I smile, and wave.

At least he didn't offer to put me up.

"Good Vibrations" is playing; the old Beach Boys song. "Good Vibrations," and I'm floating in a glass boat on a luminous yellow-green sea, it looks like dish detergent, it's terribly sad, I'm very sad all the time, and then I'm awake and I'm in Dawson's Motel, and the radio came on at 11:30 P.M., just the way I programmed it. I get up and switch off the radio and go into the bathroom, to pee and brush my teeth and wash my face and prepare to kill EBD.

Dawson's Motel is a pleasant old-fashioned place with knotty pine walls and ruffled amber shades on the lamps and a dark wood floor that squeaks as I move around. The closet has a green paisley curtain instead of a door, and many metal hangers on the pipe rod inside. The plumbing fixtures are old-fashioned and make a lot of noise.

There was a rack of skiing brochures in

the office, when I went in there this afternoon, but at this time of year they don't do much business. The old man in the office was pleased at the sight of a customer, and even more pleased at the sight of cash. "I don't much like those credit cards," he told me, "but I suppose they're here to stay."

Cash: a transitional technology.

I realize I'm hearing rain on the motel roof. When I come out of the bathroom I go over to open the door, and it's a steady rainfall out there, without much wind, coming mostly straight down, washing road dirt into patterns on the Voyager.

I shut the door, and get dressed, but I don't pack, because I expect to come back here after I do it. 11:47 say the red numbers on the clock-radio. I put on my raincoat and the cloth cap that's very much like EBD's. I take the Luger out of my overnight bag and put it in the pocket of the raincoat.

The motel door is old-fashioned enough that I have to lock it with the key when I go outside. Fortunately, there's a roof overhang here, so I don't get wet while I'm doing it. I've left the lights on in the room, and the glow against the window curtains gives it a warm and homey look. I'll be glad to get back here.

There are only two other vehicles parked

along the front of the motel, both facing in toward the rooms where their owners sleep. One is a pickup with Pennsylvania plates; I'm guessing he's a blue-collar guy, a carpenter or something like that, looking for construction work. I don't know why I think that; I guess it's just comforting to make up a story about the people around you. Invent a tribe.

The other vehicle is a big van that's been converted to a small camper. The license plate is Florida, and I'm guessing this is a retired couple. No more shocks to the system for them; winter in Florida, drive north when Florida weather turns muggy and miserable. Not bad.

But not for me, not yet, not even if I could afford it. Which I cannot. God knows if I'll ever be able to afford that kind of retirement life.

I drive north, back toward Lichgate. There's no traffic at all, and very few lights to be seen. The rain is steady and pretty heavy, once you're out driving in it. It slows me down, but it's still only five minutes to twelve when I get to the traffic light at Nether Street. It turns red just before I get there, of course.

The gas station on my left is closed, but the diner ahead to my right is open. And crossing the street in front of me, on the far side of the intersection, shoulders hunched against the rain, inadequately dressed in his windbreaker and cloth cap, is EBD!

Damn! Damn it to hell, he's leaving early! *I'm* on time, dammit!

It was going to be so easy. I would switch off my headlights as I drove into the parking lot. I would wait near the entrance, I would see him come out into the vestibule, I would drive forward, and as he came down the brick steps I would reach the Luger out the window and shoot him. And that's it.

But now he's walking, he's well away from the diner, he's already across the intersection and walking down Nether Street away from me, hands in windbreaker pockets, walking briskly because of the rain, moving along on the right side of the street past the parked cars, three blocks to walk to his house on the left.

And this damn light is still red in my face. It's going to change now; I can see the amber light come on, facing Nether Street. There's still no traffic anywhere, nobody to be seen, nobody at all out in this rain.

I switch off my headlights. Now I'm as black as the night, and when the green light switches on in front of me I turn left.

He's moving briskly. This is going to be

133

a difficult shot, out to the right from the left side of the car, me at the steering wheel, past parked cars, at a man in the dark, walking in the rain. It would be horrible to miss, to alert him, to have him running, to have him escape and at once get on the phone to the local police. (EBD would remember the phone, wouldn't get rattled like Ricks, I can tell that much for sure about him.)

Up ahead, with only the briefest glance over his shoulder, EBD comes out from between parked cars and walks at an angle, crossing the street. And now I know what I must do.

I hit the accelerator hard. The Voyager leaps forward. EBD is a dark mass against the dark masses of the night, everything vaguely glittery from the rain, everything except his wet windbreaker and wet cloth cap. The Voyager leaps at him like a fox after a mole.

He senses me. He looks over his shoulder. It's too dark to see his face, but I can imagine his expression, and then he jumps, trying to launch himself all the way over to the left curb, and the Voyager smashes into him. But he was jumping, his weight was going upward, so his body doesn't go under the car, but pastes against it, right in front of me, almost hitting the windshield, draped there like a dead deer being brought home by a triumphant sportsman.

I slam on the brakes, and he slides down the front of the car. I see his hands clutching, scrabbling for some hold, but there is none. The car is still moving, though more slowly, and he goes under it, and I feel the heavy bumps as we drive over him.

Now I brake to a stop. Now I turn on the headlights, and switch into reverse gear, so the backup lights will come on, and I see him three times, in all three mirrors, the inside mirror, the one outside to my left, the one all the way over there outside to my right, I see him three times, and in all three mirrors he's moving.

Oh, God, no. He has to stop. We can't go on like this. He's rolling over, he's trying to rise.

I'm already in reverse. Now I accelerate, and I close my eyes, and I feel the *thump* and the *thump,* and I slam on the brakes and skid, and think no, please, I'm going to hit a parked car, but I don't.

I open my eyes. I look out front, and he's there in the glare of my headlights, in the rain, one arm moving on the pavement, fingers scratching on the pavement. His hat is gone. He's crumpled, mostly facedown, and his forehead is against the pavement, his head twitching in slow fits back and forth.

This has to stop *now*. I shift into Drive, I drive slowly forward, I aim at that head. Ba-*thump,* the front left tire, yes. Ba-*thump,* the rear left tire, yes.

I stop. I shift into reverse, and the backup lights come on. In three mirrors, he doesn't move.

I'm weeping when I get back to the motel, still weeping. I feel so weak I can barely steer, hardly press my foot against the accelerator and, at last, the brake.

The Luger is still in my pocket. It weighs me down on the right side, dragging down on me so that I stumble as I move from the Voyager to the door to my room. Then the Luger bangs against my hand, interfering with me, while I try to get into my pants pocket for the key, the key to the room.

At last. I have the key, I get it into the lock, I open the door. All of this is mostly by feel, because I'm sobbing, my eyes are full of tears, everything swims. I push the door open, and the room that was going to be warm and homey is underwater, afloat, cold and wet because of my tears. I pull the key out of the door, push the door closed, stagger across the room. I'm stripping off my clothes, just leaving them anywhere on the floor.

The sobs have been with me since I made the U-turn on Nether Street and drove carefully around the body in the middle of the pavement. The sobs hurt my throat, they constrict my chest. The tears sting my eyes. My nose is full, I can barely breathe. My arms and legs are heavy, they ache, as though I'd been pummeled for a long time with soft clubs.

A shower, won't that help? A shower always helps. Here in Dawson's Motel, the bathroom contains an old-fashioned clawfoot tub. Above it, sometime later, a shower nozzle was added to protrude from the wall, and a small ring to hang a shower curtain. When you step in there and turn on the water, if you move an inch in any direction you touch the cold wet shower curtain.

But I'm not moving. I stand in the flow of hot water, eyes closed, tears still streaming, throat and chest still in pain, but the hot water slowly does its work. It cleanses me, and it soothes me, and at last I turn off the water, push the too-close shower curtain aside, step out, and use all the thin towels to dry myself.

I've stopped weeping now. Now I'm merely exhausted. The bedside clock-radio says 12:47. Exactly one hour ago I left this room, to go kill Everett Dynes, and now I'm back, and I've done it. And I'm exhausted, I could sleep for a thousand years.

I get into bed, and switch off the light, and I don't sleep. I'm so weary I could start crying all over again, but I don't sleep. The scene on Nether Street, in the dark, in the rain, in the lights of my Voyager, keeps replaying in my head.

I try to remember the last time I cried, and I cannot; sometime when I was a child, I suppose. I'm not good at it, my throat and chest still ache, my head feels clogged.

I try not to move around in the bed, I try to do things that will help me get to sleep. I count to one hundred, then back to one. I try to bring up pleasant memories. I try to shut down entirely.

But I cannot sleep. And I keep seeing the event on Nether Street. And every time I turn my head, the clock-radio shows some later time, in red numbers, just there, to my right.

I must have been crazy, out of my mind. How could I have done these things? Herbert Everly. Edward Ricks, and his poor wife. And now Everett Dynes. He was like me, he should be my friend, my ally, we should work together against our common enemies. We shouldn't claw each other, down here in the pit, fight each other for scraps, while they laugh up above. Or, even worse; while they don't even bother to notice us, up above.

When the clock says 5:19, I come to my decision. It has to end now. I have to make a clean breast of everything, atone for what I've done, do no more.

I get out of bed. My exhaustion has left me, I'm awake and alert. I'm calm. I turn on the lights and look around for writing paper, but Dawson's Motel does not equip its rooms with stationery, and I've brought no paper with me.

Paper lines the dresser drawers, white lengths of paper, in the old-fashioned dark wood dresser. I take out the paper from the bottom drawer, and find it stiff, rather thick, smoother on one side than the other. A very simple level of manufacture, this paper. (I could cry all over again, just for a second, when I notice myself noticing that detail.)

The rougher side is better for writing on. I sit at the table, I smooth the paper in front of me, I pick up my pen, and I write:

My name is Burke Devore. I am 51 years old and I live at 62 Pennery Woods Rd., Fairbourne, CT. I have been unemployed for close to 2 years, through no fault of my own. Since my army service, I have at all times been employed, until now.

This period of unemployment has had a very bad effect on me, and has made me do things I would never have thought possible. Through placing a false ad in a trade journal, I got the resumés of many other people who are unemployed, as I am, in my field of expertise. I then determined to kill those people who I feared were better qualified than I was for one certain job. I wanted that job, I wanted to be employed again, and that desire made me do crazy things.

I wish to confess now to four murders. The first was two weeks ago, on Thursday, May 8th. My victim was a man named Herbert C. Everly. I shot him in front of his house on Churchwarden Lane, in Fall City, CT.

My second victim was Edward G. Ricks. I only meant to kill him, but his wife mistook me for an older man who'd been having an affair with her young daughter, and in the confusion I had to kill her, too. I shot both of them last Thursday at their home in Longholme, MA.

My final victim was last night, in Lichgate, NY. His name was Everett Dynes, and I deliberately ran him down with my automobile.

I am truly sorry for these crimes. I don't know how I could have done them. I feel so sorry for the families. I feel so sorry for the people I killed. I hate myself. I don't know how I can go on. This is my confession.

My last resumé.

When I finish it, I sign it, but I don't date it. There's no need.

I'm not sure yet what I'll do tomorrow. Either I'll shoot myself with that Luger in my raincoat pocket hanging from the pipe rod in the closet over there, or I'll drive back to Lichgate, find the police station, and show my confession to a policeman there.

I just don't think I can kill myself. I think I have to atone. I think I have to pay for my crimes. And I think I'm just not somebody who commits suicide. So I think I'll turn myself in to the police tomorrow morning.

I leave the confession on the table, turn off the lights, get back into bed. I feel very calm. I know I'll sleep now.

14

I sleep like a log. I wake up refreshed, comfortable, hungry as a bear. I left no morning call, so I've slept until I was finished sleeping, and the clock-radio reads 9:27. I'm usually out of bed by seven-thirty, so this is really coddling myself. I always had to get up at seven-thirty to get to my job, when I had a job, and I did that for so many years that the habit has stayed with me.

I shower with the curtain only half closed, which is much more comfortable for me, but leaves the floor very wet. I'm sure that's not the first time that's happened.

It's still raining outside, a steady rain out of a low grayish white sky. It won't stop today. I put my overnight bag, with the Luger in the bottom, into the car, then hunker down in the protection of the roof overhang to look at the front of the Voyager.

The glass over the left parking light is gone, and so is the chrome rim around the headlight, but the headlight seems to be intact. There are dents on the bodywork in the left front. If there was ever any blood anywhere on the car, the rain has washed it away.

I go back into the room one last time, to see if I've left anything, and that's when I see the sheet of paper on the table. I'd completely forgotten about that, done in the woozy hysterics of the night. Wow, and I almost left it behind.

I sit at the table, and read what I wrote last night, and that awful dread begins to creep over me again. How terrible I felt last night. Tense, anxious, terrified, unable to sleep. I'm glad writing this made it possible at last for me to lose consciousness for a while.

I meant all of this last night, I know I did. Everything seemed so hopeless. The first one, Everly, went so smoothly, but both of them since have been absolute disasters. I'm not used to this sort of thing, it would be hard enough to do even if they all went smoothly and cleanly, but to have two horror shows in a row really ground me down.

From now on, I have to be more careful and more patient. I have to be sure the circumstances are right before I make my move.

I sympathize with the me from last night, who felt such despair, and wrote these words, and apologized to his victims. I too would apologize to them, if I could. I'd leave them alone, if I could.

I take the confession with me, folded in my pocket. I'll burn it later, somewhere else.

I don't have to go back through Lichgate, which is good. I head south toward Utica on Route 8, and as I drive I think about the damage to the car. I have to get it repaired. I have to fill out a report for the insurance company, though I'm not sure the damage will exceed the deductible. I have to give Marjorie an explanation.

And at the same time, of course, I have to remember the police will be looking for this car. Even if they don't call it a murder back there — and I have no idea if they can tell the body was driven over more than once — but even if they don't call it murder, even if it's merely a hit-and-run, that's still manslaughter, and they'll be looking for the car.

What do they have? Probably tread marks. The glass from the parking light. The rim from the headlight. One or all of those things will tell them the make and model of the car. They'll know they're looking for a Plymouth Voyager with these specific injuries to the left front. I didn't see any paint chipped off, so they probably don't have the color.

There are a lot of these cars on the road,

but there won't be many with these particular scars. Fortunately, the headlight still works, and the headlights are switched on because of the rain. With that rain falling, and with the light glaringly on, it will be very hard for any passing cop to see the small dings around the front of the car. I should be safe, until I can get it fixed, and I think I know how to do that.

I told Marjorie I was going to a job interview in Binghamton, so I have to wait until I'm far enough south to be on a route that makes sense for that to be where I'm coming from. Then, with the help of the rain, I'll take care of this problem.

My chance doesn't come until early afternoon, just short of Kingston, New York, where I will cross the Hudson River. For my route back, I continue south after Utica, and although I'm starving I wait a good long time, until almost noon, before I stop at a diner to eat what they would call lunch but I would call breakfast. While I'm in there, I make sure to put the Voyager where no one can casually see the front end of it.

After breaking my fast with lunch, I drive on down through Oneonta, where I turn southwest on State Route 28 through the Catskill Mountains, a winding hilly road, mostly only two lanes wide. It's in a little town along in there that my opportunity knocks.

There's a lumberyard up ahead on the left side of the road, with several vehicles along its front, parked facing in. A pickup truck suddenly backs out from there, too fast and too far, without the driver paying sufficient attention. I could avoid him, if I tromp on the brake, or if I drive briefly onto the shoulder to steer around him, but I do neither. I tromp on the accelerator and ram him, my left front against his left side by his rear wheel.

The pickup skids away sidewise on the wet road, taking my hooked bumper with him, and winding up just off the road in front of the lumberyard. I fight the wheel, roll to the right shoulder, and stop. I turn off the ignition, and get out of the car.

Three men in mackinaws come out of the lumberyard, staring at the destruction. The driver of the pickup truck, a skinny kid in his early twenties wearing a New York Giants warmup jacket and a baseball cap on backwards, sits in the truck, stupefied with shock. His engine has stalled, and his right hand is still high on the steering wheel, holding tight, and country music is blaring loudly from his radio. A dozen planks and a big can of joint compound are in the back of the pickup.

I cross the road and meet the three men in mackinaws. I say, sounding as dazed as that kid over there looks, "Did you see that?"

"I heard it," one of them says. "That was good enough for me."

"He came," I say, and shake my head, and point this way and that, and start again. "He came out, all of a sudden all the way across the road. I was going *that* way, I was way over *there*."

One of the men in mackinaws goes over to tell the kid to turn off his ignition, and he does, and the music stops. Another of them says to me, "We better call the cops."

"He came *right out*," I say.

Everybody agrees I am not at fault. Even the kid knows he's to blame, jumping way out into the road like that, not looking both ways, playing his radio too loud.

The state police treat me with the calm courtesy reserved for the innocent victim, and they treat the kid with the cold efficiency reserved for assholes. They take down everybody's particulars, get names and phone numbers from the three men in mackinaws in case witnesses are ever needed, and assure me they'll send me a copy of the accident report for me to give my insurance company.

I thank them all for their help, and at last I get back into the car, which still runs, though it has some new rattles, and I drive on, and when I reach Kingston I stop in a little neighborhood bar, nearly empty at this time of day, to have a beer, to quiet my nerves.

When I come back out, a Kingston city cop is looking at the damage to the front of my car, parked at the curb by the door to the bar. This damage is now considerably more severe than it was. He asks me if it's my car, and I say yes. He asks to see a driver's license, and I show it to him. Still holding my license, he says, "Do you mind telling me when you got that?"

"About half an hour ago," I tell him, "maybe ten miles back up Route 28. I was just calming myself with a beer in there."

He asks me the particulars of the accident, and then asks if I mind waiting while he calls in, and I tell him in that case I think I'll have another beer.

"Don't drink too much," he says, but he smiles, and I assure him I won't. He walks off to his own car, carrying my license.

I'm still in the bar, a warm and dark and comforting place, five minutes later, halfway down this second draft beer, when the cop comes in and says, "Just wanted you to know, it checked out." He hands me my license. "Thanks for the cooperation."

"Sure," I say.

15

We still treat Sunday as something different, Marjorie and I, although there's no reason to any more. I don't mean we go to church. We don't, though we did years ago, when the kids were young and we were trying to be a good influence. Since I was chopped, Marjorie's mentioned the idea once or twice, going to church some Sunday, but she hasn't made a real point of it, and we don't have a church in particular here in Fairbourne, don't really know any churchgoers, so it hasn't happened yet. I don't suppose it will.

No, what I mean by our treating Sunday as something different, I mean we still act as though it's the day I don't go to work. (The *other* day. Saturdays I get up early and do chores, still maintaining that fiction as well.) We sleep an hour later, not getting up till eight-thirty or nine, and we dawdle over a long breakfast, and we don't dress until lunchtime, and we spend most of the daylight hours with the Sunday *New York Times*. Of course, these Sundays I turn first to the help wanted section, so that's a change.

So today, this Sunday, is a true time-out. After my experiences last Thursday and Friday up in Lichgate, I'm ready for some time out. Tomorrow I'll take the Voyager to a body shop for an estimate on the damage, which I hope I can get taken care of very soon. I mean, urgently.

Originally, I thought I'd spend part of this afternoon in the office, to decide which of the three remaining resumés I should deal with next, and how to deal with him with less chance of the kind of disaster I've been having. But then it occurred to me, with that damage on it, the Voyager is a lot more identifiable than it used to be. I probably shouldn't use it to go after the others until it's been made anonymous again.

Which I don't like. I want to do it now, I want to get it over with, I really want to get this whole thing over and done with. While I was burning that confession in the backyard yesterday, during the time Marjorie was away at her movie-house job, I realized the tension of this situation could get to me again, that I could have more weak moments, and that some time, in dread and despair, I might even actually make a phone call to the authorities, blurt it all out, destroy myself. So the sooner I get this over with, the better.

"Burke! Burke!"

We're in the living room, Marjorie and I, in our robes, with the sections of the Sunday *Times* and our cooling coffee. I'm in my regular chair, with its view slightly leftward to the TV set on the far side wall and its view slightly rightward through the picture window to the front of our yard and the plantings that partly shield us from the road and our neighbors. Marjorie is, as usual, on the sofa to my left, feet curled up under her, newspaper spread all across the sofa beyond her.

And now I realize she's calling to me. I start, the paper rattling, and look at her. "What? Something wrong?" Something in the paper, I mean.

"You haven't heard a word I said."

She looks surprisingly tense, agitated. I hadn't noticed that before. Is this about something that *isn't* in the paper?

I'm a pretty big guy, now going to seed a bit, and Marjorie's what they call petite, with very curly brown hair and wide bright brown eyes and a wholehearted way of laughing that I love, as though she's about to blow herself over. Though I haven't heard that laugh for a while, really.

When we first started going together in '71, back in Hartford, we had to put up with a lot of not-very-witty jokes from our friends because I was so big and tall and she was so skinny and short. I was still a bus driver, then, for the city, and in fact I first met Marjorie when she got on my bus one morning. She was a college student, twenty years old, and I was an Army vet and a bus driver, twenty-five, and she had no intention of getting involved with somebody like me, and yet that's what happened. And even though I was a college graduate myself, she took a lot of ribbing from her friends at school when she started going out with a bus driver, and I suppose it was that as much as anything that led me to apply to Green Valley, and get the job selling paper, and find my life's work, that's now been temporarily lost.

And now she's telling me I haven't heard a word she's said, and it's true. "I'm sorry, sweet," I say. "I was distracted, I was a million miles away."

"You've *been* a million miles away, Burke," she says. There are little white blotches under her eyes, high on her cheekbones. She almost looks as though she might cry. What *is* this?

I say, "It's the job, sweet, I just can't —"

"I *know* it's the job," she says. "Burke, honey, I *know* what the problem is, I know how much this has been weighing on your mind, driving you crazy, but —"

"Well, not entirely crazy, I hope."

"— but I *can't stand it*," she insists, not letting me interrupt or make a joke. "Burke, it's driving *me* crazy."

"Sweet, I don't know what I can —"

"I want us to go into counseling," she says, with that abrupt matter-of-factness people use when they finally say something they've been thinking about for a long time.

I automatically reject this, for a thousand reasons. I start with the most explainable of those reasons, saying, "Marjorie, we can't afford —"

"We can," she says, "if it's important. And it *is* important."

"Sweet, this can't go on forever," I tell her. "I'll find another job before you know it, a good job, and —"

"It'll be too late, Burke." Her eyes are bigger and brighter than I've ever seen them. She's so *serious* about this, and so *worried*. "We're being torn apart *now*," she says. "It's been too long, the damage is being done. Burke, I love you, and I want our marriage to survive."

"It *will* survive. We love each other, we're strong in —"

"We're not strong enough," she insists. "*I'm* not strong enough. It's wearing me down, it's grinding me down, it's making me miserable, it's making me desperate, I feel like a . . . I feel like a woodchuck in a Hav-a-Hart trap!"

What an image. She must have been thinking about all this for quite a long while, and I haven't even noticed. She's been unhappy, and keeping it to herself, trying to be brave and silent and wait it out, and I haven't noticed. I should have noticed, but I was distracted by this other thing, concentrating on this other thing.

If only I could tell her about all that, tell her what I'm doing, how I'm making sure everything will be all right. But I can't, I don't dare. She wouldn't understand, she couldn't possibly understand. And if she knew what I was doing, what I've already done, what I'm going to do, she'd never be able to look at me in the same way again. I understand that, all at once, right now, sitting here in the living room, looking at her, in our robes, the both of us covered like bums in the park with sections of the *New York Times*. I can never tell her what I've done, what I'm doing, to save our marriage, to save our lives, to save us.

I say, "Sweet, I know what you're feeling, I really do. And you know I'm feeling the same frustration, I'm having to deal with it every second of every —"

155

"I can't do it," she says. "I'm not as strong as you are, Burke, I never was. I can't deal with this awful situation as well as you can. I can't just, just *hunker down* and wait."

"But there's nothing else to do," I say. "That's the bitch of it, sweet, there's nothing else to do. We *both* have to just hunker down and wait. But believe me. Please. I have a feeling, I just have a feeling, it won't be that much longer. This summer, sometime this summer, we'll —"

"Burke, we need counseling!"

How she stares at me, almost in terror. For God's sake, does she *know?* Is that what she's trying to say?

No, it can't be. It isn't possible. I say, "Marjorie, we don't need any third party, we can talk things out together, we've always been able to do that, even that bad time when I was . . . You know."

"When you were going to leave me," she says.

"No! I was never going to leave you, you know that. I never for a second thought or said or planned that I could ever leave you, not *you*, sweet, my God. We talked all that —"

"You were living with her."

I sit back. I put one hand over my eyes. With everything that's going on, to have to deal now with something like this. But it's important, I know it is, I have to pay attention to this. Marjorie is my other half, I learned that eleven years ago, the time we're talking about now. Everything I do is as much for her as for me, because I can't live without her.

Still shielding my eyes with my hand, I say, "We talked that out then, and that was the worst thing that ever happened. We talked it out —"

"It wasn't the worst."

I lower my hand and look at her, and I want her to see in my eyes how much I love her. "Oh, but it was," I say. "This job business is terrible, but it isn't as bad as that was. And we talked that out."

"We had help."

"Yes, that's true."

A friend of Marjorie's from her college days had been her confidante, back then, and the friend was a churchgoer, and she took Marjorie along to meet this Episcopalian priest, Father Susten, and then Marjorie brought me along, and he actually was a help, he gave us somebody to pretend to talk to when we were saying things we couldn't say directly to one another. Father Susten's church was down in Bridgeport, he probably isn't even there any more, he wasn't a young man eleven years ago.

Besides, that was a marital difficulty, that was my infidelity, the stupid mistake of a man who had to go for just one last hurrah, no matter how much it hurt. Our problem now is a job and an income; what could he say about that? What could he do to help? Give us something out of the alms box?

And what would I have to say to him about *this* problem? Discuss what I'm doing with the resumés? I say, "Marjorie, Father Susten couldn't —"

"He isn't there any more. I phoned."

So she's very serious about this. But I want to head it off, I don't want to entangle my mind with *counseling* when I have this hard, tense, frightening work to do. I say, "Marjorie, we can talk it out together, all this stuff about the job."

"I can't talk to you," she says. She looks over at the picture window. She's calmer now. "That's the problem, I really can't talk to you."

"I know I've been inattentive," I say, "but I *can* pay attention, and I *will* pay attention."

"That's not what I mean." She continues to look at the picture window. Now that she knows I'm listening, she's become very quiet, draining all the passion out of what she says. "I mean I can't talk to you about the current situation."

I simply don't understand. "Why not?" I ask her. "We both know the situation isn't —"

"No, we don't both know," she says, and turns her head, and looks at me again. "You don't know the situation at all," she says, "and that's why we need counseling."

I don't want to know what she's telling me. It's too late not to know, but I don't want to know. I feel myself trembling. I say, "Marjorie, you haven't . . . made any . . . *done* any . . . you're worried about . . . you think you might . . ."

She's looking at me. She's waiting for me to stop. But when I stop, I'll have to know. I take a long painful breath, a deep inhale, and when that breath comes out I say, "Who is he?"

She shakes her head. I'll kill him, I think. I know how, I didn't used to know how, but now I do, and I know I can do it, and I know it's easy. It's easy. With this one, a pleasure.

"Just tell me who he is," I say. I try to sound very gentle, like someone who doesn't kill people.

She says, "Burke, I called some state social services offices. There's counseling we can go to, it isn't terribly expensive, we can —"

"Who is he, Marjorie?"

How many people could he be? How many places does she go? Not many, not since we sold the Civic. Could it be the dentist, Dr. Carney, that white-coated wimp with his Coke bottle glasses, endlessly washing his hands? Or that fellow at the New Variety, the movie house, what's his name, balding, harried, slovenly, Fountain, that's it. Could it be Fountain? Somebody at one of those places.

I'll follow her, I'll trail her, I know how to do these things now, she won't know I'm there, I'll find him, and then I'll kill him.

She's still talking, while my mind races around like a dog that's lost the scent, and what she's saying is, "Burke, either we go into counseling together, or I'm going to have to move out."

That stops the questing dog in his tracks. I give her my full attention. I say, "Marjorie, no, you can't go — How could you? Where could you live? You don't have any money!"

"I have *some*," she says, and I realize I'm the one who doesn't have any money, not since the unemployment insurance ran out a few months ago. (That was so humiliating, taking the unemployment insurance, going down there, signing the forms, standing on the lines with *those people*. It was shaming and degrading, but it wasn't as bad as when it stopped.)

And if Marjorie goes away? We can't afford *one* household, how could we afford two?

She says, "I have my part-time jobs, and I can get another one, part-time, at Hurley's."

Hurley's is a liquor store, in the same mall as Dr. Carney's office. Could it be *Hurley* she's shacked up with, stinking of stale cigarettes?

I'm feeling desperate, scared, trapped. I say, "Marjorie, none of this would be happening if I hadn't lost my job."

"I *know* that, Burke," she says, as desperate and trapped as I am. "Don't you think I know that? That's what I'm saying, the strain of this, it isn't *fair*, it isn't fair for any of us, but it's getting to us, it's making you silent and secretive, I have no idea what you do in that office all the time, all those papers you're constantly going over and marking up with your pencils, all those trips you take —"

"Interviews," I say, quickly. "Job interviews. I'm *trying* to get work."

"I know you are, honey," she says. "I know you're doing your best, but it's driving us apart, it's making me feel I want to *laugh* again sometimes, I want to stop being so miserable, feeling so weighed down all the time."

"All right," I say. I have to speed up the operation, I have to finish it all very soon. Her . . . person . . . whoever he is, I'll get to him later. I have to finish the other first. "All right," I say.

She cocks her head, watching me. "All right?"

"I'll go along with you, to . . . counseling," I say, and even as I say it I feel lighter, happier. It won't be easy, I know. I'll have to hide so much from this person, and this is a person you're supposed to be seeing so you can have somebody to be *open* with. But I can't be open, not with anybody, not till this is over, and even then never about this. I'll never be able to tell anyone in the world about this, about this awful period in my life, not a single human being ever. Not Marjorie, not a counselor, not a thousand counselors sworn to secrecy.

But still, we'll be able to talk about some of it, the desperation, the resentment, the feelings of inadequacy, the shame, the feeling that somehow it is all my fault even when I know it isn't.

"All right," I say again. "Counseling. I'm sure it's a good idea anyway."

"Thank you, Burke," she says.

162

I say, "Marjorie . . ."

"No," she says. She's very firm. "Don't say anything about it."

I was going to say to her, don't see him any more. But I know she's right, I can't say that, I don't have the right to say it. "All right," I say.

16

Three hours later I am in my office. This time, I'll go after the nearest one, to make it simple and easy, and so I can make more than one trip, reconnoiter, be sure I know what I'm going to do and how I'm going to do it, and how I'm going to *keep* it simple and easy. *Then* I'll do it.

The road atlas. Here he is, in Dyer's Eddy, a dot of a town right here in Connecticut, not thirty miles from this spot.

Marjorie is reading a novel in the living room. I say to her, "I'm going for a drive, I have to think," and she nods, not looking up from the book. We're extremely awkward together.

I don't carry the Luger, this is just reconnaissance. I carry the resumé.

KANE B. ASCHE
11 Footbridge Road
Dyer's Eddy, CT 06687
telephone 203 482-5581
fax 203 482-9431

EMPLOYMENT HISTORY: Most recently, (1991-present) Product Manager, Green Valley Paper & Pulp, introduced the new product line of industrial polymer paper applications.

1984-1991, assistant plant supervisor, Green Valley Paper & Pulp, responsible for paperwork for OSHA and other Federal regulators as well as state regulators. Additionally, oversaw second shift, home products line.

1984, oversaw the dissolution of Champion Pulpwood after bankruptcy. Dismantled machinery, negotiated with purchasers, maintained records of dispersal of machinery, money, materiel.

1971-1984, various responsibilities with Champion Pulpwood, beginning on factory floor as sludge operator, moving up through various jobs to night shift supervisor, then to assistant to the manager during the period when Champion was being purchased and dismantled by Kai Wen Holding Corp.

EDUCATION HISTORY: High school diploma, 1962. Received bachelor's degree in business administration from West Texas University Extension while serving as an enlisted man in the United States Army (two tours, 1963-1971). Received master's degree, Connecticut Tech (night school) 1985. Am pursuing doctorate part-time.

I am still under 50 years of age, eager to share my experience and give a long-term commitment to a solid reliable employer.

Still under 50. The bastard. He doesn't know it, but he's going to be under 50 forever.

It's all back roads between Fairbourne and Dyer's Eddy. Last week's rainstorm has finally drifted out to sea, leaving a clean-scrubbed world behind, glistening under pale spring sunshine. There are a number of Sunday drivers out, looking at the fresh greens of spring, the colors of the tulips people plant beside their porches and around their birdfeeders. I'm in no hurry, I drive along in their wake and I think about Kane Bagley Asche.

(In my research, in that stalling period after I knew what I had to do but hadn't yet steeled my mind to do it, I used our family computer and its modem — we're online, though we can't really afford it, and I have to keep warning Billy not to spend too much time there — to access public records on my six resumés. Birth certificates, wedding licenses, property ownership. You can learn a lot about other people, though none of it did me much good. No good at all, really, except that when you know things about other people, and they don't know you know those things, you feel a sense of power over them. That's a help, if you ever intend to deal with them in some way. And one extra result of it all was that I now know every-body's middle name, and that's pleasurable in a strange way. I know their secret name, the one they don't usually tell people. That's probably the same sense of power the police feel, because they always use the middle name, you notice, when they announce a manhunt or an arrest.)

The eddy that's been named after Dyer is a small seasonal whirlpool in a little stream called the Pocochaug, a tributary of the Housatonic River. There are a lot of Indian names around this part of the country, some of them worse than Pocochaug.

This is the eddy's season, springtime, with snowmelt and the spring rains. New Haven Road, the town's main street, almost its only street, runs along the west bank of the Pocochaug, then angles right where the stream angles left, and that's where the town is. Just above that, at the north end of town and just within the town limits, is the eddy, con-sidered such a local attraction that there's even a small parking area there, between road and stream. At the moment, midafter-noon on a May Sunday, there are about seven cars there. I make it eight.

There's a footbridge across the stream here, over the eddy, which is simply water behaving, in a somewhat larger fashion, the way it behaves when you empty your sink. Half a dozen people lean on the stripped-bark log railing there, looking down at the eddy, I have no idea why. Beyond them, the footbridge, which is wooden planks over a solid iron structure, curves down to the far side of the Pocochaug, where there's a little park, some boulders sticking out of the ground, a few picnic benches, and a seasonal (like the eddy) snack shop.

It's open. I don't buy anything, but I walk around the little rustic building and the general area of the park. It's so pleasant here, as though there are no problems in the world, as though there was nothing difficult I had to do, as though Marjorie had not delivered earlier today her terrible news. Walking here, among the trees, in the neat park, I am feeling relaxed. How long has it been since I felt relaxed?

I stand in the middle of the park and look back toward the stream, where people still lean on the railing to watch the water eddy. It looks to me as though some of them are the same people as when I first got here. Beyond them is the gravel parking area, and beyond that the lightly traveled road, and beyond that a couple of white houses and a road winding away uphill.

Footbridge. KBA's address is Footbridge

Road. That must be Footbridge Road right there.

A few houses are visible, uphill, through pine trees. Can I see KBA's house from here? I've forgotten the number.

Tensing up, feeling excitement grow, I walk back across the footbridge. KBA's house. Is he home? Can he be one of these people down here, looking at the eddy? Unlikely; the eddy will be old news to him.

Why don't I walk up there? It can't be far, and people are walking today, it's a nice day. And it would be good not to drive the car past KBA's house in its present condition.

I go to the Voyager and look at the resumé, to remind myself of the house number, and it's eleven. I leave my cap on the car seat, and open my windbreaker, and start to walk.

It's a little farther than I expected, and certainly not visible from that park back there, but the road is a gradual slope, an easy climb, past well-cared-for New England houses, all of them cleverly fitted into the slant of the hill. Many retaining walls, the older ones of stone, the newer ones of railroad ties.

Number eleven uses railroad ties, and a lot of plantings. The house is on the left as I walk up, well set back from the road, the blacktop driveway walled on one side by the railroad ties, the mailbox built into the wooden post constructed at the road end of the ties.

I walk past, on the other side of the road, and as I get a little higher I can see them. Husband and wife. Digging in the garden.

Planting season. They have several gardens, all around the house, including this elaborate one on the uphill side, with a tall wire fence all around it. I look more closely, and see small green clumps growing in there, and realize those are different kinds of lettuce. A vegetable garden. They're growing their own vegetables.

They're both in blue jeans. His T-shirt is dusty rose, with words on it I can't read from here, while hers is wordless and pale blue. They both wear sweatbands around their foreheads, his white, hers the same blue as her T-shirt. She's wearing gloves, he isn't.

They're absorbed in their work, digging with trowels, inserting little plastic markers to show what they've planted. I look at him, as I walk by. It's probably only the dirt streaks on his face, but to me he looks more than 50. If they think he's lying at interviews . . .

No. That's a powerful resumé. If there were jobs to be had, in our shared industry, he would have one. Before me, he would have one. He's the most recent arrival among our group of unemployed, and even without my intercession he wouldn't be with us long.

I know him now, know what he looks like. I walk on up the slope, and a while farther on it begins to get steeper, so I stop to sit on a stub of stone wall and look back down the way I've come, and think things over.

It's just as well I didn't bring the Luger today. I am *not* going to do anything while the wife's around, period.

Rested, I walk back down the slope. I wonder, on the way down, should I start a conversation? Ask directions, something like that? But what's the point? In fact, I'm much better off if I don't talk to him. It was doubly horrible with Everett Dynes, having talked with him, gotten to know him, like him. I'm not going to let that happen again.

They're still at work, struggling toward vegetable self-sufficiency. A black Honda Accord is in their driveway; I memorize the license number.

I continue on down to New Haven Road, and cross it to the parking lot, and a state trooper's car is parked behind mine. When I get closer, a young trooper with cold eyes rises from inspecting the damage to the front of the Voyager and looks at me. "Sir? This your car?"

This far away, the alert has gone out. I'm surprised, but of course I don't show it. "Yes, it is."

"Could you tell me how you got banged up here?"

"I was just asked that question last week," I say. "Over in Kingston, New York. What the heck is going on?"

"Sir," he says, "I'd like to know what happened here."

"Okay," I say, and shrug, and tell him the story; the pickup truck backs out of the lumberyard in the rain, unavoidable collision.

He listens, watching various parts of my face, then says, "Sir, may I see your license and registration?"

"Sure," I say. While I'm getting them out, I say, "I sure wish I knew what was going on."

He thanks me for the documents, and goes away to his car, which is blocking mine. I take off my windbreaker, feeling warm from the walk, and toss it on top of the resumé on the passenger seat, with my cap. Then I sit behind the wheel, lower my window, and listen to the burbly rush of the water in the eddy. It's soothing, and the air is sweet and not too warm, and I'm actually about to fall asleep right here when the trooper comes back, trying to be less cold and formal, which is rather like watching an I-beam try to curtsey.

"Thank you, sir," he says, and gives me back my license and registration.

He's about to go away, without another word, but I say, "Officer, give me a break, will you? What's going on? This is twice now."

He considers me. This is a need-to-know guy if there ever lived one. But he decides to relent. "A few days ago there was a hit-and-run," he tells me, "upstate New York. This type of vehicle. We expect it's got some damage on the front left."

"Upstate," I say. "No, I was in Binghamton. But thanks for telling me."

Nodding at the front of the Voyager, he says, "You ought to get that fixed."

"I'm taking it in tomorrow," I promise. "Thank you, officer."

17

For some reason, I seem to do all these things on Thursdays. I didn't plan it this way, but with Marjorie working Mondays and Wednesdays, and only one car in the family, this is the way it's been happening. I dealt with the first three resumés on Thursdays, and now here it is Thursday again, and I'm on my way back to Dyer's Eddy.

Will I deal with KBA today? I hope so. Get it over with. Now that the car is anonymous again.

It wasn't possible before this. Monday, after I took Marjorie to Dr. Carney's office (I kept the radio on in the car, tuned to WQXR, the *New York Times*'s classical music station, to hide the silence in there with us), I went to the dealer where I'd bought the Voyager, five years ago, back when I was replacing my cars every three years, and I talked with Jerry in the service department. I've had the car serviced there every time since I bought it, because I have to keep it going for who knows how long, so Jerry and I know one another, and he has some idea of my financial situation. He looked at the car, and he looked at me, and he said, "Your insurance covers this?" This is the first time we've dealt with damage.

I'd brought along my policy, which I handed to him, saying, "Two-hundred-fifty-dollar deductible."

He frowned over the policy. When he handed it back, he said, "Uh huh." Giving nothing away.

"Jerry," I said, "you know my situation. I can't afford two hundred and fifty dollars."

"This is a rough time, Mr. Devore," he said, and he sounded sympathetic. "They just let my wife go at the hospital."

I didn't follow. I said, "What? She was in the hospital?"

"She *worked* at the hospital. X-ray technician. She was there eleven years."

"Oh."

"Some big health care company from Ohio bought them up," he said, "and they're cutting back. All the problems about health costs, you know?"

Funny; I don't think of hospitals as being commercial institutions, bought and sold, belonging to corporations. But of course they are. I think of them as being like churches or firehouses, but they're just stores, after all. I said, "So they let her go? After eleven years?"

"Boom, like that," he said, and poked at

his thick moustache with a knuckle. "They had nine X-ray technicians, now they'll get along with six. To do the job nine did before."

"Still," I said, "that's a skill, isn't it? X-ray technician?"

He shook his head. "They're all cutting back," he said. "She thought it'd be easy, find another job, but the placement people told her they got more people with her training than they know what to do with."

"Jesus, Jerry," I said. "I am sorry. Believe me, I know how rough it can get."

"I know you do, Mr. Devore," he said, and looked around. "For all I know," he said, "in some office somewhere, right this minute, they're deciding this place only needs two service managers, not three."

"They won't let *you* go, Jerry," I said, though of course they might. They might do anything.

He knew it, too. "Nobody's safe, Mr. Devore," he said. Then he lowered his voice and said, "We know each other, I can take a chance with you, help you out a little. There's likely to be two different estimates, you know? One for you, one for the insurance company."

"God, that'd be a help, Jerry," I said.

"Take a seat in the waiting room," he told

me, "I'll see what I can do here."

I thanked him, and forty-five minutes later he gave me the two estimates, and grinned and said, "Make sure you send the right one."

"Oh, I will," I promised, and on the drive home I thought, I could have returned that favor by telling Jerry how to keep his job, if the crunch ever came. Just kill one of the other service managers. And if his wife had chopped three X-ray technicians before *she* got the chop, she'd still be working at that hospital.

But that's not a thing you could say to anybody.

An hour after I got home, the mail arrived. I can't help feeling a little queasy these days, every time I go out to the mailbox. I can't help looking around for parked cars. I know it's silly.

The mail included the accident report from the state police; very good. I phoned Bill Martin, my insurance guy, and he said to bring my paperwork right over, and I did, and we met in the office that used to be part of the built-in garage in his home. I gave him the police report and the esti-mate, the one for the insurance company, and he whistled and said, "Boy, you really banged it up, huh?"

"It wasn't fun," I told him.

"I'm sure it wasn't." He peered at me. "How are *you*, Burke? You okay? You didn't get hurt?"

I laughed and said, "Should I claim whiplash, Bill?"

"No, for God's sake," he said, in mock terror. "They're cracking down on fraud these days," he told me, "and looking for it harder, too. Everybody's squeezing a dollar."

"I know it."

"Where is the car? At the shop?"

"It's the only car I've got, Bill," I said. "It's right outside."

"Let's look at it."

"Okay."

We went out, and he looked at it, and looked at the estimate again, and then he looked at me, and casually he said, "You get a new position yet?"

"Not yet," I said.

He nodded, and we went back inside, and he said, "I'll fax these things off to the company today. There shouldn't be any problem."

"Great," I said. "When will it be okay to get it fixed? It looks kind of ugly now."

"Tomorrow, I hope," he said. "I'll give

you a call, when they fax the approval."

"Thanks, Bill."

We shook hands, and I left, and drove home.

It's a wide-ranging conspiracy.

Tuesday was our first meeting with the counselor. Marjorie had arranged it, not through any of the state agencies, after all, but through that church where we'd met Father Susten eleven years ago. "His name is Longus Quinlan," she told me, as we drove south toward Marshal, where the office was.

I was surprised to hear it was a man we were on our way to see, expected Marjorie to have preferred a woman, but I covered whatever surprise I might have showed by saying, "Longus. That's a weird name."

"Maybe it's a family name," she said.

Our appointment was in a newish redbrick building four stories high on the edge of Marshal, called Midway Medical Services Complex, midway between what two points I don't know. Life and death? Sanity and lunacy? Yesterday and tomorrow? Hope and despair?

Columbia Family Services was on the top floor. We rode up uncomfortably together in the elevator, and found a receptionist at the top, who took our names and asked us to wait in the reception area there, a simple pastel space with simple pastel furniture, clearly designed to keep everybody calm until we can get this trouble sorted out.

We only waited a minute or two in this well-meaning but very boring place before the receptionist said, "Mr. and Mrs. Devore?"

We were the only people waiting. We stood, and she pointed down the hall to our right and said, "Room four."

We thanked her, and walked down to room four, where the door stood open. We stepped in, and a heavyset black man of about forty, wearing white shirt and dark tie, got to his feet from behind his desk, smiled at us, and said, "Mr. and Mrs. Devore. Come on in. Why not close that door there."

Had Marjorie known he was black? I shot her a quick look as I shut the door, but her profile was blank, unreadable. She didn't look in my direction at all, but went straight over to sit in the chair Longus Quinlan gestured to. I came over, then, and took the remaining chair, and now we made a triangle.

It was a small office, with venetian blinds over the wide window at the back. The desk faced the door from under that window, with the other two chairs angled to face it from the side walls, closer to the door, so that people in those chairs faced the person at the desk directly but still had a good clear view of each other.

Once we were all seated, he gave us an amiable smile and said, "I'm Longus Quinlan, as you probably guessed. Father Enver told me he didn't really know much about you two, your connection with the church was before his time. Father Susten, was it?"

We agreed it was, and he nodded and said, "Before my time, too, but I've heard good things about him." Drawing a printed form toward himself, picking up a pen, he said, "Let's just get the boilerplate out of the way to begin with, okay?"

Well, the boilerplate, as he called it, took the whole first hour. I was sitting there waiting to hear how Marjorie would describe her affair to this counselor — waiting also to hear if there would be any clues to the guy's identity — but we never got to that. We got to all the normal personal information, and we got as far as bringing up the fact that our difficulties — unstated difficulties, as yet — seemed to be caused by my having been out of work for almost two years.

Then the time was up, that fifty-minute hour, and he put his hands together on top of the form on his desk and smiled at us and said, "I'm glad you've come to me, not because it means you've got a problem, but because it means you've got the desire to *solve* that problem. And what I'm here for, as I guess you already know, is not to solve the problem for you, because I can't do that. It can only come from inside yourselves. A Band-Aid from me isn't gonna help. My job is to help you look inside yourselves and see what strengths are there, see what you really want from each other and from life, and help you find the way that's already there inside you to rise above your problems and make things come out right. But one thing."

He held up a hand and raised a finger and smiled past it at us. "We don't yet know what it is you want," he said. "You *think* you know what you want. What you probably think is, what you want is what you used to have. But it may turn out, that isn't what you want, after all. That's one of the things we'll have to discover along the way."

What he's saying, I realized, is that we may wind up ending the marriage when this is all over, and then that'll turn out to have been what we wanted all along, and he'll have turned out to have done his job. Pretty good. How do I get into this line of work?

It was agreed we'd come to see him every

183

Tuesday at this same hour, and he'd bill the insurance company — we're still covered, for a while longer — and after he was paid by them we'd make up the difference, the twenty percent deductible that was our responsibility.

Then we left, shaking his hand and thanking him, and in the elevator going down, I said, "I've had a lot of job interviews went just like that."

"Oh, Burke," Marjorie said, and put her arms around me, and we kissed very warmly. But that was it, just that one instant. I pulled back, and so did she.

We listened to WQXR in the car again, going home. Along the way, I decided I didn't think much of Longus Quinlan, but I'd go along with the program, because maybe it could help after all, some, along the way. And eventually I'd find out who the man is.

And if these sessions are the price to keep Marjorie in the marriage, I'm more than willing to pay. After I've killed her boyfriend, and after I've got my new job, things will be all right again.

Then, on Wednesday, Bill Martin rang up in the morning to say I could go ahead and get the car fixed, and when I phoned Jerry at the dealer he said he'd expected the call and had the necessary parts waiting, so after I dropped Marjorie at Dr. Carney's office I drove on over to the dealership and they gave the Voyager its plastic surgery, to make it look like everybody else.

And now it's Thursday again, and I'm on my way to KBA.

18

That's where I sat the other day, the first time I came here, and walked up Footbridge Road. Now I sit in the Voyager, parked by the side of the road, next to that stub of stone wall where I caught my breath, last Sunday, after the climb. I sit in here, unnoticed, and I watch KBA and his wife put stakes in the ground, bring out flats of seedlings, dig and plant and fill. How they garden.

How they believe in togetherness, in fact. From this vantage, from the height of the Voyager, I can see down over the slope, the uncleared land above their house, and I can see them moving around together, working together, handing each other things, talking and sometimes laughing together. They're goddam irritating.

I got here a little before nine this morning, and they weren't yet out, but the Honda Accord was in the driveway, just as it had been last Sunday. I waited, sitting here, and at about nine-thirty out they came, dressed for gardening again, and they've been down there ever since, as the morning has slowly passed.

It's like watching a Japanese art movie,

seeing those two in the distance, putting in their crops, not knowing the bandit is in the hill above them, watching. This time, he isn't waiting for the harvest, to steal it. This time, he's waiting for them to separate, just for a few minutes. That's all I need.

But it doesn't happen. They brought a cordless phone out with them, and twice this morning I've watched the wife answer it. Once it was for her, and once she handed it on to him, but neither call made one of them go off alone into the house.

That's what I need, for *her* to go in. If she does, and if it looks as though she'll stay indoors for a while, I'll get out of the Voyager and take the Luger from under the raincoat on the passenger seat, and I'll walk down there and shoot him.

Or why doesn't one of them take the car, and go on an errand? If he leaves, I'll follow him and shoot him. If she leaves, I'll walk down to him in his garden and shoot him.

But neither happens. They keep working, and I suppose they're taking advantage of the cool and cloudy day to get all this hard laborious donkey labor done.

At twenty to twelve the mail delivery arrives, a youngish man in a small green station wagon with US MAIL posters in the windows. I suppose this is a second or third job, these days, for a lot of those people. At work most of their waking hours, and only sliding backward a little more every day.

Isn't there something in *Alice in Wonderland* about that?

They put down their tools and walk down to the mailbox *together*. What are they, Siamese twins?

I could almost do it, shoot them both, but the memory of Mr. and Mrs. Ricks holds me back. How horrible that was. It's enough I'm going to take this woman's husband, I can't take her life as well. I have to wait it out.

I'm very visible, parked just up the road, when they come out to the mailbox, but neither of them looks up in my direction at all. They're very involved in one another. He opens the mailbox, pulls out the little messy stack, distributes some to her, keeps some for himself. I see her ask the question, I see him shake his head in response; no job today. Then they go up to the house, together, put their mail on the table on the side porch, and walk back out to their garden.

Twelve-thirty. They compare watches, and go inside, hand in hand. Lunchtime; of course.

I'm hungry, too. Just north of town, I

noticed this morning, there's a small mall, with an extensive garden nursery and an Italian restaurant. I wait two minutes after they disappear into the house, just in case he has to go to the store for something, but when he doesn't emerge I drive on down to New Haven Road and turn left, and have a not very good spaghetti carbonara in the Italian restaurant, with coffee.

When I drive back up Footbridge Road, they're in the garden again, still together. I'm reluctant to park in the same place as this morning, because sooner or later they're bound to notice me, or neighbors farther up the hill will notice me. I drive another quarter mile, and pull off the road to consult my road atlas, and I see that this road is no use to me at all in this direction. It merely curves around and heads south, away from home. So I make a U-turn and drive slowly back down Footbridge Road.

Yes; there they are. There's no point watching them any more today. They'll simply keep on doing what they're doing, and then they'll go indoors together, and that will be the end of it.

Not a Thursday this time, then. Maybe Friday.

I drive on down to New Haven Road and turn left, and drive past the place where I had the not very good lunch — tomorrow, if I'm still on watch, I'll have to find somewhere else to eat — and I head home.

One strange advantage to this miserable experience with Marjorie is that I no longer have to tell her where I'm going. We aren't talking to one another that much any more. This morning, after breakfast, I simply got into the Voyager and drove away.

Not having to make up destinations and job interviews and library research is a great burden lifted. Not the greatest burden, of course.

Driving homeward, I can't help but contrast KBA and his wife with Marjorie and me. It's true he hasn't been out of work as long as I, and he could have a much thicker financial cushion. His resumé didn't mention children, and I saw no sign of children around the house, and come to think of it, that togetherness of theirs is something I associate with childless couples.

Children are the great expense in life, or one of the great expenses. If KBA and his wife have no children, and if they have a bigger nest egg, and I know he hasn't been jobless as long as I have (and he's still under fifty, the son of a bitch, as he likes to tell us), then naturally he'll be calmer about his situation than I can be, he'll be more patient, less worried. It won't affect his marriage as much, not yet. But wait till he's out of work for two or three years, *then* see how much togetherness they show.

Well. We won't be testing that, will we?

19

I can't sleep, at first, tonight. Marjorie and I are polite with one another now, even concerned about one another, but neither of us has much to say. We watched television together this evening, and at ten o'clock there was some sort of talking-heads special on about the millennium, which we watched by unspoken mutual agreement, but neither of us made any comments during the program, as we always used to do.

I missed that, the little disrespectful remarks about the TV show in front of us, and I'm sure Marjorie missed it, too, but there was no hope that either of us could break through.

Being in bed together is grim. We don't touch. We don't acknowledge each other's presence. The lights are off, and because today's cloud cover has continued, the night is very dark, and we lie here next to one another like parcels to be delivered, and for a while I can't sleep. I don't know if Marjorie's dropped off or not, I only know that I am awake, and my mind turns this way and that.

I think about many things. I think about

the job to come, in Arcadia. I think about killing the boyfriend, when I find out who he is. I think about the circumstances that have led me here, to this thorny place. And I think about the millennium.

Strange, that. I'd never thought about it before, that the simple arbitrary numbering of years could have an effect on us, but it turns out to be so. Having the number of the year change from 1 to 2, which will happen just two and a half years from now, has a great effect, it seems, on people's minds and actions, and on society itself.

It's ridiculous, of course. There couldn't be a more arbitrary number in life than the number of the year. The one we use is dated from the birth of somebody who possibly existed, and if he did exist his birthday was either four years or six years earlier than the date chosen when the year was being worked out. So even if you go along with Jesus Christ — yes, he's God, yes, he was born, yes, we number our years from his birth — even then this can't be 1997, the way we think it is. No, it has to be either 2001 or 2003, and the millennium's already gone past, so it's too late to worry.

The Chinese think the year's a different number from us, and the Jews go with yet another number. But none of that matters.

The generally accepted idea in *our* society is, the world is going to reach the magic number two thousand very soon now, and therefore people are going a little nuts.

It happened last time, a thousand years ago, as the program explained. Strange religions came along, mass suicides, strange migrations, all kinds of milling around, pushing and shoving, all because the year 1000 was on its way.

Even the hundred-year anniversaries have an effect, the same way the full moon is supposed to. But the thousand-year marker is the big one.

One reason, the program said, is that it seems that many people, even intelligent, educated, sophisticated people, believe way down inside themselves, down at some instinctive level, that the millennium is the end of the world. They believe somehow the world is going to blow up or vanish or melt or spin out of the solar system or do *something* cataclysmic. That's why there's more and more religious fanaticism at the moment, and more and more strange cults, and more and more group suicides. The millennium is shaking us up, the way a high-pitched tone shakes up a dog.

Lying here, unable to sleep, in the darkness, I find myself wondering if that's why

I'm out of a job. They didn't suggest this on the program, it's my own idea, which I'd never thought of before, but what if that's what's happened? All these hard-nosed executives, all these tough businessmen, making their brutal decisions, firing people from healthy companies, stripping everything down, ignoring the human cost, ignoring their own humanity, what if, without their knowing it, without their even being able to accept the idea, what if they're doing it because they believe the world is coming to an end?

2000; and it all stops.

Maybe that is what they're doing. It's as good an explanation as anything *they've* offered. They're trying to make everything neat and perfect for the end of the world. When the hammer crashes down, when everything comes to a dead stop, they want to be in the very best position possible.

This kind of business management that has never been seen in the world before, trashing productive people from productive careers in productive companies, is happening because of the millennium. Because of the year 2000. I'm out of work because the human race has gone mad.

On that thought, I fall asleep. It's only later that I wake up to terror.

20

I get a late start, having had trouble rousing myself this morning, after last night. But I'm on the road finally a little after nine, and make the turnoff to Footbridge Road at quarter to ten.

Last night. After the trouble I had getting to sleep, with all those thoughts circling, suddenly I woke up in the middle of the night, in pitch-black darkness because of that cloud cover — which is still here today, but not as though it's going to rain — and I woke up into that blackness with a sudden feeling of terror.

At first I couldn't imagine what it was that had me so terrified, and I lay there rigid, on my back, staring up at black emptiness, listening to the tiny inhabited silences of the house, while my brain tried to find its way back from panic, tried to sort out what the problem was. And when at last it did, and I figured out what it was that had so frightened me that it had driven me up out of sleep, what I was afraid of was me.

The boyfriend. Somehow, in my sleeping mind, the boyfriend had appeared, or I mean the *idea* of the boyfriend; I still don't know who he is. But that thought, the idea of the boyfriend, was circling in my sleeping brain, along with the idea that I was going to kill him when I found out who he was, and how easy that idea was, how unlike the angry way that people say, "I could kill him!" or "I'll kill that guy!"

Mine hadn't been like that. What I had said, in my mind, calmly, was, "Oh, okay, he's a problem, so I'll kill him," and I had absolutely meant it. Absolutely.

And that's why I woke up in terror, thinking, What am I becoming? What have I become?

I'm not a killer. I'm not a murderer, I never was, I don't want to be such a thing, soulless and ruthless and empty. That's not me. What I'm doing now I was forced into, by the logic of events; the shareholders' logic, and the executives' logic, and the logic of the marketplace, and the logic of the workforce, and the logic of the millennium, and finally by my own logic.

Show me an alternative, and I'll take it. What I'm doing now is horrible, difficult, frightening, but I have to do it to save my own life.

If I kill the boyfriend, it will be something else. Not exactly casual, but *normal*. As though killing has become a normal response for me, one of the ways I deal with a problem. Simple; I murder a human being.

The untroubled *ease* with which I'd thought that thought — kill him, why not — is what's frightening, what scares me. I'm harboring an armed and dangerous man, a merciless killer, a monster, and he's inside me.

That's another reason why I have to get through this process very soon, I can't let it drag on. It's changing me, and I don't like the change. The sooner this business is *done,* and the sooner I'm in that job in Arcadia, then the sooner this new change can start to bleach away, like the most recent fat melting off when you first go on a diet.

Which is why I just can't accommodate the Asches' togetherness forever. They're going to have to move apart from one another soon, or else. I have a horror of killing the wife, very like the horror of that decision to kill the boyfriend, but my greater horror is in staying in this swamp too long, being changed permanently by it, becoming forever somebody I wouldn't be able to stand to be around.

So I've come to that decision this morning, as I drive toward Dyer's Eddy. It wasn't an easy decision, a blithe decision, like deciding to kill the boyfriend, but it's solid, and it's

unswerving. If those two insist on living together, every second of every day, they'll just
have to die together.

Footbridge Road. I make the right turn,
and drive slowly up the easy slope, and the
first thing I notice when I reach their property is that the Accord is gone from the
driveway. Have they driven off somewhere
together? Will they be out all day? Damn; I
should have got an earlier start.

I continue to drive upward, slowly, and
there she is, the wife, in the garden, in a
pale yellow T-shirt and white headband. She
has a clipboard and seems to be doing a
drawing. A chart of the garden, I suppose,
to show where everything is.

She's there. The Accord is gone. He's in
it. Damn, damn, and double damn, if only
I'd been here earlier, when he left.

The nursery. It comes to me in a sudden
leap, an immediate understanding. The garden nursery down there in the mall, across
the parking lot from the Italian restaurant
where I ate yesterday. He's there, I know he
is.

I make my U-turn at the same place as
yesterday. I drive more rapidly down the hill.
It won't do me any good to meet him coming
back. If I'm ever to come across him on the
road, it will have to be when we're both

traveling in the same direction, so I can pull up next to him and shoot him. Not to meet him head-on.

I certainly can't do what I did to Everett Dynes in Lichgate, with the car, if KBA is in a car.

Traffic delays me at the turn into New Haven Road. Why does it have to be a left? Cars come from one direction, then cars come from the other direction, then back to the first direction. There's never quite enough space in between for me to get out there, and I expect at any second one of those cars coming down the main road from the left will be a black Honda Accord.

No. A space at last, and I take it, jerking out into New Haven Road, swinging to the left, then running along in convoy with all these other cars. What is it about Friday around here?

It's another left turn into the mall with the nursery, and again I have to wait. I'm punching the steering wheel with my right fist. I know he's in there, I know it as surely as if I'd seen him drive in. And now, in my mind's eye, I can see him paying for his purchases, coming out to the car, getting in, driving out, making that easy right turn over there while I sit *here*, stuck.

Another break; I lunge through it, make

the turn, drive into the mall.

It seems as though most of this mall is parking lot, fringed with a collar of low buildings. The nursery is at the front left, so I drive over there, slowly cruise the aisles. I know his license number.

And there it is. The black Honda Accord, sitting there, waiting, not far from the entrance to the nursery. I knew I was right, I knew it.

There isn't another parking spot near his, but I see a heavyset woman stuffing packages into a green Ford Taurus, one row over from KBA and about three slots to the right. I drive around there, and now she's being a good citizen, slowly waddling her shopping cart back to one of the collection points. Most people don't do that, lady. Most people leave the goddam cart where it is, and get into their goddam automobile, and drive *away*.

I can see the Accord over there, just the top of it. Still there. KBA isn't near it. Not yet, he isn't.

She comes back to her car, and for a second our eyes meet. I nod and smile, to let her know I'm waiting for her space, and she continues ponderously on, with no reaction, in no hurry. I wait while she finds her car keys in that great horse's feedbag she has dangling from her shoulder. I wait while she arranges herself behind the wheel just *so*, and the feedbag on the seat beside her just *so*, and the rearview mirror just *so*, and by now I'm ready to shoot her and come back to get KBA tomorrow.

I have plenty of time to think about this, waiting for her to get the hell away from here. What if I were to do such a thing, kill a few of the more obnoxious people one comes across? Then, when I kill KBA, it will just seem like more of the same. And if they draw any connection between KBA and my first resumé, Herbert Everly, it's just the work of a random killer. The famous serial killer.

People believe in serial killers these days. Movies and novels have come out populated almost entirely by serial killers, as though it's a tribe, or a fraternal organization, like the Elks. The great thing about serial killers, I guess, for the people who make up those stories, is that they never have to worry about motivation. *Why* did that person kill that person? It's unfair to ask that, in such a story, because the answer always is, he did it because that's what he does.

I have a motive. I have a motive, and a very specific category of person I have to get rid of. Which means, unless I'm very careful,

I could be vulnerable. A clever detective might begin to get me in his sights. But if Everly and KBA, my only two gunshot victims in Connecticut, were merely part of the pattern of a serial killer, wouldn't that make me safe?

And does this woman in the green Ford Taurus deserve to live, any longer?

She backs out of the parking space. She doesn't bother to look at me, or acknowledge me. She drives away, and she will never know just how close a call that was.

I ease the Voyager into the space, and stop. Still in the car, I put on the raincoat, then transfer the Luger to its right pocket. This is the kind of raincoat that in college we called the shoplifter's special, because the pockets are open at the top inside, to give access from both the inside and the outside of the raincoat, which means you can put your hand in the pocket and *through* the pocket. And that's what I do, and hold the Luger waiting in my lap, as I keep my eye on the Honda Accord.

Serial killer. That had been a strange thought. It was never serious, though.

I wait ten minutes, and then I see him. He's pushing a shopping cart, laden with small boxes and white plastic shopping bags, with a big sack of peat moss lying over everything else. The Accord is parked facing in, so he stops at the back of it and opens the trunk, while I climb out of the Voyager, holding the Luger against my right leg, and walk forward between the cars until I'm on the same row as he is, just three cars to my left.

He's wrestled the peat moss bag into the trunk, and now he's surrounding it with the rest of his purchases. He's bent forward, head partly under the open trunk lid, as he moves his new boxes and bags.

I stop behind him. I say, "Are you Mr. Kane Asche?"

He turns, with a questioning smile. "Yes?"

"I know you are," I say, and bring the Luger up past the right flap of my raincoat, the raincoat bunching up around my right wrist, and I shoot him.

The bullet doesn't hit his eye, it hits his right cheek and makes a mess there. The raincoat pulled my arm down, just that little bit. His eyes stare, as he falls backward, half in the trunk, half sagging down across the rear bumper.

This is no good. This is messy, bloody, awful. *And* he's alive. I lean closer, put the barrel of the Luger almost against that staring terrified right eye, and I shoot again, and his head snaps back, and now he lies there, mostly on his back, sprawled, mouth wide open, one eye wide open.

I walk, not briskly, back to the Voyager. I get in, leaving the Luger in my lap, covered by the flap of my raincoat. I start the Voyager, shift into reverse, back out of there, drive away.

There's very little traffic, all the way home.

21

Well, that wasn't so bad.

And I got a good night's sleep, dreamless — at least, nothing I remember or that bothered me in any way — and woke up refreshed this morning, feeling positive about things for the first time in a while.

I think what it is, in addition to the business with Asche being simpler and cleaner than the two before it, almost as clear-cut as the very first one, I think there's the knowledge that finally I'm more than halfway through this thing. At the beginning, I had to do the six resumés, and I have to do Upton "Ralph" Fallon, but then that's it, that's the end of it, forever and ever.

(I'll know how to handle the situation ahead of time, if anything like this ever looms again.)

But now I've done four of them, so there are only three to go, and that lifts my spirits considerably. It's like realizing you've finally made it past the midway mile marker in a long and grueling race.

Also, there's some sort of early indication that there might be a thaw between me and Marjorie. Nothing tangible, really, no words said on the subject, merely a difference in the quality of the air inside the house. A little conversation between us, casual, about minor things. Not like normal life exactly, but closer.

This change may have happened because she'd finally come out with it, told the truth, or at least partly, and doesn't have to keep her burdensome secret any more. (If only it could be that easy for me.) And also probably because I'd agreed to the idea of counseling, and because the first session has happened, however little might have been accomplished so far, and because it looks as though the counseling can continue.

And maybe, just maybe, even more than all of that, it could be there's been a change in me as well. Maybe, when I was determined to kill the boyfriend, when I wasn't even turning it over in my mind but just accepting it as a fixed and certain thing to be done, maybe during that time I was clenched and tense around Marjorie, stalking her, watching her, searching for a trail to my prey. And now that I've caught on to myself, stopped myself, now that I've realized how awful that idea was and given it up completely, maybe she can sense a new ease in me, and my relaxation helps her to relax.

Long-term joblessness, it hurts everything. Not just the discarded worker, but everything. Maybe it's wrong of me, snobbish or something, to think this hits the middle class more than other people, because I'm middle class (and trying to stay middle class), but I do think it does, it hurts us more. The people at the extremes, the poor and the very rich, are used to the idea that life has great swings, now you're doing well, now you're doing badly. But the middle class is used to a smooth progress through life. We give up the highs, and in return we're supposed to be protected from the lows. We give our loyalty to a company, and in return they're supposed to give us a smooth ride through life. And now it isn't happening, and we feel betrayed.

We were supposed to be protected and safe, here in the middle, and something's gone wrong. When a poor person loses some lousy little job that had no future anyway, and has to go back on welfare, that's an expected part of life. When a millionaire shoots the works on a new venture that falls flat and all of a sudden he's broke, he knew all along that was a possibility. But when *we* slip back, just a little bit, and it goes on for month after month, and it goes on for year after year, and maybe we're never going to get back to that particular level of solvency and protection and self-esteem we used to enjoy, it throws us. It throws us.

And what's happening is, because we're family people, it's throwing the families, too. Children turn bad, in a number of ways. (Thank God we don't have that problem.) Marriages end.

Do I want my marriage to end? No. So I have to realize that what's happening to us now is only happening because I've been out of work for so long. If I were still at Halcyon Mills, Marjorie wouldn't be running around with somebody else. She wouldn't be working two stupid jobs. I wouldn't be killing people.

I didn't play the radio in the Voyager when I drove Marjorie to the New Variety just after lunch, for her afternoon cashier job, and that's because we were talking, we were in an actual conversation. It felt good. We talked about whether or not we might want to go see the movie that's at the New Variety now, and that she'd try to get a sense of whether or not the movie's any good while she was there this afternoon. And we talked about dinner, what to have, should I stop at a store after dropping her off or should we shop together later when I pick her up again. We didn't talk about anything that matters

— money, jobs, the kids, marriage, counseling — but just *talking* was enough.

And now I've come home, and I'm in my office, and I'm planning my next move. Only two resumés to go. What an astonishment. What a relief.

Three weeks ago, I wasn't even sure I could do it. I was afraid I wasn't up to it. Three weeks ago. It feels like a thousand years.

I study them, my two remaining resumés, trying to decide which to go after first, which to go after second. I'll start on it tomorrow, drive to that resumé's address, check it out, see how it's going to go.

One of the remaining resumés is here in Connecticut, the other over in New York State. And of course Upton "Ralph" Fallon is in New York State, too.

The easiest ones have been in Connecticut. It was in Massachusetts that Mrs. Ricks complicated the situation and made it all so much worse, and it was in New York that I'd had to hit that poor man with the car.

Maybe it's just superstition, but I think the way for me to go is to finish Connecticut first. Do that next, then the last two are both in New York. And then it's over.

22

The phone rarely rings when we're asleep, maybe once or twice a year, and that's usually some drunk with a wrong number. But there's been a change in us, in Marjorie and me and our relationship to the late-night telephone call, and I never realized it before.

I come slowly awake, in the dark middle of the night, very beclouded by sleep. I can hear Marjorie murmuring into the telephone, and then she turns the light on, and I squint, not wanting to be awake, and the clock says 1:46. (We deliberately got a bedroom alarm-clock-radio *without* illuminated clock numbers, because we like to sleep in darkness. I'm always aware of those floating numbers at the level of my sleeping head whenever I spend a night in a motel.)

Slowly I focus on Marjorie and her conversation, and it's something troubling to her that's keeping her responses very down and quiet. "Yes, I understand," she says, and "We'll get there as soon as we can," and, "I appreciate that, thank you."

Sometime in through there, during the course of the conversation, failing to understand who she can possibly be talking to or what possible subject it could be about, I suddenly have my realization about us and late-night phone calls, and it is this: I didn't hear the phone ring.

We have phones on both sides of the bed, but it's only the phone on my side that rings, quietly. It used to be, whenever the phone rang at night, I would immediately wake up and deal with it — the drunk, the wrong number — and Marjorie would sleep right through the whole thing. I think in every marriage, that's one of the unconscious items that's worked out early on, who will wake up when the phone rings. In our marriage, it was always me, and now it isn't me any more.

Since I lost my job, Marjorie is the one who wakes up when the phone rings. She can't count on me any more; she has to be alert for herself.

I sit there, while Marjorie continues to talk into the phone and listen to the phone, and I turn this new understanding over and over in my head, to study it. I don't know if it makes me mostly angry or mostly sad or mostly ashamed. All three, I guess.

Marjorie hangs up, and looks at me. She's very solemn. "It's Billy," she says.

I think, an accident! At the same instant, I think, but he's in bed in this house, in his room, asleep. Stupid, still clearing cobwebs, I say, "Billy?"

"He was arrested," she says, astoundingly. "He and another boy."

"Arrested? *Arrested?*" I sit up, almost falling over. *I'm* the one who's supposed to be arrested! "Why would he — ? Why would they — ? For God's sake, what *for?*"

"They broke into a store," she says. "The police found them, and they tried to run away. They're at the state police barracks in Raskill."

I'm already struggling out from under the covers. The sheet and blanket cling to my legs, not wanting to release me into this terrible unknown. "Poor Billy," I say. A store? What store? "It's all my fault," I say, and go into the bathroom to brush my teeth.

The CID detective at the state police barracks, a sympathetic soft-voiced man in a rumpled brown suit, talks to us first, in a small square office painted pale yellow. Three walls are smooth shiny plastic, the fourth, an exterior wall, is bare rough concrete block. The floor is a different kind of smooth shiny plastic, black, and the ceiling is plastic soundproofing panels, off-white. Since the canary yellow paint on the concrete block was certainly put there as a very good sealer, it occurs to me that, if anything really horrible were to happen in this room, they could hose it clean in two or three minutes. From my position, in this green plastic chair facing the gray metal desk, I can't see a drain in the floor, but I wouldn't be surprised if there is one.

Did the architect plan the room this way? Do architects think in such terms, when they design police stations? Does it bother them? Or are they pleased at their professional skill?

Am *I* pleased, at my professional skill? My new skill, I mean. I've never thought about that before, and I don't want to think about it now.

It's very hard for me to concentrate on the detective, here in this deniable room. I can't even retain his name. I want to see Billy, that's all I know.

Marjorie is much better at dealing with this than I am. She asks questions. She takes notes. She's as quiet and calm and sympathetic as the detective himself. And, through their conversation, that I tune into and tune out of, over and over, I finally understand what happened.

It took place in the same mall where Marjorie works for Dr. Carney. There's a small computer store there, that sells business software and computer games and things like that. Apparently, Billy and this friend of his from school went there this afternoon — yesterday afternoon, I guess, by now — and found a moment to sneak unobserved into the back and rig the back door, the door that opens to the wide alley in back and that's used for deliveries and trash removal. They rigged that door so it would seem locked but wasn't. Then, tonight, long after we thought Billy was asleep in his bed, he snuck out of the house, was picked up by his friend — the friend has a car — and they drove to the mall, and slipped into the store from the back.

What they didn't know was, the store had already been robbed in exactly the same way three times before, and as a result they'd added a new burglar alarm, a silent alarm that alerted the state police barracks here, so that when Billy and his friend went in, the state police knew it at once, and four police cars converged on the place, two each from the state trooper barracks and the local town police.

The boys were leaving, with canvas tote bags full of software, when the police arrived. They abandoned the bags and ran, and were immediately, as the detective kept saying, apprehended.

The police have everything, or almost

everything. They have an admission from the friend. They have absolute proof the robbery was planned and the door rigged, so they can demonstrate it was a planned crime and not a spur of the moment thing. They have police eyewitnesses who saw the boys carrying the stolen goods. They have the attempted flight.

What they don't have yet, and what they want, is proof that these two boys committed the three previous burglaries.

I hear the detective, and I hear how sympathetic he sounds, and I hear him say they're just trying to wrap this all up, get all this paperwork out of their hair, get it all behind them, and I can see Marjorie nodding and being sympathetic in return, ready to help this honest unassuming civil servant, and finally I rouse myself to speak, and I say, "This is the first time."

The detective gives me his slow sad smile, happy I've joined the group, sorry we have to meet this way. "We can't be sure of that yet, I'm afraid, Mr. Devore," he says.

"We can be sure," I say. "This is the first time for Billy. I don't know about the other boy, or what he might say about Billy, but this is Billy's first time."

Marjorie says, "Burke, we're all just trying to —"

"I know what we're trying to do," I say. I look flat and level at the detective. I say, "If this is Billy's first time, the judge will give him probation. If this is Billy's fourth time, the judge will put him in jail, and my son doesn't belong in jail. This is Billy's first time."

He nods his head slightly, but says, "Mr. Devore, we can't be sure what a judge will do."

"We can guess," I say. "This is Billy's first time. I'd like to speak to him now."

"Mr. Devore," he says, "this has been a shock to you, I know, but please believe me, I've been around this sort of thing a lot, and nobody wants to persecute your son, or make life tougher than it already is for anybody. We just want to clear this all up, that's all."

"I'd like to speak to my son," I say.

"Very soon," he promises, and turns back to Marjorie, more fertile ground than I am, he thinks, and says, "I hope you'll urge Billy to come clean on this. Just get it off his chest, get it all behind him, and then the whole family can get back to normal life."

I watch him, and I listen to him, and I know him now. He's my enemy. Billy isn't a human being to him, none of us are human beings to his kind, we're all just paperwork, irritating paperwork, and they don't care a pin what happens to the people involved, so long as their paperwork is neat and tidy. He is my enemy, and he is Billy's enemy, and we know now what to do about enemies. We do not accommodate our enemies.

I always believed that I and my family and my home and my possessions and my neighborhood and my world were exactly what the police were here to safeguard. Everybody I know believes that, it's another part of living this life in the middle. But now I understand, they aren't here for *us* at all, they're here for themselves. That's their agenda. They're the same as the rest of us, they're here for themselves, and they are not to be trusted.

Marjorie has understood what I was saying, and she gives the detective less sympathy than before, and he quickly realizes he's lost her, so he brings out the forms. The inevitable forms. Before he gets to fill them out, though, Marjorie says, "Can we take Billy home with us?"

"Not tonight, I'm afraid," he says, and the son of a bitch does a wonderful imitation of sincerity. "In the morning," he says, "Billy will appear before the judge, and your lawyer can ask for his release in your custody, and I'm sure the judge will go along with it."

"But not tonight," Marjorie says.

Looking at his watch, the detective tries a smile, saying, "Mrs. Devore, tonight's almost gone, anyway."

"He's never been in jail before," Marjorie says.

Oh, please; what does this creature care? He's in jail all the time. I say, "You have some forms there? Before I get to see my son?"

"This won't take a minute," he says.

It's all the same questions, all the usual crap. Of course, it has the one zinger question in it: "And, Mr. Devore, where are you employed?"

"I'm unemployed," I say.

He lifts his eyes from the form. "For how long, Mr. Devore?"

"Approximately two years."

"And where did you work before that?"

"I was a product line manager at Halcyon Mills, up in Reed."

"Oh, is that the company that went bust?"

"They didn't go bust," I say. "They merged, two companies merged. Our operation was moved to the Canadian branch. They didn't take any U.S. employees with them."

"How long were you there?" Now his sympathy almost does seem real.

"With the firm, twenty years."

"You were downsized, eh?"

"That's right."

"A lot of that going around," he suggests.

I say, "Not in your business, I think."

He laughs, a little self-consciously. "Oh, well, crime," he says. "A growing industry."

"I wonder why," I say.

"I don't think I've ever seen them before," Marjorie whispers to me, as we follow the detective down a concrete block corridor toward whatever space now holds Billy.

I'm irritable, holding myself in. I give Marjorie an angry frown, not wanting confusion at this point, wanting clarity, and I say, "You never saw *who* before?"

"The parents," she says, and gives me her own surprised look. "Burke, they were *sitting* back there in the big room, when we came through. Didn't you see them? They have to be the other boy's parents."

"I didn't notice them," I say. I'm focused, Billy is my concern.

"They looked frightened," she says.

"They should," I say.

There's a uniformed trooper at a desk in the hall. He sees us coming, and stands to unlock a yellow metal door. Everything is yellow, pale yellow. It's supposed to be spring, I suppose.

The detective says, "If you could keep it to five, ten minutes, okay? He'll be home in the morning, you can do most of your talking then."

"Thank you," Marjorie says.

The trooper holds the door open. We go in, Marjorie first, and as I go by the trooper says, "Knock when you want to come out."

"All right," I say, thinking, it isn't that easy.

This is the cell; my God. I'd thought it would be a visiting room or something, but I suppose a small state trooper barracks like this couldn't be expected to have very elaborate arrangements. Still, it's a shock. This is a cell, and we're in it with Billy.

He was sitting on the cot, but now he stands. There's only the cot, attached to the wall, and a chair, attached to the floor, and a toilet without a seat. That's all there is.

Billy is in his socks, and his belt is gone. From the puffiness of his face, I would say he's been crying, but he isn't crying now. He has a closed, bruised, defensive, sullen look to him. He's shut himself down inside himself, and I can't say I blame him.

I let Marjorie go first, asking him how he is, assuring him she loves him, assuring him everything will be all right. She doesn't talk about the burglary, thank God.

I let her go on a while, and then I say, "Billy."

He looks at me, ducking his head, pathetically abashed and defiant, almost standing up to me. Marjorie steps back, white-faced, watching me, not knowing what I mean to do.

I say, "Billy, we are not alone." I point to my ear, and then I point around at the walls. I keep my face deadpan.

He blinks, having expected almost anything else from me; recrimination, accusation, tears, perhaps self-pity. He looks around at the walls, and then I can see him trying to gather himself together, trying to be receptive and alert instead of closed-down and mulish, and he nods at me, and waits.

I say, "Billy, this is the first time you ever did anything like this. This is the first time you ever went along with anybody at all to break into that store."

I raise an eyebrow, and point at him, to let him know it's his turn to speak. "Yes," he says, looking at my finger.

"That's right," I say. "I don't know this friend of yours, I don't know what he's likely to say, how much he's likely to want to spread the blame, but *whatever* he says, Billy, don't you ever change from the truth, and the truth is, that is the first time you ever

222

broke into that store, or any other store, or any place at all."

"Yes," he says. He's looking now like a drowner seeing the man with the rope.

"That's all you have to remember," I say, and then I spread my arms, and I say, "Billy, come here."

He comes over and I embrace him hard, feeling my heart well up into my throat. "We'll get through this, Billy," I murmur against his ear. He's as tall as I am, but not as husky. I say, "We'll get through it, and we'll come out the other side, and we'll be okay. We'll all be okay, my darling. It'll be okay, my love. It'll be okay, my sweetheart."

Then he cries. Well, we all do.

We're driving home, and it's not long after three in the morning, but I'm not finished yet tonight. Beside me, Marjorie says how good I was, how strong I was, and I say, "It isn't over. It's just starting. There's more to be done."

"In the morning, we have to call a lawyer."

"Before the morning," I say. "There's more to be done tonight. But there is that, too, in the morning. The lawyer. Who was the lawyer, when we bought the house? Do you remember his name?"

"Amgott," she says. "I'll call him, if you want."

"That might be better," I agree. "To hear from the mother."

I leave the car out, don't put it in the garage, because I'm not finished tonight. "What is it, Burke?" Marjorie asks.

"Some clean-up," I say.

She follows me through the house into Billy's room, the room that has been so much neater lately, and I thought it was because he couldn't afford to buy things any more. I open his closet door, and push the clothing to one side, and there it is. He's built a bookcase in there, or a software case, three shelves of the stuff. There must be thousands of dollars there, far more than they'd need to move the charge up from petty larceny to grand larceny.

"Oh, Billy," Marjorie says, as though she might faint.

"We have to get rid of it all," I say. "Right now, before they come around in the morning with a search warrant." I smile at her, trying to get her spirits up. "Finally," I say, "a use for all those plastic bags from the supermarket you keep saving."

We get her bag of bags from the kitchen, we load them up with the bright-colored

224

little boxes, and we carry the full bags through the house to the side door. Neither of us is at all sleepy.

Billy *should* have these things, he should know about them and have experience of them, if he's going to make it in the new world coming. I should be providing them, I should be making it possible for him to keep up with what he has to learn. This is my failure. Billy wasn't wrong to do what he did, he was right. He was wrong to go to the well too often, though.

I'll never say anything like that to him, of course. A father has responsibilities. Get him out of this mess, but don't condone, and certainly don't encourage.

Six shopping bags; they fill up the backseat of the Voyager. I thought I'd drive alone, but Marjorie wants to come with me, and I'm happy for the companionship.

I drive nearly thirty miles through the dark and empty land. We meet only two other cars the whole way. Almost every house is black dark. Every business is shut down tight.

My goal is a different shopping mall, a bigger one, that I noticed once on my drive to Fall City, weeks ago, when I was after Herbert Everly. This place also is shut tight, dark, deserted. I drive around the back of

225

it, then circle the whole complex, to be certain there are no police cars or private security cars tucked away in the shadows, waiting. There are none.

Along the way, I've observed the dumpsters, the big green truck-sized trash receivers, out behind the various stores, and I choose the supermarket's dumpster to stop next to. A faint unpleasant aroma rises from it, which is why I chose it. Boxes, bags, heads of ancient lettuce; so much stuff in there, not picked up on a Saturday night.

I throw the bags in, one after the other. They disappear, anonymous trash. No software shows.

When we drive back homeward, alone in the world, Marjorie holds my hand.

23

They're waiting for us when we finally get to the house, the police. I'd thought they would be.

It's three in the afternoon by now, the whole day is shot. It was impossible to find a lawyer this morning, a Sunday morning, so finally, at around ten o'clock, I called the state police to ask them where the court was, and they gave me an address and a phone number, and I called the court, and spoke with a woman who was determined to be nothing but efficient, not to permit the slightest vestige of individuality or personality to peek through. That might be a good strategy, I suppose, if you answer the phone at the courthouse for your living.

I kept explaining my problem to this woman, and she kept offering me no help at all, no guidance, nothing, and then all at once she asked me if by any chance either I or the defendant qualified to be taken on by the public defender.

That hadn't even occurred to me. Such things don't occur to people like me. I said, "I've been out of work for two years. I've used up my unemployment insurance. I have no income."

"You should have said so before," she said, being snippy.

I didn't bother to tell her I'm not used to offering my failure as an asset, and she went on to give me another number to call.

Which I did, and this was answered by somebody who sounded like, and possibly was, a teenage girl. I told her the situation, and that the court had given me this number to call, and she took down a lot of information — or at least asked me for a lot of information — and said someone would call me soon.

Then an hour went by, in which nothing happened. Billy was supposed to be arraigned this morning, that strange word. Arraigned. It sounds like a torture. It is a torture. But they wouldn't perform the torture until Billy was represented by counsel, so until I could find a lawyer he would remain in that pale yellow cell, or perhaps some worse cell somewhere else.

So after an hour I phoned that last number again, and this time the teenage girl calmly pointed out that it was difficult to find an attorney on a Sunday, and I said I knew that, and she said someone would call. Chastened, I hung up.

At twelve-fifteen, the phone rang. Marjorie and I were both in a state by then, not knowing what else to do, who else to call, how to get help, how to get this process *started.* We were both pacing the house, like starving lions. But then the phone did ring, at twelve-fifteen, and this was an older man, who slurred. I thought he was probably drunk.

"I've talked to the judge," he said. "Do you have anything to put up as collateral for bail?"

"The house," I told him.

"Bring the deed," he said, "the mortgage, whatever papers you can lay your hands on. I realize it's difficult, on a Sunday."

"I'll find something," I promised.

"I'll meet you at the courthouse," he said. "My name's Porculey. I'll be in a maroon suit."

A maroon suit? He slurs as though he's drunk, and he'll be in a maroon suit, and this is to be my son's lawyer.

On the other hand, he'd already talked to the judge, and it was clear from what he'd said that bail would be set, so that was good.

There's a folder in my filing cabinet marked HOUSE, and I just brought the whole thing with me, along with Billy's birth certificate and Marjorie's and my passports for identification. I didn't want to be one piece of paper shy.

When it did happen at last, it happened with great speed. First we met with Porculey, who turned out to be a much older man than he'd sounded on the phone, at least seventy, and who, from the drooping eyelid and sagging cheek, I suspected of having suffered one or more strokes, which was why he sounded drunk. It's true he was in a maroon suit, a horrible thing, with pin-stripes, but nevertheless, while this was a wreck, it was a wreck of a once-good lawyer. And what was left was good enough for the job at hand; to get Billy out of there, out of their clutches, back home with his mother and father, where he belonged.

It was mostly like going to church, some-body else's church. You watch the other congregants, do what they do, go along with the ritual as best you can, without under-standing a bit of it, but keeping in mind always that *they* take it seriously. *They* believe in it.

Oddly, Billy looked better than he had last night, when we finally saw him, in the sunny courtroom with the pale maple wood benches and altar. I know they don't call it the altar, where the judge and his vergers perform their sacraments, but that's what it is.

Billy wasn't there at first. Porculey led us to a pew near the front to wait, and then he went out, through a side door, with all our papers, to do whatever. After a while he came back into the courtroom, nodded reassuringly at us, and sat at the lawyer's table up front, with a few other people as unprepossessing as he was.

Then Billy was brought in, unshaved, wrinkled, exhausted, but looking less destroyed, less distraught. I watched him as he was led to his place up front, saw him try to scan the room without turning his head, saw him see us, and I smiled in encouragement, and he gave me a quick scared smile back.

The ritual was mostly in English, but didn't seem to have much literal meaning. It was all in the code of this church. Porculey and Billy briefly stood together before the judge, as though they were there to be married to one another. The judge, a disgruntled bald man whose head seemed too heavy for him to hold upright, listened and spoke and looked at papers and passed papers on to the verger at the little desk down to his right.

Then Marjorie and I were brought forward, and Marjorie wept a little, and so did Billy, which pleased the judge, who remanded our son to us in our custody, and actually did do the thing of hitting the block of wood with the gavel. Religious to the core.

Of course we weren't done yet. Over at a side desk, I had to sign a lot of forms, and at one point I had to raise my hand and swear an oath, I'm not sure why.

Billy was no longer with us at that point, but Porculey stayed by our side. He seemed to know most of the court employees, including the judge. I would say they all liked him and were happy to see him, but didn't take him seriously. And I would say he knew that and didn't care, just so he could go on playing the game.

I suppose he lives for Sundays, really, when lawyers are hard to find.

When they were at last done with us, Porculey shook Marjorie's hand and then my hand and told us which corridor to go down to collect our son — "You'll have to show them that paper" — and promised to be in touch with us about the court date. Then he went away, carrying a very new brown briefcase that I could imagine some proud grandchild giving him for Christmas last year, and we walked down the corridor to a coldfaced man in a brown uniform who looked at our piece of paper with contempt, went away, and some time later came back to contemptuously give us our son.

Billy was silent on the drive, abashed and ashamed and afraid. We got about halfway home, all of us silent, and then I said, "Billy, it won't surprise me if the police come around, very soon, with a search warrant."

He was riding in the backseat, Marjorie beside me in front. His startled eyes focused on my reflection in the rearview mirror. "Warrant? Why?"

"They'd like to be able to close all those other burglaries," I said. "They'd like to find something to show that you broke into that store before."

Now he looked really frightened. He knuckled his head, and said, "Dad. Dad, I — listen —"

"It's all right," I told him. I don't want to condone, and I don't want to encourage, but he had to know this much. "Everything's all right," I told him.

"Dad, no, listen —"

He still didn't understand, so Marjorie turned in the passenger seat and said, "Billy, it's been taken care of. Your father took care of things."

Then he got it, and the look he gave me was humbled and ashamed, and he said,

"I'm sorry, I'm really sorry. It was so stupid, I'll never do anything like that again, I *swear* I won't."

Marjorie said, "Of course you won't. Everybody gets to make a mistake, Billy, it's all right. It won't happen again."

"I know you can't afford," he said, and stopped, and looked away, out of the car. He was starting to cry again.

Well, that's true. I can't afford any of this. The lawyer will cost us *something*. This whole thing will cost money we don't have. And time. Time I don't have either. But you do what you have to do.

"We'll just get through this, Billy," I said, "and then it will be over and done with and forgotten."

He nodded, but he didn't try to speak, and he kept looking out the side window at the neighborhoods going by, and a little later we turned in at our driveway, and there was the police van out front. When they saw us, five uniformed policemen got out of it. Local cops, in blue.

Well, there's nothing for them to find. I did a lot of clean-up last night, even more than Marjorie knows. When we got back from that distant mall, she helped me pull the bookcase out of Billy's closet — back in there, empty, it was too suggestive — and we lugged it into the garage, where I piled it with some paint cans and old rags, so it looks as though it's been there for years. Then, while Marjorie was in the bathroom before going back to bed, I got the Luger out from the bottom drawer of my filing cabinet and put it under the backseat in the Voyager; that is, inside the seat. Under Billy, as we drove home.

And now we wait, in our living room, as the taciturn police go through our house. There's nothing for them to find. They can even paw through the folder of resumés in my office, if they want. What could it tell them? Nothing.

Sitting here, waiting, I start to think about this downsizing business again, how it affects the families, and how smug and blind I was to assume it would never affect *my* family. First Marjorie, and now Billy; it's bending our lives out of shape.

Betsy isn't with us, and now for the first time I have to think about her, too. She seems like such a good kid, so normal, so accepting of the change in our lives, so un-altered by it; but is that so?

We told her this morning, of course, what had happened to Billy, and she wanted to stay with us, come with us to the court, but

I didn't want her along. I didn't want her to have that kind of memory of Billy in her mind, the rest of her life.

Betsy attends a community college about forty miles from here. She should drive there, but we can't afford a second car, so another student, a girl she's known since elementary school, gives her a lift every day. She'd been scheduled to go with that girl to a Drama Society meeting this afternoon. She wanted to beg off, but Marjorie and I insisted she go, and I'm glad we did. She shouldn't be here to see the police pawing through her possessions, looking for stolen goods.

All at once I remember Edward Ricks, my resumé from Massachusetts. I remember how his daughter, Junie, had taken up with a much older man, a professor at her college, and how that had caused the confusion that led to me having to kill her mother as well. I felt so superior to those people at the time, with *their* daughter in such contrast to *my* daughter. I'd simply taken Junie to be an ordinary tramp, sly and vixenish.

But now I wonder. Was Junie a victim, too? If Daddy hadn't lost his job, would Junie have taken up with that other fellow, that unacceptable father substitute? What was his name . . . Ringer.

Was Ringer a victim, too, of downsizing? How it spreads. And now the police, without a word, depart. May they rot in hell.

24

It's after dinner, Sunday evening, the very first of June. Billy is definitely at home, in the living room, watching television with Marjorie and Betsy, while I am here in my office. It's time to get back to the operation, lose no more days. But I'm sitting here instead, for a minute, to look at a little 3x5 card I push-pinned to the wall over the desk a few months ago, when I first began to realize that doing it their way wasn't going to get me anywhere.

The card refers to a bit of history, in the Scottish Highlands. Until the late eighteenth century, the Highlands were populated mainly by tenant farmers, poor families in little stone huts eking out a small living from the soil and paying a small rent to the landlord. Then the landlord — or whoever acted as the landlord's accountant, in those days — discovered there was more money to be made if the human beings on all that land were replaced by sheep.

So, for the next seventy years, more or less, there was in the Highlands what came to be called the Clearances, in which families, clans, villages, everything was cleared from the land, which was then given to the sheep. The tenant farmers had lived there for generations, built the houses and barns and corrals, worked the soil; but it wasn't theirs. No one had lived on it but them, but it wasn't theirs, so what were they to do?

They left, not willingly. Some went to Ireland, some went to North America, some went to hell. Some died of cold or starvation. Some resisted, and were given the chop right there, on their own land. Well, no; not their own land.

I learned about the Clearances in college. I always enjoyed the history courses, because they were simply stories, so I did well in them, bringing my whole grade average up.

One year, another guy and I did a term paper on the Clearances, and in the course of it my partner looked up the word in the *Oxford English Dictionary*, the big one. I so loved the definition that I never forgot it, and after I got the chop, during one of my days of legitimate library research, I looked it up again, to be sure I had the phrasing exactly right. I wrote it on this 3x5 card and put it up on the wall here, in front of me.

> Clearance   2. *spec.*   The
> clearing (of land) by the re-
> moval of wood, old houses,
> inhabitants, etc.

You'll never see a clearer proof that history is written by the winners. Just think; one comma less, and the inhabitants would have fallen into the etc.

It's the descendants of those landlords that are doing the clearances called downsizing now. The literal descendants, sometimes, and the spiritual descendants always.

You like that desk where you are? You say you've given the company your life, your loyalty, your best efforts, and you think the company owes you something in return? You say all you really want is to stay at your desk?

Well, it isn't your desk. Clear it. The owner has realized he can make more money if he replaces you with another sheep.

Here's the resumé I want. The address. I'll visit Mr. Garrett Roger Blackstone to-morrow, after I drop off Marjorie at Dr. Carney's office.

Garrett Blackstone
PO Box 217, Scantic River Rd.
Erebus, CT 06397
Tel: 203 522-1201

Born Marysville, NJ August 18, 1947

Loyola Elementary School, Marysville, NJ - St. Ignatius Combined Middle School, Smithers, NJ - St. Ignatius High School, Smithers, NJ - Rutgers University, New Brunswick, NJ, receiving BA, art history 1968

United States Army, 1968-1971 - stationed in Texas, Vietnam, Okinawa

Married 1971, Louise Magnusson - four sons

Salesman, Rutherford Paper Box Co., Rutherford, MN 1971-1978

Manager, product line, Rutherford Paper Box Co., 1978-1983

Manager, product line, Patriot Paper Corp., Nashua, NH 1983-1984

Plant Manager, Green Valley Paper, Housatonic, CT 1984-present

Twenty-six years' experience in the paper industry.

Eighteen years' experience with a broad variety of paper manufacture as manager in charge of all product lines for a broad-base papermaker.

Experience includes consumer paper products, industrial paper products (including polymer paper applications) and defense-related paper products.

I am a willing worker, and am prepared to devote whatever part of my experience and expertise is of use in the new work situation.

25

At the mall, I stop in front of the entrance to Dr. Carney's office. Before she gets out of the Voyager, Marjorie leans over and kisses me, lightly, on the cheek. I look at her in surprise, and her eyes are shining. "It's over," she whispers. Then, seeming to be embarrassed, she slides out of the car, waves behind herself without looking back, and hurries into the building.

I know what she means, of course. The other man, the guy, the boyfriend, that's what's over. She won't be unfaithful to me any more.

As I drive east across northern Connecticut toward Erebus, I think about what she said, and what it means, and why she said it. I've believed the affair happened in the first place because of the general despondency around our house as my unemployment has lengthened from months into years, and I've believed that she finally told me about it *because* she wanted it to end, but she also wanted me to know what she'd been going through, what had made it necessary. And she wanted somebody neutral around, a counselor, our Longus Quinlan, to help us find our way out of this morass. If there is a way.

So the affair was a battering ram, that's all. And now the door is open, and she doesn't need the battering ram any more. And she wants me to know that, too.

But now, driving along on these little roads from little town to little town, I wonder if there isn't a second reason as well. Maybe I'm just trying to make myself feel better, make myself believe that *I* had something to do with it, too, but I can't help wonder if another factor in her change toward me is the way I handled the Billy emergency.

I handled it well, I know I did. But I also handled it differently from the way I would have a couple of years ago, back when I was a regularly employed person in what I thought of as a normal and changeless life. In that time, when I was the person I was before I got the chop, I would have been much more passive in this situation. I would have trusted the law, or society, or somebody, to do right by Billy. And the result would have been, they'd have gotten him for four burglaries instead of one, and he'd be looking at jail time. They might not even have set bail.

I did the right thing with Billy, and the

reason I did the right thing, and could even *think* about the problem the right way, is because I don't trust them any more. None of them. Now I know it; nobody will take care of me and mine but me.

Erebus is a village in the hills of north central Connecticut, between Bald Mountain and Rattlesnake Hill, just across the state line from Springfield, Massachusetts. Scantic River Road doesn't go through the actual village itself, but wanders the nearby hills, southward from the state line. I actually drive up into Massachusetts briefly, to pick up Scantic River Road at its northern end, and then I drive slowly southward, looking for PO Box 217.

This is suburbia along in through here, but a more relaxed suburbia than the areas closer to New York City. This country around here is a bedroom for Hartford and Springfield, so there's less visible money thrown around and less visible effort at high style. The basketball hoops above the garage doors look as though they're actually used from time to time. There are more pools above the ground than in it. The cars are less showy, and so are the gardens.

217 is a bit of a problem, being in the middle of a blind curve, with signs in both directions warning of their hidden driveway.

It's on the west side of the road, on the right as I drive south, and while the road itself is mostly level along here the land climbs steeply to the right and falls away to a fast narrow stream on the left. A stone wall retains GRB's land around this curve, with a narrow driveway chopped into it, leading upward toward a house I can barely glimpse.

This is going to be a very difficult place to watch. Can I do the mailbox again? It's on the same side of the road as the house, built into the stone retaining wall next to the driveway. I haven't seen a mail deliverer in my travels today, so I decide to head on south, just to see if luck is with me.

It isn't. I take Scantic River Road all the way south to the Wilbur Cross Parkway, by which time I'm surely in some other mail delivery route, so I turn around at the Parkway and drive north again, and when I'm near Erebus here comes the mail delivery, southbound.

Damn! GRB's house is still north of me, the mail's already been delivered. Is he out there now, picking up his mail?

The Luger is still inside the backseat. I keep driving, not too fast, reaching behind myself, trying to find that slit in the bottom front of the seat cover, trying to extend my arm way back and down inside there to get hold of the Luger by touch alone.

Metal, metal . . . Got it. I pull it out by the barrel, put it on top of the raincoat, then turn it so it doesn't point toward me.

The curve. HIDDEN DRIVEWAY. And here it is, on the left, with a person at the mailbox, head bowed, studying the mail. For just a second I'm very excited, staring at GRB, not looking away from him as my right hand claws for the Luger — but then I realize it isn't him. It's a woman. It's the wife, no doubt, in corduroy pants and a dark green cardigan and a dark blue billed cap with writing on the front.

I drive slowly past, trying to see up the driveway. Is he up there, waiting for the mail? Doesn't he care about the mail? He has to. Or is he ill? There's a lot of psychosomatic illness among us, we who've gotten the chop. Maybe he's in bed and won't get up until his wife finally brings him some good news. That would make him very tough to get at.

About two miles farther north, there's a parking area for a scenic view, pine-covered mountains with a valley between, stretching away to the west, full of peaceful villages. I pull off the road there, put the Luger under the raincoat at last, and study my road atlas, but it doesn't do me any good. It doesn't show any roads that might run along above and behind GRB's property. This road he's on just makes that elbow at that particular point, because of a hill, and their house is built on the slope above the road, with what looks like nothing but undeveloped hillside above them. And I already know, from looking at it, that there's nothing downhill in front of the house but scruffy woods, because of that stream.

There must be a way. I feel like a cat circling a mousehole. I know he's in there, and I know there has to be a way to get at him. But what?

Finally I decide to just drive by the place yet again, see if there's *anything* to be done. So I leave the turnoff, headed south once more, and drive along, the road atlas now on top of the raincoat, and the pressure of other traffic keeps me from going as slowly as I'd like when I go around that curve.

The house, barely seen. No sign of cars or people.

Nearly a mile later, there's a right turn off Scantic River Road. I take it, and am now on a very small residential road marked DEAD END.

There's no other traffic with me now. I drive up as this narrow road twists and turns, with very few houses visible along the way, broad forested spaces between them. Then I come to the dead end, which is clearly marked by a single width of wooden rail fence painted white, with a yellow DEAD END sign on it.

I stop the Voyager and get out to look around. According to the road atlas, this spot where the road has petered out is not that far from the elbow on Scantic River Road containing GRB's house. It should be down that way, to the right, through the woods.

I'm not a woodsman, never have been. It could be both stupid and dangerous to go roaming around in there and get lost, and eventually be found by police or boy scouts or whoever, and have no explanation for why I'm here, with a Luger in my raincoat pocket. Still, I've got to find some way to get at GRB.

I walk around to the far side of the white fence. The woods, out ahead of me, are cool and pleasant. June second; gnats come flying, to study my face. I brush them away, but they won't go. Anyway, they're merely curious. They don't want to bite me, they just want to memorize me. So long as I breathe with my mouth shut, they won't really bother me. They're just an irritation, these tiny fast dots in front of my face.

Looking past them, gradually learning to ignore them, I at last see what seems to be some sort of path, moving away to the right through the trees. Don't deer create paths sometimes, in the woods? But so do people; Marjorie and I have friends, whom we haven't seen for a while, who've made woods walks into the land out behind their houses. (We used to see more people. We used to know more people. When you can't afford to entertain, a certain embarrassment keeps you from maintaining those old friendships.)

So I come to a decision. I'll wear the raincoat, with the Luger in the pocket. I'll walk along that seeming path, which looks to be at least headed in the right general direction. I'll see where it goes, and how far it goes, and the instant it starts to fork or disappear or do anything that might make it hard for me to retrace my steps I'll turn around and come right back here.

It's a pleasant day for walking, with the airy trees protecting me just enough from the rays of the sun. The air is a bit cool, in a refreshing way, like the air near an ice cube. I walk along, following this very clear brown trail in the green woods, and the first time I look back the Voyager is already out of sight.

I stop, then. Is this a good idea? I really

don't want to get lost in here.

But so far, this path is very obvious. Also, the land slopes very gently downward here, and the path follows that downward tendency, so if I do get confused at some point, I should merely turn around and head up the slope. That's a theory, anyway.

I walk for about fifteen minutes, and for much of that time I'm not even thinking about why I'm here, what the purpose of all this is, what the function is of that weight dragging down my raincoat on the right. I'm just going for a walk in the woods, led along by this clear path and by gravity. It's nice. No cares, no problems. No hard solutions.

A noise. Up ahead, a sharp cracking noise. Something's coming.

What is it? I look to the sides, and off to my right there's a tumbled mass of boulder sticking out of the ground. It's all tangled brush and weeds between here and there, but it's the only hiding place I see, so I set off toward it at once, trying to be silent. Behind me, I hear that cracking sound again.

If this is a deer, fine, no problem. But if it's a person, I don't want to be seen. I don't want to be the mysterious man wandering in the woods just around the time GRB is done away with.

The boulders. I scramble around them,

and the crack rings out again. I crouch low, looking back toward the path, and here she comes.

The wife, it's the wife. The same woman I saw collecting the mail, still dressed in the same cap and cardigan and corduroys. She's walking alone, briskly, and she's carrying a nice thick walking stick, like a shillelagh, and as I watch she uses it to hit a tree as she goes by: *crack*.

Oh, of course. Snakes. She's afraid of snakes, and somebody's told her that if she makes a noise as she goes along they'll stay away from her. *Crack*. On she strides.

Good God, what if she'd had a dog with her? What a mess that would be. The dog would surely know I'm here, would probably come over to investigate. And then I'd *really* be in it. Not just a strange man wandering in the woods, but a strange man *hiding* in the woods.

She's gone; I hear a distant *crack*. I straighten up, behind my boulder. Is he home alone? Do any of the four sons still live with these people? If I follow this path, will I find the house?

One good thing. She announces her presence by hitting trees with that stick, so I'll always know when it's time to get out of her way.

I decide to chance it. I hurry back from the boulders to the path, my raincoat flaps catching on the thorny waving reedy branches of wild roses, and now I set a much brisker pace, walking, I hope, toward GRB's house.

It's another quarter hour, and there it is. Or there something is, some house, visible through the woods where a smaller path branches leftward from the main one. Is it the right place?

I go there to see, and find a two-strand electric fence across my route, to keep the deer out. The other side of it is an expanse of lawn, fringed by plantings of rhododendrons and other things that deer like to eat. Ahead and to the left is a smallish in-ground pool, still covered, even though this is June. But you can't afford to maintain the pool this year, can you? Not without a job.

Beyond the pool and the lawn stands the house, fairly large, stone on the first floor, white clapboard above, several dormers along the top. Yes, that's the house I glimpsed from the road. There's no one in sight.

The gate in the electric fence is just here, at the edge of the lawn. But if I go through, there'll be no cover, and GRB will be able to see me if he looks out any of those windows over there. And what if I'm still on the property when the wife comes back?

No, the thing to do is wait. First, I have to find out for sure where GRB is. There's a stone patio over there, between house and pool, with a table topped by a big umbrella, and several white metal chairs. Maybe they'll have lunch together, right there. Can I do a shot that long? Or can I hope for something to bring him closer to the fence?

Crack. Some distance away behind me. But that means she's coming back. I move away along the fence, careful not to touch it, grateful they've kept the shrubbery cleared along the fence line — for maintenance, I suppose — and as those occasional *cracks* come closer I reach at last the end of the fence, where it attaches to the small pool house. From here I can be very well hidden. And I'm somewhat closer to that patio, which is just beyond the pool, which is just beyond the pool house. Still a longer shot than I've ever tried before, but what if he has to come to the pool house, for ice or something? Then he's mine.

I see her, to my right, as she goes through the fence, carefully hooking it shut behind her. As she strides to the house, planting that walking stick firmly into the lawn at every second pace, I look at my watch: twelve forty-five. Lunchtime. But I didn't bring any.

Well, I'm getting used to not eating my midday meal. There's a tree stump about five feet back from the fence, a large one. Some big tree was once here, and probably cut down when they put in the pool house. I ease back there, gather my raincoat about myself, sit down. The Luger is in my lap.

Four o'clock. It's getting cooler now, the sun hidden behind higher hills off to the west. I'm stiff and achy, and my back is complaining about this length of time, over three hours, seated here on this stump, with no support.

He never came out. She never appeared again, either, after that walk. I can catch a glimpse of their driveway from here, and neither of them used the car today. I don't know what GRB looks like, and I don't know what his car looks like.

This day wasn't wasted, not entirely wasted. I've learned how to get near the house. But it's frustrating, nevertheless. I want to get this over, over and done with.

Tomorrow I won't be able to come here, because of the counselor, Longus Quinlan. So it's Wednesday, while Marjorie is again working at Dr. Carney's office, that's when I'll be back.

When I stand, bones crack all over my body, enough to scare any snake in the county. I'm tottering, having trouble making my feet work. But it's time to go, get back to the Voyager, drive homeward, get to the mall by six o'clock to pick up Marjorie.

Staggering like Frankenstein's monster, I make my way along the path, back toward the Voyager. In this direction, it's uphill.

26

Yesterday, at the counseling session, Marjorie said, "When Burke first lost his job, I thought it was a kind of opportunity. I thought things were too good for us, we always had whatever we wanted, and so we never had to struggle together for anything, we never had to prove ourselves to each other. I thought this was going to be some little short time, and it wasn't really going to mean anything in the long run, but I could prove myself to Burke, and I guess to myself, too, to be honest about it, just to prove I was the perfect wife, the perfect partner. We're in this together, and this is my chance to prove it. So I immediately started all these little economies and showed how we could save money here and save money there, like I was Mrs. Noah on the Ark, going around finding little leaks, plugging them up, keeping the water out. I never thought it was going to go on this long. I don't think Burke did, either. I think at first he took it a little more seriously than I did, because he knew a little more about what the real situation was, but I don't think he took it really really really seriously then, at first. I think after a while he did, and instead of turning to me and saying, 'Marjorie, we're in a jam, this is a tougher situation than I thought,' he just closed down inside himself, more and more. I thought for a while he was blaming *me* for what was going on, that he thought it was my fault he still didn't have a job, we didn't have any money, but I've thought about it some more, I've had plenty of time to think about it, and now I think Burke's been doing the same thing I've been doing, trying to prove what a perfect husband he is, perfect provider, keep the little woman safe and happy, don't let her see how bad things are. I mean, I can *see* how bad things are, but we can't talk about how bad things are, or what we're going to do about them, or what's going to happen next, so I never actually *know* what's going to happen next. Burke's gotten more and more secretive, more and more silent, more and more cold, and sometimes when he's looking at me it's almost as though he hates me, just for being there and seeing the situation he's in, it looks in his eyes as though he could kill me for being there, just because he feels like he can't protect me the way he's supposed to, and I don't *want* to be protected like that, but how can I say anything? He keeps that wall up. The wall is supposed to be his strength, I guess, but I never thought that was why he was strong. When I met him, I was still in college, I was a completely useless Liberal Arts major, but I also took typing and shorthand, and summer vacations I did temp jobs to help out, make some money for myself, and I always thought I'd work in industry someplace, as a secretary, something like that. I actually did work for an insurance company for about six months after I graduated, and got one promotion and raise, and I could have stayed, but Burke wanted to get married right away, and then he wanted a family right away, so I dropped out of the job market. The magazines I used to read were always full of pieces about women dropping out of the job market, and then what happens when you get divorced or widowed, and I was never afraid of that. *This* they didn't talk about. This is worse than divorced or widowed, because I'm still with Burke but he's wounded. I'm with a wounded man, and we both have to pretend nothing's wrong. About half the wives I know have jobs or careers, one's a speech therapist, one's a librarian, a lot of them I know, but it seems just as normal either way, if the wife works or doesn't work, and I've always thought that was the woman's decision, except with us it's mostly been Burke's decision, and he makes it plain in different ways. Like, a few years ago, at Christmastime, he bought a computer, a personal computer for the home, he said it was for the whole family. It was really for Billy, our son, but I knew why he said it was for the whole family, and why he teased me about learning it and putting the checkbook in it and all. The children were growing up, almost out of high school then, and I'd been talking about looking for a job again after all these years, wanting to do something with myself, and Burke didn't want me to. This was before he was laid off, before anybody thought he *could* be laid off. So he wanted to be the provider, the protector, the same as always, and he brought that computer into the house just to let me know I didn't have the skills any more. When I got out of college, it was typing, but the computer isn't typing, it's something else, and he wanted me to know I'm hopelessly behind. But actually, he doesn't know it, but I'm farther along with the computer than he is, because I've been doing the billing for this dentist we know, Dr. Carney, so I've been using his computer, and his regular nurse showed me what I had to know, and I've taught myself some more on my own, so I'm not so hopeless after all. But I couldn't tell Burke how happy I was and pleased that I was learning the computer, because he wouldn't like that. I had to keep it to myself, and pretend there wasn't *anything* I was happy about, or anything I could possibly be happy about, until he got a new job, and the exact same kind of job again, of course, even though we read in the newspaper every day that people don't *get* the same kind of job back, especially if they're over fifty. We know a man, a neighbor of ours, he was always considerably more wealthy than us, he was a bank executive, he only had to commute in to the office in New York three days a week, he was that important, and there was a merger, and they let him go, it must be three years ago now, and he was out of work for almost two years, wanting to be a bank executive again. And now he works at a Mercedes dealership in Hartford, he sells cars, and he works six days a week and he doesn't make anywhere near as much money, and Burke, did you notice? Their house is for sale. But a lot of houses are for sale, you've probably noticed that, Mr. Quinlan, so I don't know how long they'll have to wait. And I don't know if we'll have to try to sell our house, too, or *what* is going to happen. I can't find a full-time job now, because I was out of the job market too long, I'm too old, I'm not *that* skilled, and nobody knows when Burke will find another job or what kind of job it will be or when he'll agree to settle for it. It isn't fair for the children, but that isn't Burke's fault, even if he does take the blame all on himself, but they have to live with it the same as we do, and usually I think they understand that, though Billy did get himself in trouble. But that's not the point. The point is, it's so hard to be *happy* at home, and you have to have some place in your life where you're happy. And you have to have some person you can talk with, open yourself with, laugh with. Or even cry with, I don't care, just *something*. But Burke's been so — He's like cryogenics, he's frozen himself, he won't thaw out until he gets a job, and in the meantime I'm living with this frozen thing, and finally, four months ago, a man I know acted tender toward me and I responded, and something started between us. Burke's off on his own secret mission all the time, for a while I thought *he* was having an affair, but I don't believe that any more, I believe he's doing strange like *magic* things, like going off and reading entrails or something, I don't know, he has some kind of mysterious *project* with papers in his office and mysterious trips, and lying to me about where he's going, and I wouldn't *dream* of asking him what's going on. Because he wants to shoulder it all himself, shoulder the burden, shoulder everything, the family, the responsibility, and I'm left out here, and I turned to this other man because at least he'd *talk* to me, and he'd let me talk to him. And he has problems, too, but he isn't afraid to talk about them or say he feels weak when he gets up in the morning, he doesn't know what to do next. I could console him, he was somebody I could put my arms around, I could find some way to make him laugh. I can't do anything with Burke, he's like a rock or a dead person, he's like a stone, you can't put your arms around a stone. You can't get anything from a stone. So when I realized that it wasn't this other man I wanted, it was Burke I wanted, but it was Burke when he's alive, when he isn't all shut down and cold and waiting for a miracle, and I thought, I have to use dynamite. So I told him we needed to see somebody like you, and he fought that idea, and I knew he'd fight it, of course he'd fight it. *Talk* about things! When he fought it, I told him about the man, because I thought that would be sink or swim, kill or cure, and I thought, I can't go on like this. I either want Burke back or I want it over with. And thank God he said all right, let's come here, because I couldn't say this to him without you in the room. And he knows I'm not seeing the man any more, but the truth is, I'm not seeing Burke either, and I want to see Burke, I want my husband back, and I don't know what to do."

Quinlan looked at me, with a gentle smile. He's a great absorber, Quinlan. He said, "You'd like to thaw, Burke, wouldn't you? Knock down the wall?"

"I didn't know I was doing that," I said. "I thought I was just trying to hold myself together." But it's true; I'd caught glimpses of myself, here and there in her description.

He went on smiling, and said, "You didn't buy the computer to insult Marjorie, did you?"

"No, of course not," I said. "That never even occurred to me." That had been part of the description where I had not caught sight of myself, and I was grateful to Quinlan for calling attention to it.

His smile now moved over to include Marjorie, who was sitting there looking exhausted. No, not exhausted, not like somebody who's just run a long time, but drained, like somebody who's just had an operation. He said to her, "We're all of us paranoid, Marjorie, you know," and shrugged. "Like right now," he said, "I'm wondering how you feel about taking advice from a black man. Are you just humoring me? Do you laugh behind my back, in your car together?"

"We don't laugh about anything," Marjorie said, which I thought an overstatement, but kept my mouth shut.

Quinlan smiled more broadly; he has a very broad smile, when he wants. "Paranoia is not a good guide," he suggested, then looked back at me and said, "But Marjorie was right about the cryogenics, wasn't she? You're frozen, waiting to be thawed when there's a cure."

"That sounds right," I admitted, "though I'm not sure what to do about it. I mean, it'll be hard to retrain myself." Retrain; retraining. The sick joke of downsizing, and now I've volunteered to try it in my home.

"We're in no hurry," Quinlan told me, and looked at Marjorie again, to say, "Isn't that right? As long as we know the problem's out in the air, and progress is being made, we're in no hurry, are we?"

"I feel much better," Marjorie said. "Just being here, just talking about it."

I couldn't tell them, of course, that the situation is going to change for the better, the much better, pretty soon now, no matter what we do in the counseling. Two resumés and Upton "Ralph" Fallon, that's all that's left. I'm a short-timer now, in cyrogenics.

But I'm glad Marjorie got to say all that, and I'm very glad I got to hear it. I don't want to lose her, any more than I want Billy in jail. I don't want any of the extra bad things that happen to people in our situation, I don't want the fringe banes.

We're at sea, that's my image, not cryogenics. We're lost at sea on a raft, and it's up to me to keep the raft together, ration the supplies, keep us afloat until we find shore. That's my task, my position. If it's made me cold to Marjorie, then I'm wrong, I'm trying too hard. Hurting her can't help me, or anything else. I've been *too* focused, that's what it is. I have to try to relax, even though all I really want to do is keep my guard up twenty-four hours a day.

In any event, now we know who the guy is. James Halstead; always James, never Jim. Banker turned Mercedes salesman. Now we know, and we don't care.

That was yesterday, and today is Wednesday. I've just kissed Marjorie goodbye at Dr. Carney's, warmly, with love. Now I'm on my way to kill GRB.

27

The weight of my raincoat is more balanced today as I walk through the woods, with the Luger in the right pocket and two apples in the left. Today I'm prepared for a long wait.

It's not yet ten in the morning when I reach GRB's house and take up my position, seated on the stump at the edge of the woods, behind the pool house. The house over there beyond the lawn seems shut up tight, as though the owners have gone away forever. But she, at least, was here the day before yesterday, when I saw her hike through the woods, hitting trees with her shillelagh.

I settle down, trying to find a position that's more comfortable for my back, on this stump, and I wait. And after a while, I find myself thinking about this or that part of yesterday's session with Longus Quinlan, and how all of that history just came pouring out of Marjorie. I must be a different person from the one I always thought I was, if she had to keep so silent around me for so long, if she had to create this entire scenario, an affair, counseling, before she could suddenly blurt it all out like that, like a dam bursting.

I remember what I said yesterday about retraining, that word from when I got the chop, bubbling to the surface all at once there, and I think I'm serious about it. I've just been going along, doing my best to take care of my family, but ignoring the effect I was having on Marjorie, taking it for granted she was happy with me.

Retraining. That was part of the separation package at the mill, what *they* called retraining, and what *they* called retraining was so miserable and false that I really ought to find some other word for the reappraisal I want to make in connection with myself. What *they* called retraining was . . .

I don't suppose they actually meant it to be insulting. I think what they were trying to do was keep us all calm and hopeful until we were well out the door, and that's why we had the severance packages and the inspirational meetings and the offers of retraining, all this crap.

At first, I was even hopeful about the idea of retraining. I'd read all the stuff about it, the same stuff we've all read, how it's going to be necessary in the brave new world of tomorrow for people to move on from job to job, learning new skills along the way, and how males older than fifty have the hardest time giving up the old skills in exchange for the new skills, and I was absolutely prepared to prove that particular generalization false, here's *one* guy can adapt, just try me.

And so they tried me, all right. They offered me air conditioning repair.

Where am I, in a vocational high school or a minimum security prison, which one? Air conditioning repair? How is this a brand new skill to carry anybody into the brave new world of tomorrow? And what does air conditioning repair have at *all* to do with my entire work history? I manage assembly lines, that's what I *do*.

Okay, forget specialized paper processes, just talk about assembly lines, the management thereof, and that's what I do. Retrain me to run a different kind of assembly line, all right? I'm adaptable. The product lines are still out there, the products are still churning out the factory door. I'm happy to retrain, if it connects with *me* in any way at all, if it makes any kind of sense.

Let's say you're the owner of a company that services air conditioning units in large office buildings, and you have an opening for a repairman, and thirty guys apply (and thirty guys will apply) who have had *years* of experience repairing air conditioners, and I show up with a certificate of two months' training in air conditioner repair and a quarter century of experience in manufacturing specialized paper products. Are you gonna hire me? Or are you not that crazy?

Take James Halstead, the banker turned car salesman. Is that *retraining?* He looks like a banker, which means he looks like a Mercedes salesman. He already has the suit. Is he where he is because he actively welcomed retraining, or is he where he is because he failed? Did he seek for solace in Marjorie's arms because he'd made a successful transition to the brave new world of tomorrow, or because he was discarded like last year's computer? Can it be he's unhappy because he just found out the bank didn't need him after all? Those complacent days of plenty, riding the commuter train three days a week to what turned out not to be his actual life, but just a game they were letting him play, for a little while.

When one of his old bosses comes in to buy a Mercedes, using the money they've saved on his salary, do they recognize him? They do not. But he recognizes them. And never lets on. And smiles, and smiles, and sells the car.

That's retraining.

Eleven-fifteen; she appears, in the same hat and cardigan and corduroys, but a different blouse. The last time, the blouse was light blue, this time it's light green. She carries the shillelagh again, and she marches across the lawn like the commander of a prisoner-of-war camp on inspection. She goes through the gate in the electric fence, and strides off up the path: *crack . . . crack . . . crack . . .*

Is he in there? Do I dare try it? I have at least half an hour, probably more, before she gets back, judging by last time. I can't sit here forever, day after day, on this stump, like a leprechaun.

I rise — stiff already — and cross to the gate, and let myself through, carefully hooking it shut behind me. I thought at first I'd slink around to the right, along the fence, past the rhododendron beds and the birdbath, to where the wires of the fence are attached to the right rear corner of the house, but now I realize there's no point hiding. What if he does see me? So what? I'm a respectable looking man in a raincoat, walking across his lawn, probably got lost out there in the woods, looking for directions. He comes to the door, he asks if he can help, and I shoot him.

So I cross the lawn, not exactly boldly, but casually, looking around as though with a normal curiosity about somebody else's home. Nobody appears at a door, nobody appears at a window. I veer to the left, cross the patio, and try one of the sliding patio doors. It glides open, and I step inside.

The central air conditioning is on, discreet but apparent. If anything happened to it, I wouldn't know how to fix it.

This is a dining room, with its view through the glass doors to the patio and pool. I cross it, and now I'm definitely a trespasser, not an innocent man lost in the woods.

I move swiftly and quietly through the house, first downstairs, then up, and it's empty. GRB isn't here. At the very end, I open the door from the kitchen to the attached garage, and there's no car in it.

He's out. Where is he? Does he have a counterman job, like Everett Dynes? Is he selling automobiles? How do I find him? How do I get my hands on him?

I'm crossing back through the kitchen when I glance out the window and see her coming, still marching firmly forward, headed this way across the lawn, mashing it every second step with her stick. A shorter walk today; damn.

I don't want her to find me, because I don't want to have to kill her. For many reasons I don't want to kill her, but the primary reason right now is that her husband isn't home, and if I leave her dead and him alive he'll be alerted, he'll be surrounded by police, I'll never get my hands on him. If I kill her, and then wait for GRB to come home, what happens if he *doesn't* come home? What if he's on an overnight job interview, won't be back till late tomorrow?

I can't stay here, to wait for him. I can't kill this woman, so I can't permit her to know I'm here.

She uses the patio door, or she has in the past, the same door I just came in by. When she enters, which way will she go?

Either the kitchen, I think, or the downstairs bathroom, which means through the dining room and the smaller sitting room and the hall, *not* through the large living room facing the front of the house. So I move into the living room, and crouch behind the sofa that stands in the middle of that large space. It looks toward the stone fireplace, with its back to the large bow window showing front lawn and the driveway that recedes downward toward the invisible main road. Crouched here, behind the sofa, eight feet from that window, I'm fully exposed to anyone out front, but why would anyone be out front?

I hear her enter, as the door glides open,

and then shut. I hear the final *click* as she puts the shillelagh down, its tip striking the polished wood floor.

I crouch behind the sofa. My right hand grasps the Luger in my raincoat pocket. I try to remember to keep my finger away from the trigger, afraid I'll spastically shoot when I don't want to, probably wounding myself, certainly alerting her, surely destroying everything I've done so far.

I hear the duller *tocks* of her shoes as she crosses the dining room. This way, or the other?

The other. Across the smaller sitting room, into the hall, and into the bathroom. Yes, a brisk walk in the woods does exercise the bladder, doesn't it, and that's why the walk was cut short. And she shuts the bathroom door, even though she's alone in the house, as her mother taught her.

I rise up, behind the sofa, and take my right hand out of my pocket, away from the Luger. My fingers are stiff, like arthritis. Briskly, I cross the living room and the dining room. As silently as possible, I slide open the door, exit, slide it shut. I trot across the lawn, wanting to be well off her property before she's done in the bathroom, because next she'll surely go on to the kitchen, and from the kitchen windows over the sink she'll have a full view of this entire lawn.

The gate. I unhook it, step through, hook it. Without a backward glance, I stride up the path, almost as purposeful as she is.

On the walk back, I eat both apples.

28

About three miles before the turnoff to Scantic River Road, still inside Connecticut, there's a gas station with an outside pay phone on a stick. That's where I stop to make my call, glad to see this phone has the same exchange as GRB's. Local calls disappear more readily.

I'm phoning GRB's house because I had a sudden revelation last night. So many marriages fall into trouble among the downsized; not just mine and Marjorie's. What if GRB and his wife have split up? What if he's living somewhere else, all the time I'm crouched in the woods behind his house, waiting for him?

Or, another possibility. What if he's taken one of those time-serving jobs, say, assistant manager at the local supermarket, then he'll *never* be home during the day. For whatever reason, and there must be one, he hasn't been home the two days I've watched the place. So it's time to find out what the situation is.

Nine-forty. She won't have left for her walk yet. I dial the number from GRB's resumé, and she answers on the second ring:

"Blackstone residence." She sounds efficient but impersonal, as though she's chief of staff there, not the lady of the house.

I say, "Garrett Blackstone, please."

"He's not in at the moment, may I say who's calling?"

"It's an old friend from the papermill days," I say. "Is there any way I can get in touch with him?"

"Well, he's at work right now," she says. She sounds a bit doubtful.

I say, "Could I call him there?" I need to know where the man is, dammit.

"I'm not sure," she says, not wanting to offend an old friend of her husband's, but troubled by something. "He's just started there," she explains, "and he might not want outside calls right now."

"Oh, it's a job he likes?"

"It's a wonderful job," she says, and all at once the restraint gives way, and she bubbles over, saying, "It's *just* the job he wanted!"

Arcadia! The son of a bitch got my job, I'll kill him today, I'll kill him in an hour! Gripping the phone so tight my hand is cramping, but unable to relax, I say, "Oh? Back at a paper mill?"

"Yes! Willis and Kendall, do you know them?"

Five *hundred* pounds drops away from my

body. I could dance. I say, "The tin can labels!"

"That's right! That's just the job, do you work there, too?"

"Oh, that's great," I say, and I truly mean it. "That's wonderful. Mrs. — Mrs. Blackstone, please give your husband my, my *strongest* congratulations. Tell him I'm delighted for him. Oh, tell him I'm delighted."

"Who should I say —"

I hang up, and float back to the Voyager. I couldn't be happier if I had a job myself. It's true; well, almost true. But he's at work, he's in a *position*, he's where he wants to be!

By God, I don't have to kill him.

Oh, that's great, that's great. Starting the Voyager, making the U-turn, I'm grinning from ear to ear.

As the miles go by, as I drive closer and closer to home, the weight slowly settles down on top of me. Two to go.

29

Saturday morning. I'm in my office, and I've just taken out of the file drawer the last resumé, I'm just reaching for the road atlas, when Marjorie knocks on the door. I place the road atlas on top of the resumé, and say, "Yes?"

She opens the door. She looks worried, and a bit confused. She says, "Burke, there's a policeman here. He wants to talk to you. A detective."

Terror closes my esophagus. I'm caught, I know it, and everything was in vain. And I was so close. Standing, trying to find a reaction I can share with Marjorie, I say, "Billy? Is it something about Billy?"

"I don't think so," she says. "I don't know what it is, Burke. He's in the living room."

"All right."

I step into the hall. The Voyager is closer the other way than the living room is this way. But there's no point in that. I walk down the hall, while Marjorie goes back to whatever she was doing.

He's in the living room, a slender young guy in a gray suit, on his feet, facing the sofa as he smiles at the framed print that hangs above it. It's a Winslow Homer seascape, very turbulent, and I don't know why we have it. Marjorie saw it for sale years ago, at a frame shop, and bought it, with some embarrassment. "I just love it," she told me. "I don't really like prints, but we'll never have a *real* Winslow Homer. Is it all right, Burke?"

Of course I told her it was all right, and I drove the nail into the wall and hung the framed print, and it reminds me that other people are mysterious, no matter how much we get to know them. I will never understand why that picture spoke to Marjorie, that picture more than any other, but it's all right; that's the lesson. The surface of the print is flat, it can't hide what it is, a print and not a painting, but the subject is this roiling sea, over vast unknowable depths. That's what we all are for one another, flat surfaces on which some turbulence can be seen, but unknowable depths. It doesn't matter that I'll never know Marjorie very deeply; I know her enough to know I love her, and that's enough.

And would I like her to know my depths?

The detective turns, sensing me, and smiles, nodding toward the picture. "I grew up on boats," he says. "My father's a great sailor. Mr. Devore?"

"Yes?"

He extends a hand and we shake, as he says, "Detective Burton, state CID. I hope I'm not interrupting anything?"

"Not at all. Sit down."

He does, on the sofa, twisting around to look at the Homer again, while I sit on the armchair across from him, trying to conceal my worry, reassured a bit by his friendly manner.

He turns away from the picture at last, saying, "You a sailor, Mr. Devore?"

"No," I say, regretfully. I wish I could say yes, so we'd have a kinship. I say, "My wife loved the picture."

"I grew up on Long Island Sound," he says, taking a notebook out of his inside jacket pocket. Chuckling, he says, "And sometimes in it." Opening the notebook, he studies something written in there, then looks seriously at me and says, "Do you know a Herbert Everly?"

It *is* me he's after! How did I ever think I'd get away with it? But what can I do but pretend innocence, ignorance, disconnectedness? "Everly?" I say. "I don't think so."

"How about somebody named Kane Asche?"

"Kane Asche. No, doesn't ring a bell."

He says, "You worked for Halcyon Mills, didn't you, for a long while?"

"Were they *there?*"

"No, no," he says, grinning at the misunderstanding. "But they did work at paper mills. Different ones from you."

I spread my hands. I say, "I'm sorry, I don't know what you want."

"Neither do we, Mr. Devore, to be perfectly frank," he says, with his guileless smile. Can I trust him? He's still holding that notebook. He says, "We got a very strange call the other day from the personnel officer with a paper company called Willis and Kendall."

"I applied for a job there, a few weeks ago."

"That's right," he says. "And you were one of the people they interviewed."

"I didn't get a callback, though, so I guess I didn't get that job."

"There were four people they called for a second interview," Burton tells me, "and turned out, two of them had just been killed. They'd both been shot to death."

"Good God!"

"It's these two, Everly and Asche." Burton taps his notebook. "And *now,*" he says, "ballistics tells us they were both killed with the same gun."

I say, "Was it somebody they worked with?"

"They didn't know each other," Burton says, "so far as we can tell. There's no link we can find between these two men except they both applied for the same job."

I say, "Do you mean, you think somebody's going to come shoot *me?*"

"It's probably simple coincidence," Burton says, "those two getting callbacks for the same job. A number of people applied, and so far everybody else is perfectly fine, like yourself. They hired somebody now —"

"I thought they must have."

He grins in sympathy and says, "Sorry to be the bearer of bad news."

"No, you get used to it," I say.

"It can get rough, I know," he says. "My brother was laid off down at Electric Boat, and his wife was laid off one week later from the insurance company. They're going nuts."

"I'm sure they are."

"What we think," Burton says, "is that Everly and Asche must have met somewhere, sometime. Maybe a trade conference, or a job referral outfit, who knows. They met each other, and they met somebody else, and something went wrong. So the Willis and Kendall connection's just a coincidence."

"The man the company hired," I say. "Is *he* all right?"

"He's fine. No threats against him, no

mysterious strangers lurking around."

"So it probably doesn't have anything to do with that company," I say.

"That's right. If there's a link, it's somewhere in the past. That's why I'm here, we're canvassing everybody with any connection at all to either of the victims."

"Mine's not much of a connection," I say. "We all applied for the same job."

"But it's the phone call from that employer that got us started on this," he points out. "We don't know what we're looking for, so we've got to look everywhere we can think of. Like, if we could find some place, some time, when people like you in your industry got together, somewhere you all might have been at, a trade fair —"

"I ran a product manufacturing line," I say. "I almost never went to sales conferences, things like that."

"Would you mind," he says, "taking a look at a couple photos, see if they jog your memory? See if you ever met either of these people *anywhere*."

I say, "It's not — they're not pictures of them dead, are they?"

He laughs: "We wouldn't do that to you, Mr. Devore. They're perfectly ordinary photos. All right?"

"Sure," I say.

He has the photos in his notebook, and now he shakes them out and extends them toward me.

Here they are, my resumés one and four, with their faces intact, before I shot the bullets into them. I look at the photos and feel a great sadness swelling up inside me, so that my eyes sting. I feel so sorry for these two men. They seem like decent guys. I shake my head, and when I look toward Burton I'm aware of that stormy Winslow Homer sea above his head. "They just seem like nice guys," I say. "Excuse me, it's making me teary or something. They look so *ordinary*."

"Sure," he says. "You're identifying, I understand that. Things like that aren't supposed to happen to folks like us. Unfortunately, they do."

Handing the photos back, I say, "I really don't think I ever met them. Either of them."

"Okay," he says, and puts the photos in the notebook and the notebook away in his inner jacket pocket.

Is this it? All of it? Am I still free, uncaught, unsuspected? I say, "I'm sorry I couldn't help."

"Oh, you helped," he says, and gets to his feet, and so do I. He says, "We never like coincidence, but sometimes it happens. If it never happened, we wouldn't have a word for it."

"I guess that's true," I say.

From his side trouser pocket he takes a wallet, and from the wallet a card, which he hands me, saying, "If you think of anything, or if anything weird happens around here in the next week or so, call me, okay?"

With a shaky smile, I say, "Weird, like me getting shot?"

"Whatever it was," he says, "two seems to be it. I really don't think we're going to come across a third. I think you're safe, Mr. Devore."

"That's good news," I say.

30

I'm back in my office. Burton has gone, I've described the reason for his visit to Marjorie, I've had more conversation with Marjorie on the subject of the two murders than I wanted but I felt I shouldn't cut it short, and now I'm back in my office, and I'm shaking with the realization of the close call I've had.

These two dead men, and their link to job-hunting, could be a coincidence, that's true. Two might be a coincidence or not a coincidence, and pretty soon they're going to come to the conclusion that coincidence is the only answer that fits these two.

But not three.

If I'd found Garrett Blackstone. If he hadn't been given that tin can label job. If I'd shot him either time this week that I'd been to his house, Detective Burton and the other detectives would now have *three* job-hunting paper mill managerial types shot in the same state with the same gun, and it wouldn't be a coincidence, and they'd start thinking about possible motives, and they wouldn't rest until they found me.

The same gun. I've been incredibly stupid, and incredibly lucky. It never occurred to me that they could — or would think to — link these separate murders by showing they came from the same gun. (If Willis & Kendall's personnel man hadn't stuck his oar in, they might very well not have.)

But I don't know why I didn't think of it. I've seen so many cop shows on television, and so many movies, too, where they talk about ballistics and finding the gun that fired that particular bullet, and all that, but I never once made the connection. All I thought was, this gun has not been fired by anybody in over fifty years, it has never been fired anywhere on the North American continent, there's no record of its existence, so it's anonymous.

Even an anonymous gun, it seems, can leave a trail.

They could have four victims of that gun now, instead of two, except that the shooting in Massachusetts has already been solved, so nobody's going to compare that bullet with some bullets in Connecticut. And of course I didn't use the gun with Everett Dynes.

And I'm not going to be able to use it with the last resumé, either.

What am I going to do? I can't use the Luger any more, not ever again. I don't have any other gun, and I don't know how I could get one without leaving an ownership trail. I know that criminals have ways to do that, but I don't live in their world, and if I tried to enter their world something bad would happen to me, I know that much.

A gun is so clean, so impersonal. It separates you, just a bit, from the event.

Can I stab somebody? Strangle? I don't see how I could do such things.

And I can't use the car again. Even apart from the difficulty of rigging another covering accident, and the suspicion I might arouse by having a second accident of that kind, even beyond all that, I know I couldn't do that again. Once was enough. More than enough.

And I certainly can't walk up to a total stranger with a glass in my hand and say, "Here, drink this."

What am I going to do? I've come this far, I can't stop now. Those deaths can't have been in vain. I've been given a warning, and I'll heed it. I have one resumé to go, and then Fallon, and it's all over. One way or another, I'll do it, because I have to do it.

Not today, though. I have to deliver Marjorie to the New Variety this afternoon for her cashier job, and then pick her up this evening. It would be too difficult and too noticeable, now that we're talking to each other again, to alter our Sunday pattern by spending the whole day away; it would certainly come up in Tuesday's session with Longus Quinlan, and what would I say?

Monday. After I drop Marjorie at Dr. Carney's, on Monday, I'll drive over to New York State and study my last resumé, and see what things look like. Monday, the ninth of June; I make a checkmark on the date on my desk calendar. Not to remind myself, I certainly won't need reminding, but to express to myself my determination to see this through.

I have to think of something.

Hauck Exman
27 River Road
Sable Jetty, NY 12598
518 943-3450

1987–present - Oak Crest Paper Mills - manager, polymer paper applications

1981–1987 - Oak Crest Paper Mills - supervisor, product development

1978–1981 - Oak Crest Paper Mills - sales director

1973–1978 - Oak Crest Paper Mills - salesman

1970–1973 - U.S. Marine Corps, instructor, Fort Bragg

1970 - Graduate degree, Business Administration, Holyoke University, Holyoke, MD

Married, three grown children. Self and current wife prepared to relocate if necessary.

Reference: John Justus, Oak Crest Paper Mills, Dention, CT

31

"Self and current wife." A lot of undercurrents under that "current." A hard-nosed ex-Marine, I wonder how many wives he wore down.

The simple son of a bitch was more faithful to his employer than to any woman. Out of the Marines and straight into Oak Crest and stayed there until they dumped him. How close was he to pension; a year and a half?

Hauck Curtis Exman; my God, it's my second HCE. I started with an HCE and, except for Fallon, I'm ending with an HCE. Here Comes Everybody. Yes, and here comes a candle to light you to bed.

Sable Jetty is south of Kingston, where I had my accident with the pickup truck. It's right on the Hudson River, a little old river town of wood and brick, built up the steep slope, probably two hundred years beyond any economic justification for its existence. These places have become weekend homes for the city well-to-do because they're so quaint, and they're quaint because the people have been too poor to keep up with the latest trends. This is the sort of town movie companies use when they're shooting a film set in the twenties or thirties. Now that the city people are losing their city jobs, maybe these towns will go on being quaint.

Sable Jetty spreads up from a small cove on the Hudson's western bank, where a hillock of land extends into the river, forming a natural calm basin along the shore just to its south, downstream. The Indians launched their canoes there, long ago, and the first European explorers landed there, because it was out of the river's current. A settlement built up, and then a ferry was started, and the town prospered, and all of that eventually disappeared. Today, the old ferry office is the county historical museum, the old ferry dock is long gone, and the old brick or wooden houses built up the teetery hill westward from the river's edge seem more and more like two-dimensional flat genre paintings and less and less like places where actual human beings live their lives.

River Road runs from the square in front of the ferry dock northward, immediately leaving town, arcing around the long gradual slope of the hillock. It doesn't go right along by the water, but partway upslope, with more substantial houses on its upward side, originally meant to give doctors and aldermen and hardware store owners good river views, and less substantial shacklike houses between road and water, originally meant to give the working class a roof over their heads where they could supplement their poor incomes with fish.

27 is on the uphill side, a big brick sprawl of a house, with a broad curved porch stretching around the front, set off by thick wooden pillars painted a creamy yellow. There must have been plantings around the house and along the roadside at one time, but they're gone now, replaced by a long narrow ribbon of lawn, flowing down the smooth and gentle slope from the front wall of the house to the low white picket fence — plastic, not wood — that defines the edge of the road. This lawn is flanked on both sides by very black blacktop driveways, the one on the left belonging to 27 and the one on the right belonging to the house next door. Newer smaller houses flank 27 too closely on both sides, so that this must once have been a more gracious and spacious property, until the side lots were sold off in the fifties.

Monday morning, 11:30. I came here directly from dropping Marjorie off at Dr. Carney's, crossing the Hudson on the same bridge as when I came back from Everett Dynes. I drive by 27 River Road southbound, looking up at the house on my right.

A red-haired woman in a tan sweatshirt and blue jeans sits on a riding mower, grooming the lawn in slow ovals. The detached garage at the top of the driveway is closed, and no car is parked on the blacktop. The mailbox, oversized and silver, with the address stenciled on it in severe black, stands on a white-washed wooden post between the end of the picket fence and the end of the driveway. Its flag is up; ideal for a shooting, if I could use the gun.

I don't even have the Luger with me; what's the point?

I drive on down into town, where half the small dusty shops around the square are hopelessly for rent. I park in front of one of the empty shops to study my road atlas, and there's no comfort there. River Road sweeps out of town and north around the protruding hillock, on the other side of which it angles west to dead-end at State Route 9, the main north-south state road on this side of the river. Route 9 continues south, avoiding the center of Sable Jetty, but with no other turn-offs before it reaches the town. No other road enters or crosses the area of the hillock, which makes a sort of pumpkin stuck onto the shore of the river. A private road, sealed with an electric gate, leads from the town end of River Road up to the mansion that commands the top of the hillock; long ago a lumber baron's or a railroad baron's place, it is now a Buddhist retreat, impenetrably fenced against its neighbors.

I can't get at HCE's house from behind. River Road itself is quite exposed, a long curve with several houses always visible and with no public parking areas. I hadn't noticed any vacant-seeming houses or For Sale signs near HCE's place. Several of the smaller houses on the river side of the road had looked to me to be seasonal, summer places for today's blue-collar people, but this is June and the season has begun; a few boats bob at rickety wooden docks along there, and any or all of those houses could be occupied right now, even on a Monday.

HCE, my ex-Marine, is being harder to get at than any of the others.

The road atlas can't help me. I put it away, and start the Voyager, and drive around the square to head north again up River Road.

HCE's house is now on my left. The woman on the riding mower is making smaller ovals now, her work almost done. And the garage door is open, the interior of the garage empty.

Damn! He came out! While I was in town, he came out and went . . . anywhere. For all I know, he drove right on by me while I was parked down there, frowning at my road atlas.

I don't know what he looks like. I don't know what the car looks like.

I drive on up to the T intersection with Route 9, where there's a diner just to the south and a big covered mall just to the north. It's almost lunchtime now anyway, so I pull in at the diner, and as I have my usual BLT I wonder if he happens to be working here. Hauck Curtis Exman. HCE. Is this where he drove to, from his house? Is his car outside there somewhere, maybe next to mine? There are only female employees visible out front, but could he be in back? A short-order cook?

Or did he just go out to get the newspaper, and is he home again by now?

Finishing my lunch, I drive back down River Road. The flag is down on the mailbox, so the mail has been delivered. The garage door is still open, garage still empty. The woman and the riding mower are both gone. The mower doesn't seem to be in the garage, so they probably have a shed for it around back.

I drive into town, and through it, and several miles farther south I pull over at a parking area for a scenic river view. I sit there and try to think how to get at HCE.

297

How to find him, and then how to kill him, without using a gun.

But find him first. Identify him, so I can follow him, look for my chance.

How long will he be gone from the house? Has he a make-work job somewhere? Has he a *real* job, a paper mill job, one that takes him out of contention? Could I be that lucky twice in a row?

But what real job would have him leave the house between 11:30 in the morning and noon?

When the clock in the Voyager reads 1:30 I drive away from the scenic view, which I'd barely looked at. I go back up through Sable Jetty and up River Road, and there's no change at HCE's house. Garage open and empty. He's still gone.

There's nothing more I can do today. I feel anxious, impatient, this business is so close to being over and done with, but I know there's nothing more to be done, not today. I don't want to be careless, in too much of a rush. I don't want to cause another mess, like a couple I've had, and I certainly don't want to be caught by the police, not at this stage.

When I reach Route 9 I turn north, past the big mall and on toward the bridge and, beyond that, home.

32

I'm crossing the bridge again, in bright sunshine, high over the Hudson River, seeing towns and woodland and factories and onetime mansions along both shores, the bustling but grubby town of Kingston out ahead. Wednesday morning; my second visit to the second HCE.

Yesterday, at our counseling session, there was an uncomfortable silence for a while, partway through, none of us seeming to have much to say, as though whatever the counseling's purpose had been was now completed, but then Quinlan said to me, "When you were laid off from the mill, it wasn't a surprise, was it? Not a complete surprise."

"Not a *complete* surprise," I agreed. "There'd been rumors, and the whole industry was shaking up. But I didn't expect it so soon, and I guess I wasn't ever sure *I'd* be part of it. I was always good at my job, believe me —"

"I'm sure you were," he said, with a small smile and an encouraging nod.

"I didn't know they were going to move the whole thing to Canada," I said. "We trained them, the Canadians, and now they're cheaper than we are."

He said, "How did you feel, when it happened?"

"How did I *feel?*"

"Well, I mean," he said, "were you angry? Frightened? Resentful? Relieved?"

"Not relieved," I said, and laughed. "All the others, I guess."

"Why?"

I looked at him. "Why? Why what?"

"Why feel angry, or frightened, or resentful?"

I couldn't believe we were descending down to this kindergarten level. I said, "Because I was losing my job. It's perfectly natural to —"

"Why?"

He was beginning to annoy me. He was beginning to be one of those inspirers they'd set loose on us at the mill during the last months before the chop. I said, "What am I *supposed* to feel, when I lose my job?"

"There's nothing you're required to feel," he said. "There's not even anything that's perfectly natural to feel. What *you* felt was angry and frightened and bitter and probably perplexed, and you still do. So what I'm wondering is, why did you take it that way?"

"Everybody did!"

"Oh, I don't think so," he said, and sat

back in his chair, away from his desk, farther from me. "Do you remember your co-workers? The ones who were let go the same time as you? Did they *all* feel the way you did?"

"There was pretty general depression," I told him. "Some people put a better face on it, that's all."

"You mean some of them took a more positive view," he suggested. "Saw there might be an opportunity here —"

"Mr. Quinlan," I said, "they sent specialists around to us, the last five months on the job, people to help us learn how to write resumés and dress for a job interview and all of that stuff, people to advise us about our finances now that we weren't going to *have* any finances, and people to *inspire* us, give us all this sloganeering and pep talks and feel-good stuff. You're beginning to sound a lot like them."

He laughed and said, "I suppose I am. Well, I suppose I have the same message, that's why."

"The message is crap," I told him.

I hadn't said that to any of the inspirers at the mill. Back then I was polite and receptive and obedient, just the way you're supposed to be, but I didn't think I should have to go through it all over again, so I just told Quinlan what I thought, to get *rid* of this Pollyanna stuff forever. Every day in every way we are *not* getting better and better.

Marjorie looked at me, startled, when I said that, when I told Quinlan he was saying crap, because we'd all been gentle and polite with one another up till now, but Quinlan didn't mind. I'm sure he's heard a lot worse in that office. He grinned at me and shook his head and said, "Mr. Devore, what you're *picking up* as the message *is* crap, I'll go along with that. But what you're picking up is not what I'm sending out, and it's not what those people at the mill were sending out. The real message is, *you are not the job.*"

I looked at him. Was that supposed to mean something?

He saw that I still wasn't receiving whatever it was he was trying to send, so he said, "A lot of people, Mr. Devore, identify themselves with their jobs, as though the person and the job were one and the same. When they lose the job, they lose a sense of themselves, they lose a sense of worth, of being valuable people. They think they're nothing any more."

"That isn't me," I said. "That isn't the way I look at it."

"But you felt depressed and angry," he

reminded me. "Didn't you feel they'd taken away part of your self?"

"They took away my life, not my self," I told him. "They took away my ability to pay my mortgage, care for my children, have good times with my wife. A job is a job, it isn't *me*, but it's necessary. And I'll tell you what we all knew, Mr. Quinlan, in those last five months, the hundreds of us there, used to be best friends, working together, counting on one another, not even thinking about it, we always knew we could rely on each other right on down the line. But it was the end of the line, and we were enemies now, because we were competitors now, and we all knew it. *That's* the thing we weren't saying to each other, and the counselors weren't saying, and nobody was saying. That the tribe was bust, it wasn't a tribe any more. We wouldn't be watching each other's backs any more."

He leaned forward again, watching me carefully. "Enemies, Mr. Devore? They were your enemies?"

"We were *all* enemies, each other's enemies, and we all knew it. You could see it in the faces. People who always used to have lunch together stopped having lunch together. When somebody said, 'Do you have any leads?' you said no, even if it was a lie.

We started lying to each other. Friendships stopped. Relationships stopped."

"You couldn't trust one another any more."

"We weren't a team, we were each other's competition. Everything changed."

Quinlan nodded. He wasn't smiling, he was serious. "Every man for himself," he said.

"That's what it is. Before you get the chop, you don't have to know that, you can pretend we're all buddies here. *That's* the message the inspirers were trying to implant in us, the idea that we're still all together in this, it's still a society, and it is functioning, and we're all a part of it. But after you get the chop, you can't afford that fairy story any more. It *is* every man for himself. The big executives know that. The stockholders know that. And now *we* know it."

"And what does that mean to you, Mr. Devore?"

"It means I have nobody to count on but me." Turning to Marjorie, I said, "That's why I've been so distant, and so focused, because I'm all I've got, and I'm in the fight of my life. I'm *sorry* it's made me so cold to you, I'm sorry, I wish . . . well. You know what I wish."

"You aren't alone, Burke," Marjorie said.

"You've got me, you know that."

I shook my head, but I managed a smile as I said, "Have you got a job for me?"

She took that as rejection, of course, I could see it in her hurt reaction, but it wasn't, that's not what it was meant to be. It was just part of seeing clearly. We don't have the luxury of sentiment now, Hallmark cards. At this moment, in this condition, in this situation, we have to see clearly, there's no other choice.

I turned back to Quinlan. I said, "There's nothing out there but me and the competition, and I have to beat the competition. I *have* to. Whatever it takes."

But we were getting too close to reality here, the new reality, my own personal way of *dealing* with the competition. I'd followed the new line of reasoning all the way to the end, and acted on it, but I didn't want anybody else doing that, not around me. Certainly not these two, not Marjorie or Quinlan. So I added, "It's may the best man win, now, and all I can do is hope I'm the best man."

That was the end of the session. Quinlan had let it run on, it seemed, an extra five minutes. And when we left, I thought he looked very closely at me, trying to understand.

Better not to understand, Mr. Q.

Down off the bridge; Kingston. I turn south, toward Sable Jetty.

33

She isn't mowing the lawn today. The garage door is closed, and no one is in sight. He's home, then, and probably she is, too.

How do I get at this man? You cannot approach that house unobserved, you just can't. It's as though he's still a Marine, and placed himself where he has the advantage of the terrain; the slope up to his place, the clear line of fire, the inaccessibility from anywhere except the front.

I drive around the neighborhood, and the next time I pass the house, at 11:50, the garage door is open, the garage empty. He's gone again, and I've missed him again.

This is no good, I'm not accomplishing anything. I drive away, southbound, back to that scenic view from Monday, and I sit there brooding, staring without seeing at the river as it marches endlessly by, like weary soldiers under heavy packs, blue-gray soldiers in blue-gray uniforms bent low under the weight of blue-gray packs, marching in their tight masses downstream.

The resumé. The resumé itself; can I use it? I put my ad in *The Paperman*, I got my responses, I did my winnowing, I used the addresses from the resumés, but that's all. Is there a way to use the ad itself, the fact of the ad? If I can't get at him when he's home, or find him, or follow him from home, can I *send* him somewhere, and *then* follow him?

I begin to see how it could done. I must go home, get back to the office, think this thing through.

But first I need a restaurant.

B. D. INDUSTRIAL PAPERS
P. O. BOX 2900
WILDBURY, CT 06899

June 11, 1997

Mr. Hauck Exman
27 River Rd.
Sable Jetty, NY 12598

Dear Mr. Exman:

Three months ago, we ran a help wanted ad in *The Paperman*, to which you responded. At that time, I must admit, you were not our first choice for the position. However, since then, to our chagrin, it has become apparent that our initial decision was in error.

If you have not as yet found other employment, would you be available on Friday, June 20th, to meet with our Personnel Director, Ms. Laurie Kilpatrick, who will be interviewing in the western New York region?

We would suggest lunch at one PM at the Coach House in Regnery, which I believe is not too far from your residence. The reservation will be in Ms. Kilpatrick's name.

Please fill out and return this letter in the enclosed stamped envelope, to let us know your availability. Since the gentleman to be replaced is still on the premises, a phone call might create unnecessary distress.

If we do not hear from you, we will understand that you are no longer interested in the position.

Thank you for your time.

Benj Dockery III

Benj Dockery III, Pres.

☐ I am available.

☐ I am not available.

☐ I must suggest an alternate date.

Signature _____

BD/VK

34

This is a very dangerous letter to send. For the first time, I'm leaving a trail — other than the bullets from the Luger, I mean — and for the first time I'm doing something that might warn my resumé that he's in danger.

The phone number, that's the problem. Though contact with prospective employees is often made by this kind of letter, there's *always* a phone number on the letterhead, and almost always the employer asks you to respond by phone. Explaining that the unsatisfactory hire is still there, and a phone call might make trouble in the shop, should — I hope — calm HCE's suspicions before they arise. But what if he notices there's no phone number on the letterhead?

I thought of putting a fake number on it, any number at all, but what if he disobeyed the letter and made the call? That's unlikely, since job hunters don't disobey prospective employers, but what if he did? He would not reach B. D. Industrial Papers. And, no matter what happened in the course of that call, I could be sure his next call would be to the police.

He and they would probably suspect a con

game of some sort, and they would follow the trail of the letter to my post office box, where the postmistress would certainly give them a description of me. She's seen me several times, so the description would probably be a good one.

Also, since the letterhead would lead them into Connecticut, how long would it be before it connected them with Detective Burton, the man investigating the coincidental murders of two unemployed paper mill midlevel managers? Come to think of it, what are the odds that HCE applied to Willis & Kendall for that can-label job? Which would mean Detective Burton has already interviewed him.

But the telephone number is the only problem. The meeting I've arranged isn't unheard of, and shouldn't raise suspicion. Personnel directors do sometimes go on the road, to meet with a number of applicants in the same geographical area, and one of the appointments each day will include lunch, or otherwise lunch is a waste of time.

I've made the personnel director a woman, with a name that suggests she's young, and I'm hoping that the prospect of a good meal (the Coach House has a first-rate reputation) with an attractive young woman (he'll naturally assume she's attractive), one that could lead to a prime job, will throw enough dust in his eyes to keep him from thinking about telephones.

Still, it's frightening. At this point, so many things could go wrong. For instance, I've told him to countersign the letter and send it back, so it won't be found among his effects after I kill him, but what if he makes a copy, what if he's that kind of completist? (I reassure myself that, if he's *that* kind of completist, there'll be so much paper bumf stored among his effects that no one will ever look through it all.)

I've also done the best I can with both envelopes, the one I'm mailing to him and the one included for his return. I had a few sheets of my fake letterhead copied onto extra-heavy paper, and then, carefully, with a straight-edge and a razor blade, I cut out the letterheads from three sheets and glued them as the return address on both envelopes and the destination address on the inner envelope. They do look like printed labels.

This whole move scares me. I've been very careful up till now, I've done my best to control the situations, to keep myself anonymous and separate. Now I'm, at least potentially, leaving a trail. But what can I do? I'm so close to the finish, so close. HCE is all that stands between me and Upton "Ralph" Fallon, who will be easy, easy, easy.

Now I'm desperate. I can't use the gun, and I can't get at, or even find, HCE. I have to try something, anything, and this is all I can think of. So I drive up to Wildbury, to the mailbox outside the post office, and I send the letter, and I'm terrified.

From time to time, the next few days, I'll drive over to Sable Jetty and go past HCE's house. And if I see a police car parked outside, I don't know what I'll do.

B. D. INDUSTRIAL PAPERS
P. O. BOX 2900
WILDBURY, CT 06899

June 11, 1997

Mr. Hauck Exman
27 River Rd.
Sable Jetty, NY 12598

Dear Mr. Exman:

Three months ago, we ran a help wanted ad in *The Paperman*, to which you responded. At that time, I must admit, you were not our first choice for the position. However, since then, to our chagrin, it has become apparent that our initial decision was in error.

If you have not as yet found other employment, would you be available on Friday, June 20th, to meet with our Personnel Director, Ms. Laurie Kilpatrick, who will be interviewing in the western New York region?

We would suggest lunch at one PM at the Coach House in Regnery, which I believe is not too far from your residence. The reservation will be in Ms. Kilpatrick's name.

Please fill out and return this letter in the enclosed stamped envelope, to let us know your availability. Since the gentleman to be replaced is still on the premises, a phone call might create unnecessary distress.

If we do not hear from you, we will understand that you are no longer interested in the position.

Thank you for your time.

Benj Dockery III

Benj Dockery III, Pres.

☑ I am available.

☐ I am not available.

☐ I must suggest an alternate date.

Signature _*Hank Brhm*_

BD/VK

I look forward to the meeting!

35

I sit in front of the Wildbury post office,
Tuesday, the 17th of June, at the wheel of
the Voyager, and I hold the letter in my
hands. It has orbited back to me. I look at
what HCE has written there, along the bottom, and the letter feels warm, heated by his
hunger.

He sent it back immediately, the instant
he got it. Clearly, he didn't worry about
telephone numbers or anything else.

Another possible snag, I'd realized after I
sent the letter, was that he might cut off the
bottom part of it, the part for him to fill out,
and just send that back, retaining the main
body of the letter for himself — and the
police. But HCE wants this job; he snapped
at the bait like a trout.

Now that my gamble seems to be paying
off, I can admit the other aspect of this move
that I don't like. I have killed people. I've
hated doing it, but I had to do it, and I did
it. But I haven't been cruel to them, I haven't
toyed with them. In a way, I'm toying with
HCE, I'm tantalizing him with a nonexistent
job interview with a nonexistent attractive
woman. I'm sorry to do that, I wish there'd

been some other way.

The letter got back to Wildbury yesterday, but I couldn't check the box until this afternoon, because yesterday was Billy's day in court. We had to be there, Marjorie and I, of course. We were scheduled for ten, and we arrived a few minutes early, with Billy, to find Porculey the lawyer waiting for us. His suit this time was not maroon, thank God, but a neutral gray. It was his tie that was maroon, with little white cows jumping over little white moons. He shook our hands, Marjorie's and mine, and said, "We think it will work out here," and took Billy away for a discussion with the judge.

A lot has happened in the two weeks since Billy's arrest. It turned out that Billy's partner in crime, somebody named Jim Bucklin, had been less quick-witted than we, and so had his parents. In the police car after his arrest, he'd said things that might be construed as confessions that he'd robbed that same store several times before, and apparently he'd said similar things to other detectives at the police station, and kept blabbing away until finally, the next day, he met the lawyer his parents had hired (unlike Billy's poor needy folks, the Bucklins didn't qualify for Legal Aid). That lawyer finally got Jim Bucklin to shut up.

The general feeling was that all of Bucklin's earlier loose talk would not be admissible in court, and after the lawyer arrived, Bucklin too started to claim that this burglary was his very first, so that he and Billy were at last telling the same story.

Which broke down when the police searched the Bucklin house (the same time they were searching ours) and found all that computer software.

Of course, they hadn't found any illicit software at our house. So, if finding stolen goods at Bucklin's house meant Bucklin was lying, then *not* finding them at Devore's house must mean Devore was telling the truth, or at least that's what Porculey was maintaining, and why he was doing his best to sever the two cases. Let Bucklin, the long-term master criminal, fend for himself, while Billy, the innocent youngster lured into a life of crime by Bucklin, faced the judge alone.

In chambers. We weren't there for it, having to sit out in the corridor, but apparently it went well. Over the assistant district attorney's ferocious objections — I saw her, from a distance, a hawklike woman in her thirties, thin and sharp-faced and ruthless — the judge did agree to separate the two cases, and to proceed in chambers with Billy's case.

By then, a jail term was no longer at issue.

In fact, as Porculey later explained it to us over diner coffee, the issue had become whether or not Billy would have a felony conviction on his record. He had never been in trouble before, he was a good student in school, he had a bright future, and he came from poverty. (Ah, well.) In chambers, Porculey had suggested the possibility of a sealed indictment, and the judge had said he'd think it over.

Over that coffee, as it cooled, all of us too keyed up to add caffeine to our systems, he'd explained what a sealed indictment was, and it's an unexpected bit of mercy in the judicial system. If the defendant would plead guilty, and if the circumstances warrant giving him a second chance, the judge can choose to seal the indictment, keep it unpublished and unacted-upon, in his court, for whatever length of time he decrees; usually a year. If, in that time, the defendant is arrested for *another* crime, the indictment is unsealed and he faces prosecution for both the old crime and the new one. If, however, he stays clean until the term is up, the indictment is quashed as though it had never been. There is no police record; the defendant walks away pure.

Well, that's what we were hoping for, of course, and Porculey expected we'd know before the end of the day, but first the matter of Jim Bucklin had to be dealt with. We stayed away from court during that time, but apparently Bucklin's lawyer joined the assistant district attorney in struggling to keep the two cases together, and the argument was a lengthy one. He wanted his client, of course, to coast along on Billy's cleaner coat-tails.

But eventually the judge ruled against both the defense lawyer and the assistant district attorney, and Bucklin's case was held over alone for trial — or a plea bargain later on, more likely — and at three in the afternoon we were brought back in. Marjorie and Billy and I stood before the judge, who was a different one from that original bail hearing, in a different but similar courtroom. And again it was exactly like some religious ritual, full of arcane language, and we the penitents before the high priest.

Porculey had advised us against talking to Bucklin's parents, so we'd avoided them, though they desperately wanted to talk to *us;* to convince us to re-yoke our boy to their doomed son, no doubt. I was aware of them at the back of the courtroom when our session began, remorseful, resentful and reproachful. I didn't look back at them.

The judge sealed the indictment. I thought

Marjorie would fall down when she understood what he'd just said, and I held tight to her arm. The judge spoke severely to Billy about his thoughtlessness — lovely word — and Billy kept his head bowed and his responses short and respectful, and soon it was over.

At twenty to four yesterday afternoon, Billy's troubles with the law were done. So long as he stays honest from now on, that is. And there isn't much doubt of that. This experience has frightened him, and he's aware of just how lucky he is. He has the vision of Jim Bucklin right in front of him, to show him how serious it might have been. And he's grateful to us, and doesn't want to let us down.

We shook hands with Porculey, and tried to express our gratitude, and our awareness that we might well have drawn a much worse attorney, and then I took Marjorie and Billy home. What a relief it was, almost as big a relief as if I'd finished all this other business and had my real job back. And what it showed me was, if you just keep going, keep determined, don't *let* the system grind you down, you can prevail.

I will prevail.

Well, that experience used up all of yesterday, and today was another counseling session. Today I kept my mouth shut, since I'm worried I might have exposed myself a little too much last week and I don't want to risk doing that again. Quinlan tried to probe into me two or three times, I could sense his curiosity about the direction we were heading last week, but I gave him flat answers, greeting card answers that he couldn't do a thing with. And Marjorie wanted to steer the conversation toward our roles within the marriage, which was what we were supposed to be there for anyway, so I think I did myself no damage.

When we got home, I did something I've been planning for a while, and now I think the time is right. I prepared seventeen of my resumés, my own resumés, addressed seventeen envelopes to paper mills I'd already approached in the past, plus Arcadia Processing, and I wrote a covering letter to each, saying I'm still here, I'm still available, just in case any job has opened up since you last heard from me. If the timing is right, my resumé will be the most recent one in Arcadia's files, and possibly still fresh in Arcadia's personnel director's memory, when a job over there unexpectedly does become available. And since I'm sending this whole batch out, and it's a week or two before URF's death, there shouldn't be any suspicion raised.

After I mailed those resumés at my local post office, I drove on up here to Wildbury, to find HCE's answer waiting in the box. And now I sit here a minute, in the sunshine, outside the post office, and I smile at how well things are coming along.

Friday. Three days from now, I'll find HCE at last. Will I be able to deal with him immediately? Find him and just *do* it? Then next week URF and it's all over.

I can see the job, the work, the commute. I can *feel* being in that job, like a warm bath.

Friday.

36

I am parked down the block from the Coach House. It is five to one, Friday afternoon; almost time for HCE's lunch with Ms. Laurie Kilpatrick.

Nine days ago, when I realized I couldn't get at HCE directly, and began to think about this other way to do it, I drove all around this part of the state, looking at restaurants, and decided that, for my purposes, the Coach House in Regnery is ideal. It's fairly upscale, the kind of place where the local gentry goes, and it's right on the main street of town, so there's no problem parking or being anonymous. And there are large mullioned windows on the street, Colonial style, through which a pedestrian can easily see the front part of the restaurant, where the maitre d' greets the customers and where there's a small seating area of two benches for people to await their lunch companions.

Will HCE be early? I'm sure of it. At five before the hour, he's probably in there already; time for my first walk by.

I get out of the Voyager, which I've parked half a block from the restaurant, and stroll down the sidewalk.

Yesterday afternoon, I phoned here, to make a reservation for two in the name Kilpatrick, so he'll be told the reservation does exist but the other party hasn't arrived as yet, and naturally he'll take a seat in the waiting area.

And is that him? I stroll by, and one man is on the bench there, sitting back, looking confident, one leg crossed over the other. A very good dark suit and dark figured tie, close-cropped gray hair, a squarish face; that's all I can see in that first glimpse.

I walk on, pause at an appliance store, study the VCRs and fax machines in the window for a few minutes, then turn and stroll back the way I came. A longer look at him now, and I'm sure this is my man. He has a blunt way of sitting, a square-jawed, take-command expression on his face, and just a hint of excited anticipation. HCE, at last.

I go back to the Voyager, get behind the wheel, sit watching the entrance to the restaurant. It's pretty popular; well-dressed people keep going in, usually in pairs, usually men together or women together, occasionally a mixed couple, but all middle-aged or older. I don't see another singleton who matches my idea of HCE.

1:10. Time to confirm my guess that the

military-looking man in the suit is HCE. (The suit, which looks to me very good and very expensive, is the one small cause of doubt here.) Is he still waiting? Or is someone else there in his place, the *real* HCE?

No. Still him. He's still my man. The former Marine instructor who spent his entire working life with one company. He's looking less confident now, slightly distressed, and when I walk back toward the Voyager I see him looking at his watch.

Again I sit behind the wheel. The only question now is how long it will take him to give up.

1:45. He's still in there. He must know by now that Ms. Kilpatrick isn't coming, something's gone wrong. But still he waits, hope against hope, the faithful soldier.

I hate doing this to him, the elation and then the humiliation, the terrible feeling of wretchedness and no way to strike back at the unfairness. If there'd been any other way . . .

Well. This situation has its grim moments.

2:05. Is he *never* going to give up? He can't sleep in that restaurant, he'll have to leave sometime. Did he decide to eat lunch there anyway, pay for it himself?

Unlikely. HCE and I can't afford places like the Coach House any more.

Should I get out of the car, go see if he's still seated there? If somehow he's gone out some back way, left the restaurant, I should know it. But what if I do get out, and I'm halfway there, and he —

There. At last, he comes out into the sunlight. Standing, he's shorter than I expected, but compact, a stocky man in good physical condition. He stops on the sidewalk, at a loss, looking up and down the block, and then he shakes his head and turns to walk in my direction.

My face is turned away, I'm looking at the bank directly across the street, when he walks past me. Then I turn back and watch him recede in the right side mirror, ramrod stiff. When he's a little farther along I watch him in the inside mirror, and remember poor Everett Dynes, and briefly close my eyes. I don't need that memory now.

He's turned, he's stepping between cars, he's turning again, he's unlocking a car door. When he opens it, I see the car is black; I would have expected that from him. I start the Voyager's motor, sit there with it idling.

Now nothing happens. What is he doing in there? Probably, come to think of it, with the relative privacy of the interior of his own car, probably he's allowing himself a minute to be unglued, to be angry and unhappy and frustrated and afraid. But, if I know my man, he won't need long.

No. Here he comes. It's a Ford Taurus; HCE would buy American.

I switch on my left turn signal. His Taurus drives by me, then a gray Chrysler Cirrus drives by me, and then I pull out.

We drive out of town, me keeping at least one other car between us, his black Taurus always clearly visible up ahead. Out of Regnery, this secondary road takes us over to State Route 9, where he turns north toward Sable Jetty, as expected.

There's more traffic on this road, but he's still easy to follow. I'd thought his anger and frustration might make him drive too fast or too aggressively, but he's a law-abider, and we stay respectably just above the speed limit whenever we aren't slowed by trucks.

I expect him to take the right turn that leads into Sable Jetty, but he doesn't; instead, he continues on up Route 9. I follow, keeping well back, wondering where he's going. North of town, he'll meet the other end of River Road, but that would be the long way round to his house.

Here's River Road, with the diner beside

it and the big mall just beyond it, on the other side of the road, and *that's* where he's going, the mall. He signals for a left, moving into the special mall lane there, and the three cars between us all go straight ahead, and I too signal for a left as I come to a stop behind him.

There's no traffic light at this spot, but there is one some distance ahead, and shortly after that one turns red the southbound traffic peters out, and then we can both make our turn, and so can the two cars that have come along behind me.

It's harder to follow him in the parking lot, without being noticeable. I stay well back, seeming indecisive about which lane I want, while he heads confidently forward and then to the right, and parks some distance away from the main building, half a dozen empty spaces from the nearest parked car. Is he afraid of dents and damage from other people getting into their cars next to his? I think that would probably be like him.

I find a slot closer to the building, and stop, and take out my memo pad and pen, as though I've chosen this moment to do my shopping list. I'm aware of him walking this way, then see him clearly first in the right mirror, then the inside mirror, then the left mirror.

Please. Let this one not be as awful as Everett Dynes.

When he's almost to the end of the row of parked cars, I finally get out of the Voyager, lock it, and follow. He's crossing the lanes between the parking area and the mall building, and I'm not very far behind him. Other people are walking here, too, from their cars. We all enter the building.

This is an enclosed mall, with a long broad corridor from these doors, flanked by chain stores of all kinds, and with a three-story Dolmen's at the far end, Dolmen's being a line of suburban department stores, mostly or maybe entirely in malls. In front of Dolmen's, the corridor Ts left and right, with more shops facing the fashion windows of the department store. Only the part of the building containing Dolmen's is more than one story high.

HCE walks briskly down the long corridor. He certainly seems to know where he's going. Could he be planning to buy himself something, some small luxury to soothe his feelings? He doesn't seem the type.

Dolmen's, that's where he's going. The sliding doors open for him, then close, then open for me, and I see him moving just as briskly as ever toward the escalators in the middle of the store.

I keep well back. There are a good number of shoppers in here, but it isn't really crowded, and I wouldn't want him to become aware that he's seeing me every time he looks around.

Not that he does look around, really. He's clearly concentrated on his destination. Up the escalator he goes, and I can tell he would step briskly upward except that the large family in front of him, everybody but Dad, is standing still.

I hang back, and hang back, and don't board the escalator until he's nearly to the top. Then, as I am rising upward, I just glimpse him make the U-turn and march back toward the second flight.

Yes. As I come off the first escalator and turn toward the second, I just spy his hand and part of his dark suit moving up. I follow.

He's at the top when I reach the bottom, and I see him angle left. I walk up the moving steps, gliding rapidly upward, and when I can see the third floor he's nowhere in sight.

That's all right. I saw him go leftward, toward the left rear of the store, and there aren't that many sections up here. I'll spot him any second.

But I don't. I move along that leftward aisle, looking both ways as I go along, as though searching for something to buy, not a man to kill, and he isn't anywhere. The final department up here is menswear, racks of suit jackets and sport coats along two right-angled walls, and he isn't here, either.

Where the hell did he go? I'm not worried yet, because whatever he's come here for will take him at least a few minutes to choose and buy. He's in this quadrant on this level of the store; I'll find him.

I'm still standing in the middle of menswear, frowning one way and another, deciding which route to take first, when HCE himself comes out from a doorway in the very corner, between the racks of suits and coats. He sees me, and smiles, and marches toward me, and I'm bewildered and frightened and ready to run. Then I realize, he's now wearing an oval blue-and-white nametag. It says DOLMEN'S in the upper half, and below that it says "Mr. Exman."

He works here. He's a suit salesman, that's why his own suit is so good. He's a suit salesman and I'm a customer.

"Yes, sir?" he says, hands clasped together, beaming at me in a way I know to be false to his nature and probably abhorrent to his soul.

I can't just stand and stare. I have to be quick-witted, I have to move things along smoothly, I have to not seem astonished, or guilty, or afraid. I have to be nothing at all, a blank customer, in front of a salesman. "Just looking," I say. "Thank you."

"If I can be of help," he says, with that smile, "you'll find me around."

There are no other customers in this section at this moment, and no other salesmen visible. We're alone here, but not usefully. "Yes, yes, thank you," I say. I don't want him to remember me.

Or, wait. Yes, I do. I'm thinking now, I'm seeing the possibilities all at once. I return his smile, I don't turn away, and I say, "It's a sport jacket I need, for summer, but I can't pick it out for myself, my wife has to be with me. So now I'm just looking around."

"Yes, of course," he says, nodding, sharing my male experience. "We always have to listen to the wife."

"She's a teacher," I explain, "so she's working today, but I could come back with her tomorrow."

"Good idea," he says, and slides two fingers into his inner jacket pocket and produces a business card. "I'll be here," he tells me, extending the card. "If you don't see me, ask."

This sort of job is mostly commission, of course. I take his card and look at it, and it's like his nametag, with the store name prominent above and his own name printed below. On the card, on the lower right, it also says, "Sales Representative." I nod at the card, and at HCE. "I'll be back," I promise. Then I switch the card to my left hand, stick out my right, and say, "Hutcheson."

"Mr. Hutcheson," he says, pleased.

We shake hands.

I walk away from him, my mind suddenly full of ideas. I put his card in my pocket, telling myself I must remember to throw it away soon. In the meantime, I have things to do, beginning with a telephone call.

There's a bank of phone booths just inside the main entrance of the store, next to the large sign giving Dolmen's opening hours; on Friday, it's "12 till 9." I throw HCE's card away in the trash barrel there, check my pockets to be sure I have enough change, and step into a booth, where I phone Marjorie, at home. We both say hello, and I say, "Could we eat dinner early tonight?" We usually eat around seven or seven-thirty.

"I suppose so," she says. "How early?"

"Well, I ran into a guy I used to be at Halcyon with. He's got some sort of idea, some business he thinks we could go into."

Sounding dubious — quite rightly — she says, "Do you think it's any good?"

"Don't know yet. He wants to show it to me at his house this evening, the specs he's done and everything."

"Does he want you to invest something?"

"Don't know that yet, either," I say, and laugh, and say, "If he does, he's barking up the wrong dead tree."

"He certainly is," she says. "What time would you want to leave?"

12 till 9. HCE started late, nearly two-thirty, so he'll surely stay till the store closes. "Seven," I say.

"We'll eat at six."

"Thanks, sweet," I say, and hang up.

And now, I have shopping to do. If you want to kill somebody, you can find everything you need for the job down at the mall.

37

Five minutes to nine. I open the driver's door beside me, and the interior light goes on.

I am back at the mall, and this time I am parked only four spaces from HCE's Taurus, where he'll have to walk by me. The left side of the Voyager is toward the mall building, and the long sliding door on the right side, away from the building, is open. The stubby hood is open, too, in front of me, exposing the chunky little engine. The new hammer rests on the depression between windshield and hood, where the windshield wiper lies when not in use; the hammer's business end is pointed downward, and its handle is out toward the side of the car.

My other purchases are all in the vehicle with me. Over there at the main entrance, the last shoppers trickle out. The parking lot is less than a quarter full, and none of the remaining cars are close to HCE and me.

What I'm planning has some risk to it, but without the gun anything I do must include some risk, and this plan has as little as possible, I think. The long June twilight is nearing its end, so, even though darkness hasn't really settled in yet, it's that tricky time of evening light when you're never quite sure what you're seeing. Also, no one but HCE is going to walk out this far across the parking lot, because our two vehicles are the only ones this far from the building. I expect to have the element of surprise on my side, and I have my purchases from the various shops in the mall.

Four minutes to nine. Three minutes to nine. Still three minutes to nine.

I keep looking at my watch, I can't help myself. My hands clench and clench the steering wheel, no matter how hard I try to relax, no matter how much I tell myself I shouldn't exhaust these hands, I'm going to need them soon.

Someone coming. A man, in silhouette against the lights of the mall behind him. In a dark suit, I think, and trudging as though he's tired, or discouraged. Or both.

He's passed every other parked car now, and he's still coming. Is he going to be so caught up in his own gloomy thoughts that he won't even notice me here?

No. He's a man who notices things, and he does see my open car door, the soft yellow interior light shining down on me, the open hood. "Trouble?" he calls.

I sigh, theatrically. "Won't start," I say, and then I lean partway out of the car, as though I've just recognized him: "Oh, hi!"

He'd still been walking toward his own car, but now he veers in my direction, squinting at me, finally getting it: "Mr. Hutcheson?"

Yes, you'll remember the name, the hot prospect for a sport jacket, going to come back tomorrow with the wife. I say, "Yes, hello. Didn't expect to see you until tomorrow."

"What's wrong?" He frowns at the open hood. I've read him to be a take-charge kind of guy, somebody proud to be there in an emergency, and he's certainly acting the part.

I say, "I hate to admit it, but I don't know a goddam thing about car engines. I called my wife, she's going to have the garage send somebody out. God knows when."

"That'll cost you," he says.

"Don't remind me," I say. "And I really can't afford it, not now." I step out of the car, keeping my right hand down by my side, and gesture at the engine with my other hand. "There goes my new sport jacket."

Now it's personal. "No, no, Mr. Hutcheson," he chides me. "Never say die, that's my motto."

"I wish it was the car's motto," I say.

He laughs and moves toward the front of

the Voyager, saying, "Let's just take a look. Do you mind?"

"Not at all," I say. "If you can save me a tow and a repair . . ."

"No promises." He picks up the hammer and raises an eyebrow at me. "Going to fix it with *this?*"

I move my hands, showing helplessness. "I thought I might have to loosen a wing nut."

Shaking his head, he puts the hammer back where I'd placed it, and leans over the engine, his head close to the open hood. "Try to turn it over," he tells me.

"Sure. Do you want a flashlight?"

"You've got one? Perfect," he says, and turns his head toward me, right hand reaching out for the flashlight, and I Mace him in the face. He cries out and slaps both palms to his eyes, as I drop the Mace can on the ground and reach for the hammer. I hit him on the temple as hard as I can, feeling his skull crack. Quickly, I hit him a second time, same spot.

He's falling. I jump forward, dropping the hammer, and throw my arms around him, holding him up. We must look like drunks dancing, but no one is close enough, with a clear enough view, to see anything going on here at all.

I crab-walk forward, carrying him, staggering under the weight, his limp feet dragging along the ground between mine. Moving like that, I hustle him around to the right side of the car and *lunge* him in onto the clear plastic tarp I've spread over the seat and floor. I hunch him up, hunch him up, and he's completely in.

Now I flip the excess tarp over the body, grab the dark green new blanket from the floor behind the seat, shake it out from its manufacturer's creases, and fling it over him. Then I step back and slide shut the door.

Brisk now, but not too fast. I walk around the front of the Voyager, closing the hood, picking up the Mace and hammer. I toss them across onto the passenger seat, climb in behind the wheel, and shut the door. Turn the key. Surprise; the engine works just fine.

I join the other laggard traffic rolling toward the exit, turn left, head up Route 9 toward Kingston and the bridge and home.

The only lights showing at my house are one table lamp in the living room, the reading light in Billy's bedroom, and the light at the head of the stairs. It's a little after eleven and Marjorie, as I'd hoped, has gone to bed. Otherwise, I'd have to drive around until she did retire, which would make me very nervous. Billy's awake, but he won't be coming out of his room.

I don't like it that I still have this body with me, but I was afraid to stop anywhere along the way to do the necessary preparation. You can find a spot that looks perfectly safe, dark and deserted, and be right in the middle of what has to be done when other people show up, or lights go on, or the police drive by. I'm safest at home, in my own garage, with the family safely tucked in for the night.

I thumb the remote control on the visor and the garage door opens, the light switching on in there. I drive in, hit the remote control again, and wait till the door shuts before I climb out and go over to turn on the main garage light. (That first one automatically switches off again three minutes after the garage door closes.)

Now to take care of the body, at least for tonight. I open the box of plastic bags I picked up at the mall, the very large kind called lawn-n-leaf, dark green, with a tie at the top. I then put on the white cotton gloves I also bought at the mall, open the Voyager's sliding side door, and look in at that mound of green blanket.

First I pull the blanket off and stuff it into the plastic bag. The hammer and the Mace

I drop in there, too, and then I set aside that bag and pull another one out of the box.

This is the difficult part. I fold the clear tarp away from the body, and am relieved to see there's almost no blood, just a little around his crushed forehead and leaking from his nose and ears. Very little bleeding means he died the instant I hit him, which is better for both of us.

The body is still limber, but it won't be for long. I move his arms down across his body, elbows nearly straight, so his hands, the fingers partly curled, lie just above his crotch. Then I take the roll of heavy-gauge picture wire — another mall purchase — and loop the end of it around his belt, twisting the wire around itself to hold it secure.

The legs are sluggish, they don't want to move, but I press and push and force the knees to bend and the legs to fold up toward the body, until his knees are against his chest, his legs pressing down on his fore-arms. I cross the picture wire over his legs, snap off that length by bending it quickly backward and forward, and then secure this end also to his belt.

Now he's a compact package, legs and arms and torso all folded together. But I want to be sure nothing goes wrong, so I put my shoulder against his shoes and push

343

upward, to make it possible to slide the next section of wire beneath him, wriggling it up as far as his waist. Then I let the body settle back down, as I snap apart this length of wire by bending it, and twist its ends together over his shins until it's very tight around him, pressing into him and becoming impossible to twist any tighter.

Getting this trussed body into another of the lawn-n-leaf bags isn't nearly as difficult as I'd expected. Of course, I might just be running on adrenaline, I don't know. In any event, in what seems like no time at all I have the second bag standing on the cement floor.

Now I open the first bag again, and stuff the plastic tarp into it. The idea is, the body never touched any part of my car, so if they do find it — which I hope they don't — there will be no fibers or paint or anything else to connect that body with this vehicle. And the parts that did touch the car, like the tarp and the blanket, go into a separate bag.

Also into this bag goes the rest of the roll of picture wire, the box of plastic bags and, at last, the gloves. When I tie this bag, I smear the plastic with my palms. No fingerprints.

It's my own work gloves from the workbench in here that I use when I wrestle the two full plastic trash bags into a corner of the garage, surrounded by the rest of the detritus that just naturally seems to grow there, particularly since we sold the Civic. The bags are both bulky, but one is much heavier than the other.

I look around the garage. Everything is normal. Nothing is amiss. I turn out the light and go in to bed.

38

Driving toward the recycling center, I find myself thinking about the concept of the learning curve, and how far along it I've come. And how very lucky I was that first time out, with the original HCE. What was his name? I'm having trouble remembering it.

Herbert Everly, that was it.

How simple that one was, simple and smooth and fast and clean. It encouraged me, it made everything else possible, because it made me believe the whole thing could be that impeccable. If I'd had the second HCE to do first, none of this would ever have happened. I just wouldn't have been up to it.

The idea of the learning curve is, the first time you do something you aren't very good at it, but you learn something about how the job is done. Then the second time, you're better, but still flawed, and you learn a little more. And so on, until you're perfect. The learning curve is an arc, beginning with a steep upward sweep, because you're learning a *lot* each time in the early days, and then gradually it flattens out to a level, as you learn in smaller and smaller increments the nearer you get to the ideal.

Well, I'm not perfect at this yet, God knows, I haven't attained the ideal, but I've come a long way up that learning curve since Herbert Everly. Of course, the irony in this one is, as the arc of my learning curve flattens toward complete competence, I'll have mastered a skill I'll never use again.

I certainly hope I'll never have to use it again. But it is, I admit, a useful skill to possess.

Earlier today, I took Marjorie to her Saturday job at the New Variety, and when I backed the Voyager out of the garage even I couldn't readily see anything different in there. The dark bulky bags leaned together well in the back, away from daylight, amid birdseed bags and paint cans and winter boots and all the rest of the stuff garages breed when no one is looking.

On the way to the movie house, I told Marjorie the story I'd made up in bed last night, before falling asleep, about the friend's moneymaking scheme that had caused me to go out for several hours after dinner. The story I told her was that my friend reminded me that the United States government shreds its old paper money to destroy it, and it was his idea to talk the government into letting us make fresh paper out of the shredded pulp. We would make paper bags, colored green, with dollar signs on them, and market them under the name Money Bags; they would be both useful and a great novelty item.

I told Marjorie I'd thought it was a clever idea — she seemed less sure — but that I'd asked my friend what were *we* supposed to do with it? We're both knowledgeable about turning pulp into paper, but that's all. His scheme needed a politician, to talk the government into letting us have the paper, and a marketer, to get the Money Bags out there. "I told him," I explained to Marjorie, "if he could find a couple of people like that, and they were serious about it, I'd be happy to join in."

"Not in a million years," she said, and I had to agree.

When I came back home, after dropping Marjorie at the movie house, both Betsy and Billy were out, she at a rehearsal of a play she's doing at college — *Arsenic and Old Lace*; she's one of the aunts, in much makeup — and he off at a friend's house, engrossed in the friend's new computer software (he'll make do that way until life improves around here).

I opened the garage door, drove the Voyager in, shut the garage door, moved the rear seat of the car out of the way, and loaded the two plastic bags. And now I'm on my way to the recycling center.

The recycling center, of course, is what used to be called the dump, and part of it still is that. There's private trash collection in our neighborhood, but it's considerably cheaper to sort the trash yourself and bring it to the recycling center. Glass and tin and paper and cardboard they take for free, and garbage they take for fifty cents per large plastic bag. The bags are tossed into a chute, and from there they go into a compacting garbage truck, and from there they're taken to a landfill operation down on Long Island Sound.

A sea voyage for Hauck Exman. He's a Marine, he'll like that.

39

My friend with the Money Bags idea turns out to be named Ralph Upton, in honor of Upton "Ralph" Fallon, the last obstacle between me and my new job. It became necessary for this friend to have a further existence, I realized, once Hauck Exman was out of the way and it was time to think about dealing with URF.

Here's the thing: URF is employed. He's got my job, which means he's at work at the mill five days a week, which means I won't be able to ever get at him until the evenings. Weekends are complicated by Marjorie's job at the New Variety and by our own fixed weekend rituals, the Sunday *Times* and all that. So it's a work-night or nothing, and it isn't going to be nothing.

And that meant the creator of Money Bags had to go on being a presence in my life. "He has more ideas," I told Marjorie, when I picked her up from Dr. Carney's office at six on Monday, yesterday, three days after I dealt with Exman. "He has a million ideas, and who knows, one of them might turn out to be something. Anyway, he likes to bounce his notions off me and show me the presentations he's done and all that, and to tell the truth, sweet, I'd rather be doing something than nothing."

"I know you would," she said, and gave me a tender smile, and that was that.

This morning, we drove down to Marshal to spend our hour with Longus Quinlan, and to my surprise I'm enjoying these sessions now, finding them more valuable than I would have guessed. I think any marriage, after a while, falls into routines and automatic responses. Time goes by, and you no longer *see* each other clearly, you just act as though the other person's a robot, with machined and well-known responses to everything, and then *you* act like a robot, and all the life has drained out of the relationship.

Now that the awfulness of Marjorie's affair is finished, and now that Quinlan has given up trying to probe into my personal view of the world, we're dealing with what we went there to deal with, the marriage, and I think it's helping. We're becoming surprised by each other again, we're remembering why we liked each other in the first place.

If only I could tell her about this other business . . . but of course I never can. I know better. There are some strains you don't put on a person, no matter what.

Anyway, that was this morning, and this

evening we ate dinner at six-thirty, and now, at quarter past seven, I am on the road, heading west toward Arcadia, NY.

The long days of June, the long bright evenings. I'm driving along, crossing into New York State, and it's still sunny and nice. It occurs to me, as I drive; I'm beginning my commute. My new commute.

40

There's still daylight along the top of the slope, but the road into Arcadia descends into the blackness of night, decorated with neon from the town's two bars (but not from the closed luncheonette), brighter white and red light from the Getty station atop the farther slope, and the glary yellowish worklights around the mill. There are no lights visible inside the mill buildings; they're a success story, but they're only working one shift.

As I drive down the slope toward town and the dam and the quick black stream running through it, a stray thought occurs to me. What if Arcadia's success story isn't quite as glowing as the magazine made it seem? What if, even though they might not have gone all the way to downsizing, they're doing a reduction in staff through attrition, not taking on any new hires when people leave? What if I've gone through all this, and I deal with URF as well, and they don't replace him? The joke would certainly be on me, wouldn't it?

But, no. They're going to need an experienced man to run that line. If they had a night shift, then maybe the night shift man could move to days while he trains an assistant, already on the payroll, to take over at night. But this way, with only one shift, they'll hire.

I know what URF looks like, from having seen him that one time in the luncheonette, so now my first job is to find out where he lives. I don't expect much from this visit, just a little reconnaissance, to get an idea of the situation.

The Voyager's gas gauge shows just under half a tank, so I drive down to the bottom of the slope, cross the bridge on the dam, drive up the other slope, and stop at the Getty station. I fill the tank, pay the stocky woman at the counter inside, and ask if she has a phone book.

Yes, she does, though she doesn't say so. Without a word, she pulls a tattered thin phone book from under the counter, and I move off away from her a bit, as though to keep the counter clear for other customers — there are none — while I leaf through and find FALLON U R Cty Rte 92 Slt.

I don't care about the phone number, at least for now. I look at the map on the back cover of the phone book, to see what town "Slt" might be, and it's probably a place called Slate, that looks to be not very far from here.

I thank the woman as I return the phone book, and ask her where County Route 92 is, and now she has to speak, though minimally. Pointing up the road, out of town, she says, "Six miles. Where you going?"

"Slate."

"Take the left."

I thank her, and go back out to my full vehicle, and take it six miles and a little more to the county road, where green signs with cream letters at the intersection direct me toward various villages. Slate is the third one down on the sign pointing left.

This is a winding hilly road. It's hard to see what's alongside it, except for the occasional lit window of a house and once, well back from the road, the brightly lit interior of a barn.

I may not find URF's house at all tonight, unless his name is on the mailbox. Driving along through this darkness, I try to think of some way to get here on the weekend, in the daytime, either while Marjorie's cashiering at the New Variety on Saturday afternoon, or while we're normally lying around with the newspaper on Sunday. My new friend Ralph Upton may come in handy here.

FALLON.

That was so abrupt I almost missed it. I'm alone on the road, so it doesn't matter that I slam on the brakes. I hadn't seen house lights for a while, so I hadn't expected anything, and I wasn't looking for a mailbox. Then all at once there it was, on the right side of the road, in the shape of a fake log cabin, with a red metal band running along above the roof with the name in white letters.

I back up to take a second look, and that's it, all right, with a blacktop driveway leading in toward darkness next to it. I squint and lean toward the right window, and now I do see a dim light back in there.

How much do I do tonight? Is this the right Fallon? I drive on, looking for a place to stop, and just a bit farther along there's a broad metal cattle-gate leading into a field on the left, with blacktop from the gate out to the road. I turn around and leave the Voyager there, and walk back.

If I'm questioned? I'm lost. I'm looking for Arcadia.

At first the evening seems almost pitch-black, but as my eyes adjust to life without headlights I realize there's a sky full of stars, giving a cool but soft gray light, like a powder over everything. There's no moon, at least not yet. I walk along, completely alone, no traffic, nothing in sight, and here's the mailbox. I turn and walk in along the blacktop driveway, and up ahead I see the house obscurely, through a thick necklace of trees.

This must have been part of a working farm at one time. Whatever woods had been here were long ago cleared, except for those immediately around the house, which looks to be a couple of hundred years old, small but sprawling. One light gleams deep inside, not very brightly.

There's nobody home. You can tell that sort of thing. People leave a light on to discourage break-ins, but they leave too dim a light, too unimportant a light.

On the other hand, many country people have dogs. Has URF a dog? Cautiously, I approach the house. I am still, if need be, the lost traveler seeking directions.

The house has been added to over the years, mostly with rooms attached on the same side as the driveway, making the house increasingly wide. These first rooms I pass are dark, and don't suggest that anybody ever enters through here. The driveway continues on and widens in front of the house, where two vehicles are parked; a tall large pickup truck, its hood as high as my chest, and an old Chevy or Pontiac, very wide and long, that sags in a way to suggest it hasn't been moved in several years.

And here is what is probably the main entrance, at the windowed door of an enclosed porch, through which another windowed door can be seen and, dimly, a kitchen, with the light source somewhere beyond that.

If there were a dog on the premises, wouldn't he have made his presence known by now? Yes; dogs are not shy about announcing themselves. As a further test, I rattle the front door, which is locked but very loose in its frame. No reaction from within.

A professional burglar would, I am sure, get through this locked door in about ten seconds. I would rather try to find some other way in, so I leave that entrance and continue along the front wall, and when I turn the corner at the end I discover that originally *this* was the front of the house. With all the additions, and the driveway and the twentieth century, it has become the back instead, but this is the original section, facing the other way.

It's a standard Colonial center-hall design, a formal entrance door with two large windows on each side, and a second floor above with five windows, directly above the windows and door below. Inside, when it was first built, there would have been a hall and a stairway beyond this door, and four large rooms; to left and right downstairs, and the same upstairs. With the addition of electricity and indoor plumbing and central heating, all of these old places have been changed and changed and changed again, so that by now you never know what you'll find when you open one of these Colonial doors.

Not even if you're an invited guest.

In most of these old farmhouses, though, this original main entrance is no longer much used, and I see the stone landing in front of this door still has some of last fall's leaves mounded on it. I step up there, turn the handle, and push, and it seems to me it isn't locked, just stuck. I don't want to break anything, alert URF that anything is going on here, but I want to get in if I can. With the handle completely turned and my feet braced among the fallen leaves, I lean my weight against the door, not hitting it but just exerting steady pressure.

I feel it give, and I ease off, but it's still stuck. I lean again, and all at once it makes a quick sound like a sheet of paper ripping, and pops open.

Darkness. A musty smell, like laundry. The air inside is a little cooler and a little damper than the air outside. There isn't a sound. I step in.

I push the door closed behind me. It resists the last inch or so, with small compression sounds, this time like paper being crumpled, but I heave against it with my shoulder and finally hear it click shut.

And now the house. The faintest of light shimmers somewhere off to my right, more than one room away. By its hints, I can see the large doorway just here, and then what might be furniture, and then another, slightly more defined, doorway twenty feet or so away.

I move toward the light, cautiously, not wanting to trip over or disturb anything, and my knee does find a sofa arm. I detour around it, touch nothing else, and reach this next doorway.

Which leads to a corridor. The light source is a room on the left, and when I inch forward and look in, it's a bedroom. A quilt has been thrown somewhat carelessly over a double bed. The small lamp on the left bedside table is lit. There's a wide mirrored dresser, a chair piled with clothing, a lot of shoes scattered on the floor.

I'm beginning to think URF isn't married. I was wondering where his family was, thinking they might all have gone out to a movie or something, but this bedroom has the look of a man who lives alone.

When I get to the next doorway on that side, though, from the little I can see into it, it's a children's bedroom, for two kids. Bunk beds, low dressers, posters on the walls, toys on the floor. Is he a widower?

A bit farther along on the opposite side is the kitchen I saw from outside. I enter it, and cross to look out past the enclosed porch at the road. When he comes home, I'll see his headlights. If he's with his family, I'll have time to ease myself out the door I came in, far from the route they'll take. If he's alone, we'll see what happens.

I check the refrigerator, and it contains milk and cold cuts and soft drinks and beer and very little else. It just doesn't look like a family refrigerator.

I open and close kitchen drawers, because I know there'll be a flashlight here somewhere. There's a flashlight in every country kitchen, because country electricity goes off with fair frequency. Yes, here it is.

Now I can explore the rest of the house, and I do, and find several empty rooms, and underfurnished rooms, and it seems to me URF lives in four rooms out of ten, all on the first floor. He lives in the bedroom with its attached bath, and he lives in the kitchen, and he lives in the first room I went through, with the sofa I kneed and a TV set and a

361

coffee table and an end table and a floor lamp and a telephone and nothing else, and he lives in a room beyond the kitchen, originally a guest room, that he's turned into an office, the same as I have at home. In this office he keeps his tax records and work records and all the paperwork of normal life.

I spend some time in this office, using only the flashlight, because I want to learn as much as I can about URF, and in his case I haven't had the advantage of a resumé, nor did I ever bother to do a public records check. The windows here face the driveway and the road, so I'll know when he comes home.

It takes me half an hour to go through all the stuff in here, or at least to go through it enough to get a reading on the man. He's divorced, that's the first thing, and it looks to me as though he's been divorced three times. He has three grown-up kids who live in California and write him the occasional not-very-personal letter, and he has two younger kids who come to visit him in the summer and at Christmastime. He makes a good living at Arcadia — though not, I notice, quite as good as I used to make at Halcyon — but he's constantly in debt, with an entire manila folder of dunning letters. He's usually behind in his child support, but scrambles to make it up twice a year, just before they arrive for their visit.

The other thing about him, which surprises me a little, is that he's very serious about his job. From that article where I first read about him, I'd thought he was more of a lightweight, but I see that he keeps a file of articles torn from the newspapers and our trade journals, having to do with our line of work, and that he underlines sections and makes mostly sensible remarks in margins, and seems very intent on keeping up with the industry.

Well, that's fine. I'm good at the job, too, and I'd like my new employer to have somebody first-rate to compare me to, so he'll know what a valuable man he's getting.

The other important fact is, those two younger children always seem to start their summer visit just about the first of July, which means a week from now. So that's a deadline; much better to get all this taken care of before they arrive.

There's nothing else for me to look for in the office, and nothing more to learn. When I leave there and return the flashlight to its drawer, I see by the illuminated hands of the kitchen clock that it isn't even ten. Wherever URF is, tomorrow's a workday, so he'll probably be home fairly soon.

And he won't have his family with him.

My guess is that URF's in one of those two bars in Arcadia. That's where he'll spend his evenings after work, having a hamburger or some pizza for dinner. When he gets home, I don't imagine he'll be completely sober.

There's no point my driving to Arcadia to look for him. I'd be halfway there when he would pass me, coming home, and I wouldn't know it.

I go back into the office, from where I get the best view of the driveway and the road. I sit at his desk, in the darkness there, and after a while lean back in his swivel chair and put my feet up on the desk, and I keep an eye on the windows.

From time to time, a vehicle passes along the road out there, but not often. I sit here at URF's desk, with nothing to do but wait and watch and think, and I can't help but go over and over all the things I've had to do the last two months. Some of them were much harder than others. Some were very hard indeed.

On the other hand, some were easy. And I truly think, more recently, I've gained more confidence, and that makes it easier yet.

Oh! I'm falling asleep. No good, no good.

I get to my feet, stamping around in a

circle in this dark room. I can't be *asleep* when he gets here.

I leave the office and go down the hall to his bedroom, just to be near some light, to beat off that sleepiness. And now for the first time, as long as I'm in here, and to have something to do, I make a quick search of the bedroom, and the one thing I find of interest is the pistol in his bedside drawer, next to the flashlight and the Tums. Of course I don't know guns, except my father's Luger, but I can tell this is some kind of pistol, with that round cylinder to give it the pregnant look. It's black, and the handle is a bit worn as though it's old. It looks like the starter gun used in a race.

I don't touch it. I close the drawer, and merely remember it's there.

Back in the hall, I glance into and through the kitchen, and out the porch windows, and I see the headlights just as they make the turn into the driveway. Weaving, slow-moving, hesitant.

URF is coming home.

41

He's drunk. I can tell that much before I even see him, from the way he drives his car, the excess caution with which he steers this dark-colored Subaru station wagon around the driveway curve toward his house.

There are half a dozen methods, right in this house, by which I can finish him off with no trouble, and even make it look like accidental death. Which would be a lot better than yet another murder of a paper mill manager.

The Subaru jolts to a stop, out front. I'm not watching from the kitchen, I've moved on to his living room, his TV room, whatever he might call it. In one of the windows there, I can stand without any light behind me, and watch. I was afraid, if I'd stood in the kitchen doorway, he might see a silhouette.

Everything he does is in slow motion. Some time after he stops, the lights go off, so I suppose the engine went off then, too; I'm not sure I can hear it, through the glass. And then, a little while after that, he opens his door and climbs wearily out. The interior light goes on, but my concentration is on URF — I'm thinking of him now as a kind of dog, named "Urf" — as he slams the car door and makes his way around the front of it.

Come in, come in. Come home, go to bed, rest, sleep. I'll wait here. Or farther back, in the unused room on the other side of the unused entrance, just in case you decide to come on in here and fall asleep in front of the television set.

He makes his way around the front of the car, leaning on the hood, and then he turns right again, and opens the passenger door, and a woman gets out.

Damn! I stare at her, and she's about as drunk as he is. A large woman in sweater and slacks, weaving. I see her stand beside the car, holding on to the open door, and I hear her voice, quite loud: "Where the hell is this?"

"*My* place, Cindy! Damn! *You* know my place!"

She grumbles something, and moves forward. He slams the Subaru's passenger door and follows her, and in a minute I hear him fumbling with his keys.

Not tonight. He picked her up at the bar, and he's done it before. So not tonight.

But he doesn't pick up a woman *every* night, not Urf. There are nights he sleeps alone.

As the stumbling sounds of them move across the kitchen, I fade back across the TV room into the hall and to the door I used when I came in tonight. I tug on it, and it opens more easily this time, more quietly. Not that they'd hear much. I slide outside.

There are more lights on now, in the kitchen and in the bedroom. I skirt around all three vehicles parked here, staying out of the lightspill. I walk away down the driveway. I am not at all discouraged.

42

I park the same place I did on Tuesday, and walk back down the dark country road toward Urf's house. It's nine-thirty, Thursday night, the 26th of June, and I am here to kill him. He could have an entire harem with him tonight, I don't care. Tonight he dies.

I'm feeling such time pressure now. It's not only that I've been at this for nearly two months, though that's part of it. Having to think about these deadly things all the time, do these deadly things, it's wearing me down. I take less pleasure in life, and for that I don't blame the downsizing, the chop, the *adjustment,* whatever you want to call it; I blame this grim hell I'm living through. Food doesn't taste as good as it used to, simple pleasures like music or television or driving or just feeling the sun on my face have all flattened and become drab, and as for sex, well . . .

Though that problem *did* start with the downsizing.

Once I'm out of this. Once it's over. Once I'm out of this and safe on the farther shore, with the new job, with my life back. Then the colors will be bright again.

So that's a reason to want it over, but now there's an even more compelling one, and that's Urf's children. If they follow their normal pattern, and why shouldn't they, next week is when they'll arrive for their summer visit with their father. The 4th of July is on Friday this year, so they'll surely want their travel to be finished well before the weekend, which means I have less than a week before they show up to complicate my life beyond imagining.

No time at all. Weekends are impossible. Mondays and Wednesdays are impossible as well, because of Marjorie's job with Dr. Carney. By the time I pick her up at six in the evening and drive her home, with dinner still to come, it's far too late to set out for Slate, New York. So if I don't get him tonight, I won't have another try at him for five days, not until next Tuesday, and by then his children could already be here.

I'm a little later tonight, deliberately, assuming his pattern is never to come home directly from work. And I seem to be right; his house is as dark as it was when I arrived on Tuesday. The nightlight in his bedroom, nothing more.

There's a learning curve with this house, as well. Tonight, I walk past the two parked vehicles and the entrance to the enclosed porch, go directly on down to the end and around the corner, then straight through the original front door. I walk through the TV room without kneeing the sofa, glance in at the lit bedroom and the dim kitchen, and make my way to the dark office, where I sit again at his desk.

Not home yet. Out drinking his dinner. Anesthetizing himself, just for me.

It's a little warm in here, but I keep my windbreaker on. In the pockets are the things I've brought, just in case. The coil of picture wire. The small roll of duct tape. The four-inch length of heavy iron pipe, one end wrapped with electric tape for a better grip. The cotton gloves.

I don't have a particular plan, not yet. It all depends what the circumstances are, when Urf gets here.

I put my feet up on the desk, and cross my ankles. A car drives by, southbound, out there on the road. Then nothing. I sit and wait for Urf to come home.

43

Light. I blink.

"Wake up, you!"

"Oh, my God!" I twitch, and my feet fall off the desk and thud to the floor, jolting me forward in the swivel chair. I stare in the harshness of the overhead light. My eyes are gummy, my mouth sticky.

I fell asleep.

He's in the doorway. His left hand is still across his body, fingers touching the light switch. His right hand holds the revolver I last saw in his bedside table. He stares at me. He weaves left and right in the doorway. Even as I'm realizing the horror of the situation, I can see that he's pretty drunk. "Mister . . ." I say, trying to remember his name. Urf, not Urf. Fallon.

"Don't move!"

My hand has started upward, to wipe my sticky-feeling mouth, but now I freeze, hand in midair. "Fallon," I say. "Mister Fallon."

"What are you doin here?" He's aggressive because he's afraid, and he's afraid because he's bewildered.

What *am* I doing here? I have to have a reason, something I can tell him. "Mister

Fallon," I say again, stuck at that part of it.

"You broke into my house!"

"No! No, I didn't." I protest that in full honesty.

"The door was locked!"

"No, it wasn't." Even though he told me not to move, I do move, pointing away to my right as I say, "The big door by the living room. I knocked, and . . . *that* wasn't locked."

He frowns mightily, and I see him trying to think about that door that's never used. *Is* it locked? He doesn't know. He says, "It's trespassing."

Fair enough. Break in or walk in, it is trespassing, he's right about that. I say, "I wanted to wait for you. I'm sorry I fell asleep."

"*I* don't know you," he says. I'm not being particularly threatening or intimidating, so his aggression and fear are becoming less, but he's still as bewildered as I am as to what reason I'm going to give for my being here.

Is it because we're both paper line managers? Polymer paper? I've just come by for some shoptalk, a little chat about our fascinating employment? At this time of night? Unannounced, walking into his empty house?

And then I see it, all at once, and I turn my honest face up to him, and I say, "Mr. Fallon, I need your help."

He squints at me. The revolver is still pointed in my direction, but he no longer touches the light switch. That other hand is pressed against the doorframe now, to help him keep from weaving. He says, "Did Edna send you, is that what this is?"

I remember, from his tax returns, that Edna is an ex-wife. I say, "I don't know anybody named Edna, Mr. Fallon. My name is Burke Devore, I'm the production line manager for the polymer paper line at Halcyon Mills over in Connecticut, over in Belial."

Again he squints. "Halcyon," he says. He keeps up with the trade journals, but how closely? Will he know it's all over at Halcyon? He says, "Didn't they get merged?"

"Yes," I say. "That's the whole trouble, it looks like they're gonna move the whole goddam thing up to Canada —"

"Cocksuckers," he says.

"I just don't want to lose my job," I say.

"Lotta that goin around," he says.

"Too much of it. Mr. Fallon," I say, "I read about you in *Pulp*, remember that piece a few months ago?"

"They got some stuff wrong in there," he

complains, "made me look like a damn fool doesn't know his own job."

"I thought it made you look terrific at your job," I tell him, lying. "That's why I'm here."

He shakes his head, befuddled. "I don't know what the *fuck* you think you're talkin about," he says.

"I'm good at my job, Mr. Fallon, believe me I am," I tell him, with great sincerity, "but these days you can't just be good at the job, you've got to be perfect at it. I don't have much time. They're going to decide pretty soon this summer, do I stay on, does the line stay here or does it get pulled to Canada —"

"Fuckin bastards."

"I thought," I tell him, "if I could talk to Mr. Fallon, if we could just *talk* about the job, I could maybe pick up some pointers, get to where I could — I can *do* the job, Mr. Fallon, but I'm not that good, talking about it, I can't express myself. In that piece in *Pulp*, you could express yourself. I was hoping, my idea was, we could just talk, and then maybe I'd be better at it on the job. There's gonna be an interview, I'm not exactly sure when."

He studies me. The revolver now dangles at his side, pointing at the floor. He says, "You sound desperate."

"I am desperate. I don't want to lose that job. I keep thinking about it and thinking about it, and today I finally made the decision to come here and ask you for help, and after dinner I drove over here from Connecticut."

"Whyn'tcha use the phone?"

I give a wry grin and a little shrug. "Be some nut on the phone? I figured, if I come here, I can explain myself. But then you weren't home."

"So you busted in."

"The door isn't locked, Mr. Fallon," I say. "Honest, it isn't."

He thinks about that, nodding slowly, and then says, "Let's go see."

"All right."

He steps back from the doorway, and makes a waving gesture with the revolver. It's not pointed at the floor any more, but it's not quite pointed at me either. "You first," he says.

I go first, through the house, which now has lights on in every room, all the way to the door beyond the TV room, which I open onto the black night outside. I turn to him and say, "See?"

He glares at the door. "The goddam thing isn't supposed to be open like that." He comes over, switching the revolver to his left hand so he can slam the door, open it, slam it again, and then peer closely at the lock mounted on the inside of it. He tries to turn the lock's little handle, but it won't move. "Damn thing's painted stuck," he says. "Stuck open. Be a son of a bitch."

During this, I could hit him about seven times with the iron pipe in my windbreaker pocket, but I don't. I think things are going to work out better than that.

He slams the door again, turns to me, shakes his head. "I gotta get that fixed," he tells me. "Anyway, you see how it looked, I come home, there's *you* right there, asleep in my den."

"I'm sorry I fell asleep."

"Well, you had a long drive. Wha'd you say your name was?"

"Burke," I tell him. "Burke Devore."

"Burke," he says, "I know you won't mind if I have a look at your wallet."

I say, "You still think there's something wrong with me? All right." And I take out my wallet and hand it to him.

He takes it from me with his left hand, gesturing again with the revolver in his right. "Whyn'tcha have a seat on the sofa in there?" he suggests.

So I do, and he walks across to the other side of the room, weaving a little, to put the revolver on top of the TV set while he looks at all the cards and papers in my wallet, peering owlishly at them, having trouble focusing, I suppose, because he's had too much to drink.

Well, this can only help. Not only will he see I've told him the truth about my name, but I now realize my old employee ID from Halcyon is still in there, I never did find a moment to throw that away. (I probably didn't want to throw it away.)

I see the instant he finds the ID; his brow clears at once, and he's grinning in a much more friendly fashion when he next looks over at me. "Well, Mr. Devore," he says, "it looks like I owe you an apology."

"Not at all," I say. "I'm the one to apologize, walking in here, falling asleep . . ."

"Over and done with," he says, and crosses the room to hand me my wallet. "You want a beer?"

"Very much so," I say, and *that* isn't a lie.

"You want a little something in it?"

"Only if you are."

"Come on to the kitchen," he says, then looks at the revolver on the TV set as though surprised and not pleased to see it still around. Picking it up, pointing it away from me, toward the hall, he says, "Let me get rid of this."

"Fine by me," I tell him, with a shaky smile.

He laughs and starts off, saying, "I'm Ralph, by the way. You're Burke?"

"That's right."

I stand in the hall while he stows the revolver in his bedside table drawer. Coming back out, he says, "Be damned if I know what help I can be, but I'll try. A lot of these owners — Come on along."

We walk toward the kitchen, and he continues, "A lot of these owners are what I would call pricks. I've heard about them. Got no more loyalty than a ferret."

"That's about right," I say.

"Fortunately," he says, slurring the word, "we got good owners at Arcadia."

"That's good to hear."

In the kitchen, he pulls two cans of beer from the refrigerator and hands me one, then opens an upper cabinet door and brings out a bottle of rye. "Sweeten to taste," he suggests, putting the bottle on the counter.

I follow his lead. He opens the beer, takes a deep swig, then fills up the can from the rye bottle. I open and drink, and when he hands me the bottle I do a trick a bartender showed me at a company party years ago. One of the people on my line was getting drunk on vodka and grapefruit juice, and when I had a word with the bartender he told me, "I already cut him off." "But you're still pouring," I objected, and he grinned and said, "Next time, watch." So I did, and if you weren't looking for it you wouldn't see it. He put in the ice cubes and then tipped the vodka bottle over the glass, slipping his thumb over the open top just before it would pour, and pulling the thumb back again as the bottle came upright, all in one easy sliding pouring movement. Then he filled the glass with grapefruit juice and handed it to the drunk, who didn't get any *more* drunk at that party.

So that's what I do now. I drink some of the beer, and then, half turned away from Fallon, I tilt the rye bottle over the hole in the top of the can, keeping the rye in the bottle with my thumb, then stand the bottle on the counter.

Fallon wants to click beer cans, so we do, and he says, "To the bosses, the rotten ones. May we piss on their graves," and we drink. "Come on and sit down," he says, and staggers a bit as he pulls a chair out at the kitchen table.

We sit across from one another at the table, and he says, "Tell me about your line there. What kinda extruder you got? No, wait a second." And he gets up and reels over to the counter to grab the rye bottle and bring it back and plunk it on the table between us. Then he reels to the refrigerator and gets two more beer cans and smacks them down at our places. "For later," he says, and sits down and says, "So? Tell me whatcha got."

44

I'm sorry when, at last, he does fall asleep. I shouldn't be sorry, because it's very late, past midnight by his kitchen clock, but to tell the truth, I enjoyed our conversation. He's okay, Ralph Fallon. More crude than most of the people I know, because he came up from the laborer ranks instead of out of college like most of us, but a bright guy and very knowledgeable about the job. In fact, he told me a couple of things he's done on the line there at Arcadia that are very interesting, methods I'll certainly keep in place when I take over.

And he can definitely drink. He was already drunk when he came home, and since we've been seated together here at his kitchen table he's had eight more beers, each of them well laced with rye. I haven't kept up at all (I don't think he expects people to keep up with him), having only five beers and not adding any whiskey — though I did fake it every time — but I'm feeling it. I'm feeling a lot of things, really; the beer, the lateness of the hour, the knowledge that I'm almost at the end of this series of trials, and a stupid sentimental attachment to Ralph Fallon.

In my wooziness, my weakness, I even try to imagine scenarios in which Fallon lives and yet I get what I want. I talk him into retiring, or I explain my situation and he offers me a job as co-manager on the line, or he suddenly wakes up and tells me Arcadia is going to two shifts and will need a night manager on the line.

But none of that happens, or is going to happen. My long pleasant beery shoptalk session with Ralph Fallon is over; it is time to be serious.

Weary, feeling as though I weigh a thousand pounds, I get to my feet and reach for my windbreaker, on the back of the chair to my right. In the right pocket is the small roll of duct tape. I take it out and look at it, and then look at Fallon, slumped in his chair across the table from me, chin on chest, left hand on the table, right hand in his lap.

I don't want to do this. But there are always things we don't want to do, and we do them.

I walk around the table, go to my knees beside Fallon, and very gently tape his right ankle to the chair leg. Then I crawl around him on all fours — it's too much effort to stand and walk and kneel again — and tape his left ankle to the other chair leg. Then, with a small groan, I do stand.

It would be safer, surer, if I could tape his wrists together, but I'm afraid if I tried to move his arms he would wake up, so instead I run tape around the chair back and his torso, just above the elbows. It's tricky doing this without letting the tape make too much noise when I pull it from the roll, but at last I get it around him twice, snug and secure. He'll be able to move his hands and forearms, but not, I think, effectively.

With what I do next, he's certainly going to wake up, so I'd better do it fast and clean. I pull off two small lengths of tape, stand over him with a piece of duct tape in each hand, then with an abrupt motion slap the first piece against his mouth, pressing it against the flesh.

He does wake up, startled, eyes popping open, all of his limbs jerking. He's still trying to understand what's happening and why he can't move when I press the second piece of duct tape over his nose, squeezing the nostrils shut. Then I step back from him and turn away, to search the kitchen drawers while he dies.

What I need is a candle. Like the flashlight, and for the same reason of unreliable electric service, every country kitchen keeps a stub of candle somewhere.

Yes, here it is, in the drawer with the balls of string and the extra twisties and the spare keys, a short fat candle of the kind people light in church when they want their prayers answered. I take down a saucer from an upper cabinet, put it on the counter near the stove, put the candle on the saucer.

Meantime, Fallon is making terrible noises. Now that I've found the candle, now that there's nothing to distract me, I hate those noises, and so I leave the room, carrying my windbreaker with me.

I put on the windbreaker as I walk through the house. The gloves and the iron pipe are in the other outer pocket. I won't be needing the pipe, but I will take it away with me; in the meantime, I put on the gloves. Starting at the far end of the house, at the front door, I use my gloved hands to wipe everything I can think of that I touched, and I turn off the lights as I go, except that I leave the bedside lamp lit in his bedroom.

Fallon is quiet now, slumped again. I remove the duct tape from his ankles and then his torso, and he falls forward so his head hits the table. I have to lift his head, trying not to see those staring eyes, and when I pull the last two pieces of duct tape away I discover he's thrown up, into his mouth and then into his nose and lungs because it couldn't come out through the tape. So he didn't suffocate, he drowned. A miserable end, either way.

I use one of his small plastic trash bags for the pieces of duct tape, then put the bag in my windbreaker pocket. I use one of his wooden kitchen matches to light the candle.

In New York State, gas stoves don't have pilot lights, they have electric igniters. I switch on the front two burners of his stove, leave them on high, and blow out the flames. I then leave the kitchen, closing its inner door behind me, so there are now no openings from the kitchen.

By the light from the bedroom, I make my way back through the house and out the door that Fallon hadn't known was unlocked. I walk briskly past the front of the house, seeing the low winking light of the candle flame, and the four tall skinny metal bottles of propane gas tucked into the corner of the outside wall where the enclosed porch ends. I continue on out the driveway and down the road to the Voyager.

I have no idea how long it will take. I don't want to be here when it happens, but I want to be close enough to know it did happen. And I assume, when the stove blows, it will set off the propane bottles as well. There shouldn't be too much of Fallon or the kitchen left, but there should be just enough to make it clear what happened. A drunk fell asleep, unaware that he'd miscalculated in turning on the stove. I don't suppose anyone who knows Ralph Fallon will be surprised.

I get into the Voyager and drive slowly past the house and on the few miles to the intersection where I should turn right for Arcadia. I stop there, and look in the rearview mirror, and then make a U-turn in the middle of the intersection. There's no other traffic at all.

I'm about half a mile from the intersection, on the way back to Fallon's house, when the sudden yellow light switches on some distance ahead of me, showing woods and houses in silhouette. It begins to die down, as though someone had switched on a bright light and then smoothly rotated the dimmer, but then it flares brighter than before, with red and white mixed into the yellow, and again dims down, and the double blast rolls over the car like a wave, like a physical thing.

I stop the car. I make another U-turn. I drive home.

45

Every era, and every nation, has its own characteristic morality, its own code of ethics, depending on what the people think is important. There have been times and places when honor was considered the most sacred of qualities, and times and places that gave every concern to grace. The Age of Reason promoted reason to be the highest of values, and some peoples — the Italians, the Irish — have always felt that feeling, emotion, sentiment was the most important. In the early days of America, the work ethic was our greatest expression of morality, and then for a while property values were valued above everything else, but there's been another more recent change. Today, our moral code is based on the idea that the end justifies the means.

There was a time when that was considered improper, the end justifying the means, but that time is over. We not only believe it, we say it. Our government leaders always defend their actions on the basis of their goals. And every single CEO who has commented in public on the blizzard of downsizings sweeping America has explained himself with some variant on the same idea: The end justifies the means.

The end of what I'm doing, the purpose, the goal, is good, clearly good. I want to take care of my family; I want to be a productive part of society; I want to put my skills to use; I want to work and pay my own way and not be a burden to the taxpayers. The means to that end has been difficult, but I've kept my eye on the goal, the purpose. The end justifies the means. Like the CEOs, I have nothing to feel sorry for.

The weekend following the death of Ralph Fallon, I spend in a kind of contented daze, not thinking, not worrying, not making plans. The call will come, I know it will. The position is open, and the call will come.

But the call does not come on Monday, and by midafternoon, alone in the house, Marjorie at Dr. Carney's, me pacing and pacing, listening for the phone that doesn't ring, I'm beginning to picture troubling alternatives. Was there some other resumé I didn't pay close enough attention to, and he got the call instead of me? Are they promoting from within their work force, over there at Arcadia?

Am I going to have to go back over there and kill some other son of a bitch? How much do I have to do before I get my fair chance?

I'm not going to stop, I know I'm not. I'd love to stop, I want desperately to stop, but I'm not *going* to stop until I've got that job.

I know how to protect myself now. I will not be made a victim, never again. Anyone who tries to make trouble for me, from now on, with what I now know, anyone at all, corporate or personal, is in for a surprise.

It would be better all around if that fucking phone would ring.

46

Tuesday, I'm very distracted during the counseling session. Unless Quinlan or Marjorie speaks to me directly, I don't listen to what they're saying, and I add nothing. Fortunately, they're both involved enough in whatever they're discussing not to notice my absence.

What I'm thinking about is Arcadia. I'm thinking I'll have to go over there tomorrow, find out what's going on. It seems to me the best way is to get to the luncheonette when the workers come in at noontime, and listen to what they have to say.

Of course, the danger there is that I might be recognized later. I'm wondering if there's any theatrical place around where I could buy a mustache that wouldn't look fake. Or should I start growing a mustache, and be clean-shaven tomorrow and mustached when I finally get the job?

I haven't decided, about the mustache or anything else, by the time the counseling session is over. Marjorie and I drive back home in silence, me continuing to brood, only vaguely aware that she's looking at me, wondering about me.

There's a message on the answering machine, in the kitchen. Marjorie pushes the button and I pause in the doorway, disinterested, and the female voice says:

"This is Mr. John Carver's office at Arcadia Processing, calling for Mr. Burke Devore. I'm calling on Tuesday, the first of July. Could Mr. Devore please return Mr. Carver's call no later than Wednesday, the second of July? His number here is five one eight three nine eight four one four two. Thank you."

Marjorie looks at me, and I know I'm smiling so broadly my cheeks should split. She says, "Burke? What is it?"

"My new job," I say.

47

He was very good, on the phone, Mr. John Carver, amiable and interested. He told me they had an unexpected need for a product line manager of just my history and experience. He told me there'd been a tragic accident: "The funeral was yesterday." Which, of course, was why no phone call on Monday.

He said more. He said I was their first choice, that my resumé made it look as though I was just the manager they were looking for, but that their need is immediate, and when I wasn't home at the time of their call — unfortunate, very unfortunate — they couldn't be sure I was still available, and so of course they'd made a few other calls, which meant he was already seeing three applicants on Wednesday, the day after our conversation. But he promised they wouldn't make a decision before talking to me, and we made an appointment for Thursday at eleven in the morning, and today is Thursday, and I am having a very good time deciding what tie to wear.

Marjorie comes in while I'm knotting the tie, a maroon one in honor of the good lawyer Porculey, but without cows jumping over moons. The last two days, Marjorie has been as smiling and elated as I am, believing I really will get this job, believing it only because she sees *I* believe it so thoroughly, but now the smile has been replaced by a confused and questioning look: "Burke," she says, "that detective is here."

I'm blithe, I barely hear her: "Who?"

"The detective who was here before. Burton."

Detective. The one investigating the two mill managers shot by the same gun.

No. Not now. After all this, after all I've been through? To be stopped *now*, as though none of it had ever mattered?

Go through the process. It could be something else, or he could have nothing more than suspicions. All I have to do is remain firm and constant. All I have to do is remember my own advice to Billy; choose the best story available, and stick to it, no matter what.

"Okay," I tell Marjorie, smiling at her in the mirror. Then I finish knotting my tie, and, wearing tie and shirt and trousers and slippers, I walk out to the living room.

He's studying the Winslow Homer again. Are we going to have another discussion of sailing before we get to the subject? He turns when I walk in, nods and smiles, extending his hand. "Mr. Devore. Good to see you again."

Is this friendliness real, or a lie? I smile back, lying, and shake his hand. "Mr. Burton. Or do I say Detective Burton?"

"Either way," he says. "I can see you're on your way somewhere, I won't take a lot of your time. I have another name and another photo to try on you."

Which of my resumés will this be? One of them, that's for certain. I say, "If I can help."

"Sure." He's taking his notebook out of his inner jacket pocket, opening it, finding the color photo he wants. "The name is Hauck Exman."

My Marine, gone on a sea voyage. You could talk sailing with *him*, Detective Burton. I shake my head. "Doesn't ring a bell."

He hands me the photo, and I look at it, and it's a formal shot, him in a tuxedo somewhere, looking mostly like the President's bodyguard. "No," I say. "Tough-looking guy. Who is he?"

"At the moment," he says, as I hand him back the photo, "he's our prime suspect."

I am astonished, and I don't mind showing it. "Suspect! How did that happen?"

He's pleased with his detective work, that's obvious, and he'd like nothing better than to share it. "It took some digging," he says, "but we —"

I say, "Oh, excuse me. Won't you sit down?"

He's willing, but doubtful. "You've got time?"

"Plenty," I tell him.

"Okay, then."

We both sit, in the same positions as the first time, and he says, "We finally linked up the other two, Everly and Asche. Four five years ago, there was a government contract for some kind of special paper, I apologize, I don't really understand all that stuff —"

"That's okay," I tell him, "most people don't."

"It was the Treasury Department," he says, "but it wasn't money, it was something else. The bidding companies all sent reps to Washington to talk to the Treasury people —"

"I remember that," I say. "Or I think that's the one. It had to do with import forms, and we didn't bid. I mean, the company I was with then. It wasn't quite our line, anti-counterfeit stuff, and we weren't looking for extra business anyway."

"Well, these other companies did," Burton tells me. "And among the company representatives down there, all at the same time, were Everly and Asche and Exman."

"Ahhhh," I say. "And they met."

"We haven't been able to prove that," he says, "but I don't think we have to. I spoke to Exman a couple weeks ago, the same way I spoke to you, and I have to tell you, I didn't like the way he acted."

I can see it. The haughty Exman, so involved in his own problems, feeling so intensely the humiliation of being a suit salesman, and how easy it was to give short shrift to this earnest detective. No, they wouldn't have hit it off. I say, "Did you arrest him?"

"Didn't have the evidence," Burton says, and shrugs. "But now, it looks like, my visit spooked him. He ran away."

"Ran away!"

"Disappeared completely," Burton tells me, with clear satisfaction. "Left his car behind in the parking lot where he worked, didn't say a word to anybody, just took off."

"I can't imagine it," I say. "Didn't he have a family? You say he was working?"

"Not easy for most people to do," he agrees, "suddenly up and leave your entire life behind. But now we're looking into it, and what do we find out? Exman's been having trouble at home. His wife had already seen a lawyer about a divorce, he'd been playing around, she caught him, all the usual stuff. And she's not the first wife, she's the fourth."

"Making trouble in his own life," I suggest.

"And everybody else's." Burton puts his notebook away, the photo inside it. "When we searched the house, it was full of guns. *Full* of guns. Maybe a dozen weapons of all different kinds. We're testing them all now, against the bullets we have, but the feeling is, he probably disposed of the gun that did the killing."

"Where do you think he is?"

"We're talking to his girlfriends," Burton tells me, "both of them, and the place he always seemed to talk about most was Singapore."

"You think he's in Singapore?"

"Well, he didn't take his passport. On the other hand, he just might have another one." Burton gets to his feet. "I shouldn't keep you any longer. We'll track him down, sooner or later."

Standing, I say, "Once again, I haven't been much help."

"Well, your company didn't bid on that contract. Otherwise, you might have met all three of them down there in D.C."

"And been shot by Exman last month," I suggest, with a wry smile.

He chuckles. "Consider yourself lucky," he says.

"Oh, I do."

He gestures at my tie. "You're off somewhere this morning."

"A job interview," I tell him. "This time, I think it's going to work out."

"Very good," he says. "I hope you're right."

"Wish me luck," I say.

"Good luck," he says.

We hope you have enjoyed this Large Print book. Other Thorndike Press or Chivers Press Large Print books are available at your library or directly from the publishers.

For more information about current and upcoming titles, please call or write, without obligation, to:

Thorndike Press
P.O. Box 159
Thorndike, Maine 04986 USA
Tel. (800) 223-2336

OR

Chivers Press Limited
Windsor Bridge Road
Bath BA2 3AX
England
Tel. (0225) 335336

All our Large Print titles are designed for easy reading, and all our books are made to last.

LARGE TYPE
Westlake, Donald E.
The ax